MW00929961

CLAIMED
by the
WARRIOR

By
Eliza Knight

He came to conquer…

A widower, Laird Torsten Mackenzie, has worked long and hard to regain the respect his clan deserved after his older brother turned traitorous. Even in death, Cathal's crimes remain a mar on Torsten's conscience. Setting aside his grief, Torsten devotes his life to his people, and to his young, motherless daughter. When a rival clan attacks his lands unprovoked, he's determined to put them in their place once and for all. Marching on their gates, he's taken by surprise when Lady MacDonell steps through the opening instead of her wayward husband. Reacting impulsively, Torsten exacts his revenge by whisking her away.

But she laid claim to his heart…

Headstrong and fierce, Éabha MacDonell's true nature has been buried for six long years in a marriage that fills her with shame, and has kept her tucked in the shadows. But the death of her husband, and being forced from the only home she's ever known, brings freedom in a way she'd never imagined. Free to rediscover parts of herself she'd thought never to behold again—her love of art, fencing, and her desire for children. But most of all, the tug at her heart, the warmth of a secret glance and the heat of a passionate embrace.

In the arms of her captor, Éabha's more liberated than she's ever been before and Torsten might just have found the one person who can make him whole again.

DEDICATION

For you, dear reader. Thank you for reading my stories!

Dear Reader,

I'm thrilled to bring you the next book in the Conquered Bride series! In this story, you're going to meet Éabha (pronounced Ava) and Torsten. Torsten is the brother of the villain, Cathal, from book 2.5, *Taken by the Highlander*, which appeared in the *USA Today* Bestselling anthology, *Captured by a Celtic Warrior*.

Also of note, Strome Castle was originally the seat of the MacDonell Earls of Ross. It wasn't until 1602 that it was invaded by the Mackenzies, but for fictional purposes and for this series, I moved that up a few hundred years.

I do hope you enjoy this story!

Best wishes and happy reading,

Eliza

CHAPTER ONE

Strome Castle
Scottish Highlands
Spring, 1308

Damned MacDonells.

Why the hell did those bloody fools have to keep raiding? Had they not yet learned their lesson?

Laird Torsten Mackenzie crouched just out of arrow's reach from the high, thick walls of the MacDonell's castle. The fortress loomed up in the moonlight, but despite its fortifications, he planned to breach it this very night. A promise he'd made the last time the bastards had dared to cross onto his land.

Torsten was certain he'd been clear that any further raids on his lands would not be tolerated. Another raid from the

MacDonells was a declaration of war, he'd even put it in writing so the imbeciles would not be confused. Yet, despite his warnings, the arseholes had done so again, trampling crops, burning crofter's homes, beating tenants and violating women.

Rage lanced hot through Torsten's veins. He gripped the reins tighter, his body stiffened, and his mount, Lucifer, tossed his head in irritation. When he got ahold of Donald MacDonell, that sorry excuse for a laird, he was going to beat him to a bloody pulp, until the last of his breath escaped and his face was unrecognizable.

His warhorse snorted and Torsten loosened his grip, concentrating his fury on the castle just beyond.

"My laird?"

Torsten glanced at Little Rob, his second-in-command, a man not so little in personality or size. He, too, had steel-studded leather armor covering his leine shirt, his green and blue plaid muted in the darkness.

"Wait." Torsten glowered at the wall and keep, imagining the men inside celebrating their latest raid, and reliving every horrifying moment. Well, Torsten, wasn't celebrating, and his people surely weren't. They were trying to pick up the pieces of their lives, while desperately trying *not* to relive it. Donald MacDonell had better start praying now, for Torsten would show no mercy.

Mackenzie lands were vast. Torsten's castle, Eilean Donan, sat on an island perfectly situation between three lochs—Loch Alsh, Loch Duich and Loch Long—on the south-western end of his territory. The MacDonell's had crossed through their own territory traveling north into Mackenzie lands, but been careful to stay as far away from

12

the castle as possible, riding more than half a day, longer than needed, until they reached a small village built along a river. Torsten had a small garrison stationed there, but the MacDonells had more men and despite the Mackenzie superior strength and skill, the men were killed or left for dead. By the time a messenger had arrived, and Torsten had brought reinforcements, the MacDonells were long gone.

Torsten set out immediately, sending word to Eilean Donan for more of his men to meet him at Strome Castle. They all gathered now, nearly one hundred and fifty strong.

The idea of any warrior tormenting an innocent sent his guilt soaring fast. He'd dealt with enough of that with his own brother, God rest his soul. Whenever Cathal had gone raiding, Torsten stayed home, just waiting for someone to seek vengeance on his brother until the day it actually happened. Torsten thought himself a defender of the weak. A protector of those who needed it. He was laird and chief of a vast and powerful clan, it was his duty, and he was honor-bound, to keep every single one of them safe.

And yet, he was still dealing with the fallout of his brother's choices. One day, one battle, one victory at a time.

"They'll be expecting us," Torsten growled.

Little Rob nodded, the leather of his armor making a stretching noise as he shifted on his mount. "Do ye want to meet them on the field, or breach their walls?"

Torsten surveyed his warriors, each had painted a black stripe in the shape of cross down the center of their forehead, himself included. His men had lost friends this night. Loved ones. And Torsten had once more failed to protect his people.

"I want to kill them all." Torsten fingered the hilt of his sword. "But I won't. Not the innocent. We'll not stoop to MacDonell's level."

"Aye, my laird."

"Give the order. No woman, child or person of aged years is to be harmed. If a man surrenders, tie him up, dinna dispatch him. And most of all, remember that MacDonell is mine."

"And his wife?"

"His wife?" Torsten frowned, he'd not considered the lady.

Most likely she was a vile wench. Anyone married to MacDonell, their choice or not, had to be dreadful.

Torsten was not married, though he had been once. His wife had died several years ago in childbirth. He'd not remarried, first, because of grief, and then, because of his brother's traitorous actions. The imbecile had sought to marry in order to betray his king. A coup it had been, and he'd been killed for it. Torsten mourned the loss of his brother, but had spent the last two years trying to salvage the reputation of his clan, and himself as a leader and loyalist to King Robert the Bruce. There'd been no time for women, and he wasn't certain any would have wanted him anyway.

"She's to be left unharmed." Torsten gritted his teeth and eyed Loch Carron, mesmerized by the way the moon glittered on its dark depths. Across the loch was his beloved Eilean Donan. How he wished he was there right now. Worry free and drinking a whisky behind the stone walls. Lord, how he could go for a drink presently—another thing he'd resisted since his brother's death.

Instead, he was leading an attack because some arseholes were too stupid or greedy for their own good. Donald MacDonell was both. To gain some ground Torsten and his men had to ride around the loch, which had taken four hours, but they'd been hot on the heels of the bloody bastards the entire way. They were lucky for a clear sky and bright moon, else they'd have a harder time fighting, and he wasn't willing to wait until morning.

His charger shifted beneath him, restless to engage, just like his master. Torsten's gaze followed the line of the battlements. He was unsure of exactly what he was looking for, a sign perhaps, but what? Every time they went into battle, he felt it. That subtle hint that it was time to launch forward. Call him superstitious, mayhap, but he refused to begin a battle without it. And so, when dawn was on the brink of arrival and no sign had presented itself, he'd not yet advanced.

'Twas bad enough that he had to worry about the English and their constant attacks, but he shouldn't have to worry over neighboring clans as well. He supposed this was just another mess his brother had left for him to clean up. Cathal hadn't been good at making allies, only enemies it would seem.

A prickle rose along his spine, tingling the back of his neck. *Finally.* "'Tis time," he said.

Little Rob nodded. "We are ready."

Torsten slid his sword from its scabbard and raised it over his head. Then pointed it forward, remaining silent. The enemy might suspect that they would soon be upon them, but they wouldn't announce their arrival with a resounding battle cry just yet. Besides, if the MacDonells were stupid enough to continue raiding Mackenzie lands, 'haps they were stupid enough to leave their gates wide open for invasion.

They advanced quietly over the mist covered heath, their horses' steps silenced by the fresh spring growth of grass and wild flowers. The horizon winked purple and pink, but left shadows across the land. They kept a slow, steady pace, not wanting the pounding of galloping hooves to alert the guards.

But, even the most well intentioned plans sometimes had to be modified. Halfway across the heath, the sound of an alarm went up over the battlements. They'd been spotted.

Excellent. Torsten's grin grew wide, excitement and anger boiling together into a potent fire that thrummed through his veins.

"Forward!" Torsten bellowed, leaning over Lucifer's withers, urging him into a full gallop.

His men followed suit.

Torsten kept his gaze keen on the castle walls, seeing men line up one after another, their weapons and armor glinting. The gate master called for archers. 'Twas too late to turn around now.

"Shields!" Torsten shouted to his warriors, recognizing the whistle as the arrows flew through the air.

The Mackenzies wouldn't let a few arrows stop them. They continued at a full gallop, shields raised. Nothing could stop them, they advanced toward the gates, not slowing down even as arrows rained down upon them. Only a few men fell, and Torsten prayed for them, his vow for revenge only growing as his losses increased. Four down. Five.

Donald MacDonell was a dead man.

Just as suddenly as the arrows had sang through the air, they ceased.

As odd as that was, Torsten forged ahead. This was all out war.

Then something even odder occurred. When they were only yards from the wall, his warriors ready to throw up their hastily made ladders, the portcullis slowly started to raise.

Warriors. The MacDonells were sending men out to battle. Torsten let his battle cry tear from his throat, ready to sink his blade into the first man who stepped through.

But then he was stunned, almost paralyzed, when a willowy figure walked through the gates carrying a torch. A woman.

What in bloody hell?

Her skirts blew against her ankles, and clung to her thighs. Her eyes searched his, challenging him to stop, mesmerizing him for a moment until he realized just what was happening.

"Halt!" Torsten roared, bringing Lucifer to a standstill. "What trickery is this?"

Was the MacDonell such a coward he would send a woman out as bait? A consolation prize?

Torsten glowered at her, his stomach twisting in burning knots of rage.

The woman was tall, thin. Her light hair billowed in the breeze and shimmered in the moonlight. Her features were obscured half in shadow and half in golden light from the torch. She was beautiful. Cheekbones high, jaw strong, nose regal and her mouth, well, he had to tear his gaze from the lush sight.

She held up her hand, a silent entreaty for him to stop. "My laird," she called. "There is no need to attack."

Her words, spoken with such calm strength only made him angry. His back stiffened, and Lucifer let out an annoyed

17

snort when he tightened the reins. "No need? There is much need, my lady. Go back inside and send out your laird. He will pay for what he's done."

She looked at him with sadness in her gaze and shook her head. "He'll not be coming out."

Torsten resisted the urge to leap from his horse in order to throttle the woman for her insolence.

"Go back inside, woman. This is a man's business, and I intend to speak with your laird."

She straightened her shoulders, lifting her chin. "I am speaking in his place."

"I'll not speak with MacDonell's bait. One last warning— send out the laird."

Or else what?

Her raised brow seemed to dare him to answer that question as well. And how could he? He'd not hurt her. Torsten had never harmed a woman, he'd never ill-used one, and he wasn't about to start now.

"Do it," he demanded, inching his horse just a step forward, hoping to intimidate her.

"I canna. Please, let us settle this between the two of us," she pleaded, her free hand beseeching. "There is no need for a battle, or for more to get hurt."

"So 'tis all right to kill and torture my people, but we must stop at your doors? Ye beg for the lives of your people, your laird, and yet what mercy was given to my people today? The past month? The past year? None. MacDonell has killed my people, ruined our crops, stolen our cows. I warned him that the next time he came raiding, he was inviting war to his door. And here I am, lassie. I am war. I am revenge."

Why was he explaining all this to a wisp of a woman? To any woman for that matter.

His tirade only seemed to make her stand taller. If her chin grew any more obstinate she'd be staring at the sky. "If ye are war, then I am peace."

"Peace? Who are ye?" Torsten asked. "What gives ye the authority to negotiate? Send out a man."

Her hand fisted at her side, and the torch flickered against her tight hold. She glowered up at him with such ferocity, Torsten was certain to remember the look for years to come. No woman that he'd ever known had exhibited such strength. For a moment, he was actually impressed.

"I am Éabha MacDonell."

The name should have rung familiar to him, but it did not. The laird's sister? Daughter? Wife? He had no idea.

"And?"

"I am the Mistress of Strome."

Ah, MacDonell's wife. "Send your husband then, my lady, for I will not negotiate with ye."

She stood her ground. "Ye will have to."

"And if I refuse?"

Now he was challenging her to come up with a different answer.

"Then it is a battle ye shall receive." Disappointment flashed in her eyes.

Torsten grunted. "Then ye shall watch your people die as I have had to watch mine."

Sadness filled her flame-lit features. "I am sorry for the loss of your people."

Torsten grimaced. "I do not care if ye are sorry. Sorry will not bring them back. Sorry will not stop me from seeking vengeance."

"Neither will battle."

"But ye see, my lady, this is not why we do battle. We battle for revenge. For payment. We battle to teach your husband and his men a lesson."

"What lesson will they learn?"

Torsten growled. He'd had enough. If MacDonell wanted to send his wife to do a man's job, then fine. He'd teach the bastard a lesson in diplomacy.

Leaping from his mount, Torsten sheathed his claymore, held up his hands, and slowly approached Lady Éabha. She watched him warily, taking a few steps back. On the battlements, her guards scrambled, shouted and wrenched back their bows. She held up her hand, and called for them to stand down.

"What are ye about?" she said, her voice strong, though her eyes seemed to fill with fear the closer he came.

"Ye want to negotiate." Torsten kept his voice low, smooth, the way he talked to a colt he was trying to break. He held his arms out to the side, disarming her.

"Aye." She stopped moving backward, her shoulders relaxing slightly.

"I dinna negotiate from atop a horse." He continued slowly moving forward.

She cocked her head as if trying to decipher just what that meant. Her guard was down for less than a moment. But it was enough. And Torsten took full advantage. Moving with lightning speed, he grabbed her by the arm and whipped her round. Her back slammed against his chest, and he pulled a *sgian dubh* from inside his sleeve, holding it at her throat.

"Dinna shoot, unless ye want your mistress to die," Torsten hollered to the men on the walls, pressing the tip of his blade against her flesh.

"Do as he says," Lady Éabha called, using much of her strength to try and launch herself away from him. Failing miserably, she gripped onto his forearms and held on for dear life. "I will be all right."

"If your laird wants her back, he knows where to find me." Torsten backed toward Lucifer, the woman incredibly calm in his grasp, though her nails dug into his flesh.

He breathed in her sweet scent, annoyed that he'd even noticed at all. She smelled of sugar and spice, like decadent baked treats that had him salivating.

As they reached Lucifer's side, he said, "Get on the horse."

"But I—"

Torsten didn't wait to hear her protests, he simply shoved her up where she belonged and climbed behind her. Lord, her body felt nice settled between his thighs. Disgusted with himself, with her, for certainly she was a wench, he held his blade at her throat.

"Dinna speak," he ordered.

Slowly he backed his horse away, his men eyeing him as though he'd just told them to find a dragon in the field.

"Ride," he shouted, irritated at their censure. Perhaps mostly because he was irritated at himself. What in bloody hell was he thinking?

They raced over the moors. No battle waged.

He'd abducted the wife of his enemy. Only a man truly mad would do such a thing. This was something Cathal would do. Not Torsten. But it was too late to turn back now. He couldn't very well return her to Strome with his apologies, nor could he just toss her to the ground and ride away.

What had he done?

He'd invited the enemy to his own doorstep, *and* there was a woman on his lap that made him want to lick every inch of her to see if she was as sweet as she smelled.

A double blow.

Revenge could not have gone any more wrong.

CHAPTER TWO

What in heaven's name had she been thinking?

Lady Éabha MacDonell vacillated between rage and fear. The warrior—whom she'd rightfully assumed was Laird Mackenzie—was a fearsome man to behold, and wrapped up tight on his lap with his warped steel of an arm, she had no doubt he'd hold onto her should she attempt to leap from his massive warhorse.

At least he'd put away the *sgian dubh* he'd held to her throat.

That was incredibly rude, if her opinion mattered. Which apparently it did not. What a boar he was! She tried to offer peace and he'd abducted her instead. Had no one taught the man any manners?

Well, who was she kidding?

No man she'd ever met measured up to her Da, he was he only one she ever deemed a hero, and he'd been sadly taken well before his time. Why should she be surprised that one more disappointed her?

Éabha shifted on her captor's lap. The wooded landscape spread out alongside them in a blur of dark leaping shadows, freshly spring tree leaves not being generous at all in giving them enough light to see what they were passing. *Devil take it!* If he thought she was going to be an easy capture, he had another thing coming. She'd spent enough years daydreaming about the day she'd be free of her husband and she wasn't ready to give those fantasies up, especially to a brute like the giant laird behind her.

Mackenzie's height rivaled an oak. She was quite tall herself, and still he towered over her. The top of her head came just under his chin. Peculiar, since she was able to look most of the men in her clan right in the eye.

Just what kind of man was he? Obviously not one she could trust given her current situation. She was surprised he'd not tied her up, and dragged her behind his horse for all he'd been willing to listen.

Éabha glanced behind her, squinting her eyes as he narrowed his gaze down at her. A black smear of war paint started at the center of his forehead, just below his dark hairline, and stroked a formidable path over his masculine nose, and wide, frowning mouth, then an equally disturbing smear went from one cheekbone to the next. A cross. Blasphemous considering his mission was war. His skin, darkened by the sun, had flushed red with anger when he spoke about her husband, demanding she send him out. Demanding retribution for the awful acts he'd committed. The rise and fall of his proud and angry chest, the clenched fists, the bunched and brooding muscles beneath his shirt and plaid all made her shiver.

"Turn around," he growled.

Ignoring his command, she frowned, attempting to match his ire. She should be angrier than she was, but truly, she'd been longing to escape the oppressive walls of Strome for some time. Now, she had to figure out how to get away from this buffoon. "Dinna want to look at your latest victim?" she goaded.

When he found out the truth about Donald, he was not going to be pleased. Worse still, she would likely bear the brunt of his displeasure. But she would put him in his place, and remind him of the peace she'd offered. Not that she thought that would work... He was clearly a man of rash thought, else he'd not have taken her. Men of rash thought were often dangerous and acted on impulse. Still, she had to try.

The danger she was in, or perhaps 'twas the pure strength of his muscles pressed against her thighs, buttocks and back, made her face forward once more, repressing a shiver. She wasn't exactly afraid, though. Given what had happened in the last few hours, how drastically her life had changed, mayhap it was causing a collapse of her mind. A temporary spell in which she found herself feeling things she shouldn't, and not feeling things she should.

"Will ye leave me in the woods?" she asked, hoping he'd say *aye*.

"Nay."

Drat. "I would prefer it."

"Ye'd prefer the woods to what?"

"Wherever it is ye've decided to take me."

Mackenzie grunted. "Eilean Donan is far superior to Strome Castle."

Éabha chose not to respond to that. She'd heard of its beauty, and didn't doubt it. That was not the point. "And its dungeon?"

"Far fiercer."

She swallowed around the lump forming in her throat. Strome's dungeon was just a wide hole in the earth beneath the castle's foundation. A man was tossed inside, the wooden lift-lid slammed shut and that was the end of it. What did *far fiercer* mean? Was their dungeon filled with spikes that would see her impaled before she hit the dingy floor?

Éabha blew out a resigned sigh. So, she had until they arrived to escape? This wasn't boding well. Mackenzie's castle was only a few hours' ride... Suddenly she wasn't longing for adventure anymore. "Do ye intend for me to die then?"

"Die?" Mackenzie sounded startled. Behind her, he stiffened as though she'd just insulted him.

Why should he be shocked that she would bluntly ask what he planned to do with her? He must think her feeble-minded. She again, wasn't surprised. Sadly, most men did. "Will ye torture me first? Or am I to simply starve, alone in the dark, impaled by your dungeon's machines of torture?"

Mackenzie made a sound that very much reminded her of a rabid dog. They'd had one at Strome some years before, rather sad when it had to be put down.

"Ye insult me, madam."

Éabha grimaced, crossing her arms over her chest in defiance, despite the fact that he sat behind her. "I say ye've done more than enough to warrant it."

His grip around her waist tightened, momentarily cutting off her air until he seemed to realize what he was doing. She'd held herself very still, part of her praying he'd just toss her to the ground and be done with her. The other, much smaller part, fearing that hitting the ground would not feel very nice at all.

"Do it," she said. "End it now."

"Ye know not what ye ask."

"I know verra well what I ask."

Éabha was no stranger to hardship and pain. She was a MacDonell by blood. Orphaned when she was only a lass, her uncle, brother to her father, Laird MacDonell, had taken her in on the pretense of marrying her to his son, her cousin Dugal. But his son had died, and so her uncle had decided to marry her himself when she was fifteen.

She'd spent the last six years in the kirk praying and asking forgiveness for the sin she lived in. Praying for her soul, for the soul of her uncle. Hoping that her mother and father—both killed in a hunting accident—weren't rolling in their graves at the vast offense she committed by being married to her uncle.

And now, she'd been compelled to defend her uncle, her husband, against the man who'd taken her. Abducted from the only place she'd ever known as home. Aye, she'd wanted to leave, but on her own terms. These were not her terms, nor exactly the timeline she'd envisioned. She did not have only herself to worry about, but those she'd left behind, the people she felt obligated to protect, especially since her shame had given them such bad luck. Aye, she knew exactly what she asked for when she'd prayed. Night and day she'd prayed for over two thousand sunrises for an answer, for a sign.

Was this it? Was this the Almighty's way of telling her she was not supposed to live? Not meant to give back to the clan she'd taken much from?

Éabha arched her back, attempting to wrench herself from Mackenzie's hold.

"Be still," he commanded.

Éabha didn't listen. If he was only going to kill her then he should just do it now. She couldn't take it any longer.

She wriggled more in earnest now, fighting the iron hold around her middle. "Let me fall beneath your horse's hooves."

"What?" Again that annoying shocked tone.

Why did the man have to continually sound as though he'd only just now woken?

"End me. Now."

He held her tight, the studs of his leather armor poking into her back. "My lady, please, ye're being a bit dramatic. Did ye not hear me say I was holding ye for ransom? I've no intention of seeing ye harmed."

What was he saying? "Ransom?" She stilled a moment, shaking her head. "No one will pay it. No one will come for me."

That was the sad truth. While she'd tried to help them all, they were probably thanking their lucky stars she was gone.

"Bah. Your husband will."

She clenched her teeth, pressed her lips tightly together. He would not come for her, and neither would anyone in the clan. She was alone in this, and as soon as Mackenzie realized it, he'd put her out of her misery. Och, but she'd not seen her life going this way. This was not what she wanted. Not by a long shot. She envisioned herself living in a far off

28

land, a woman happily wed with a bairn or two, a goat, a sheep. Living a quiet existence full of happiness and love.

Nay, this was not at all going according to plan.

Mackenzie wanted her husband. But Laird MacDonell would rather chase a ring of fire in Hell than risk his own hide to set her free. Well, that and the Devil probably wouldn't let him go.

And yet, Éabha said nothing, kept her truths sealed in the locket at her chest. Perhaps that was her sign. Maybe she was not yet ready to die. For if she was, wouldn't she simply tell Mackenzie the truth and let him dispatch her?

After all, how many opportunities had she had in the last six years to see the deed done? Plenty. She could count each and every time she'd run up the stairs to the battlements, or to an open window, prepared to toss herself free, and the exact moment when hesitation sunk in.

"I promise ye, he will not come for me. Not now. Not ever," she said quietly, and that was all she offered him. Angry, helpless tears burned her eyes, and she clenched them closed, not wanting anyone to witness her vulnerability. She hugged herself tighter, willing away the emotions that bombarded her.

Éabha held her breath, willing herself to gain some control. She was no simpering fool. She was no weak chit, but a strong woman. A formidable one, at least she liked to think so.

Growing up within the clan, Dugal as her constant companion, she'd learned to fight. That was what she needed to remember. This was simply another battle. One she'd have to wage with her wits until she could figure out how to conduct it with a stolen weapon. No more attempts to entice her captor into killing her. What had she been thinking? More proof she might be losing her mind.

"Ye can say whatever it is ye wish to attempt to sway me, but it will not work. I'll not let ye go." As if to prove the point he tucked her closer to him, every line of his hard body pressed to hers, sparking a foreign, yet alluring, awareness.

She sucked in a breath, never having felt the sensations that her captor's closeness brought. For in truth, she'd only ever been intimate with one man. A vile abomination. Her uncle—a touch that always left her nauseous.

And now she felt even more ashamed. Damn her traitorous body. Why did her heart pound when Mackenzie's fingers curled near her hip? And why did she feel the hardness of his thighs on hers and wonder at the rippling strength of him? To make matters worse, she could feel the heat of his body sinking into hers. Warming her. When he spoke, his breath caressed her ear and made her entire body tingle, even though his words were threats and not endearments. What a confused disgrace she was.

She stiffened. This wouldn't do. Riding in his arms was chipping away at her defenses, making her mind muddled, causing her to question everything she held to be right and true. "I wish to ride with another."

"Nay."

Éabha clenched her fists in front of her.

Mackenzie leaned low, whispering against her cheek, "I want to make your husband suffer."

Her captor would have a long line to wait in, one that only ended in dissatisfaction. "Ye are only making me suffer."

His hold loosened, and he sat taller, pulling slightly away from her. "I am not a monster."

Now it was Éabha's turn to grunt. She believed him. She wasn't certain why. Perhaps it was his indignation that she suggested he would hurt her. Or the fact that he could have tied her up and didn't. Or that when she said he was making her suffer, he loosened his hold. At any rate, she sensed that he was most likely a man of integrity. Honor. Even if he wanted to kill her. He only meant to do so out of revenge, since her husband and his men had been responsible for the deaths of so many in his clan.

"Then let me go," she said, playing on what appeared to be his weakness—his pride, and place as a protector against monsters. "Dinna force me to suffer as so many already have."

"Ye are married to the devil."

"That may be so, but it does not make me a devil myself, even if it made me a sinner."

"What?" he asked, his tone low, and filled with confusion.

Éabha shook her head, the action causing her to bump against his chin.

"What sins have ye committed?" he asked, an edge to his voice that made her shiver.

Would he exact punishment on her? Make her pay?

"Will ye take me to an abbey? Allow me to absolve myself?"

"Ye shall absolve yourself as my prisoner. I'll not be simply handing ye over. To anyone."

"Ever?"

"That remains to be seen. I have an infinite amount of patience and I will wait for MacDonell to fetch ye."

Éabha threaded her fingers together in front of her. "How long will ye wait?"

"As long as it takes."

"A sennight? A fortnight? A month? A year?"

"What nonsense is this? Your MacDonell will be right upon our heels."

Éabha shook her head, again bumping him. "I assure ye, he will not."

"Are ye not his wife?"

"I am." *Was.*

"Then he will come for ye. He is duty bound, even if he has no honor."

Éabha sighed. Mackenzie didn't know the truth. She couldn't blame him for not believing her when she said that Donald wasn't coming. For how could he know that her husband was dead? He wouldn't know that when Donald had returned from the raid, he'd died, bloody, wounded and pain-filled on the floor of the great hall, for only a few had borne witness, and there had not been enough time for them to spread the news. Mackenzie's men had given him the fatal wounds, news of which must not have reached their laird.

Éabha could have told him the truth. Could have explained that her husband was dead. When she'd come through the gates to negotiate, that had been her plan. To inform him there was no need for war, because their battle had already been won. But he'd been so filled with rage and indignation. She'd not anticipated him stealing her away, a blunder she would likely spend the rest of her days—however long they were—regretting.

As mistress of the castle, in light of her husband's death, was it not her place to suffer in his stead? 'Haps. 'Haps not. No one had argued when she'd asked them to open the gates.

Aye, they'd made a half attempt to cock their arrows when he grabbed her, but would they have truly let them fly?

She thought not.

They'd blamed her and her sinful marriage for the wrongs within the clan. When crops dried up—it was her fault. When game could not be found and brought home to the table—her fault. When their cattle came down with an illness—her fault. When their laird went off raiding—her fault.

And this time, it *was* her fault. For Éabha had asked Donald to steal a few cows and sheep to feed their clan.

But she'd not asked him to be violent. To rape or kill. And she never imagined that with her simple request to help feed their people that he would burn a whole village and their crops. She'd not said to engage in battle. That was Donald's choice, and he'd paid for it with his life.

And 'haps that was where she was most a fool, for when had he ever agreed to one of her requests before? She'd merely given him the excuse he needed to commit such atrocities.

Now, she needed to pay for her many sins. To atone and bring prosperity back to the people.

"Ye'll regret not listening to me," she said softly. In the distance she could hear the trickling sounds of water, gently lapping against a shore.

"I regret nothing. Do ye make a habit of threatening men?"

Éabha obstinately set her jaw. "I make no habits unless they are worth having."

"Ye deliberately avoided the question." His tone was no longer as irritated as it had been, but there was a hint of intrigue within.

"And ye have deliberately avoided heeding my warning."

Mackenzie made a disgruntled sound in his throat. "Keep quiet then. Ye frustrate me."

Éabha pursed her lips. "I *do* make a habit of saying what's on my mind."

That was true. No matter what, she'd always spoken her mind. Her uncle had indulged her as a lass, and when she was made his wife, he simply ignored her.

"Ye're a woman who does not know her place."

"I know my place verra well."

"Then ye've been taught the wrong of it. I shall endeavor to put ye back where ye belong."

Éabha's mouth fell open in shock and outrage. "Hard to do when I am being taken in the opposite direction."

Mackenzie squeezed her tight again, and Éabha couldn't help the wicked shiver that feeling his hard body on her back brought. Unconsciously, she sank against him, eyes widening when she felt the hardness of his arousal against her buttocks.

Abruptly he let her loose, and she clutched onto the pommel, afraid she'd fall forward.

"'Haps ye should ride with another." Mackenzie whistled, and a massive man with ginger-colored hair and light eyes rode up beside him. "Little Rob, take her, her incessant chatter is irksome."

Éabha was lifted from his lap and deposited on that of a man who was not so little as his name implied.

Before she had a chance to breathe, Mackenzie was racing ahead and away from her. What had spooked him? Had he sensed her wicked, and unwanted, attraction to him? Or maybe she was reading too much into it. Perhaps he truly was annoyed with their conversation. But she could still feel the burn of his touch.

"I dinna like chatter," Little Rob said. "Ye'd do best to rest."

Rest when she'd just been abducted? Was the man daft? "Has anyone ever told ye that your name was indeed about size, but that of your brain and not your body?"

Without replying Little Rob let out a whistle, and another warrior rode up beside him. This one less intimidating. Éabha raised a brow at him and the warrior shook his head.

"Laird wants ye to hold onto his bounty. Careful, she talks a bit much."

And once more, she was being tossed to another lap.

Well, fine then, if they were going to play *pass the lass*, then she was going to play *slight the knight*. Let them see who would win.

CHAPTER THREE

With the rising dawn, Torsten realized his battle was only just now beginning.

Approaching the gate tower arching over the bridge to the island where his castle proudly stood, Torsten bellowed for the portcullis to be raised. He didn't slow as he crossed beneath the jagged ends of the metal grate, his horse galloping over the wooden structure and toward the second gate, which was also opening.

Behind him, his prisoner sat with perhaps the eighth or tenth warrior she'd been passed to as they traversed the woods and heath in haste.

The woman was a nuisance to be sure, and already Torsten was regretting his decision to steal her away. She'd somehow, single-handedly, been able to find the one weakness of every warrior she'd sat with. As if the wench was keen on what would hurt most.

He refused to even think about his own weakness when it came to her, or any woman for that matter.

In the bailey, he leapt from his horse, tossing the reins to a stable lad and assessed the faces of his clan who waited to hear the result of their retaliation. They stood in vast numbers, men and women of all ages and positions. Children who'd lost their parents. Everyone looking to him to be their leader, their savior.

They scanned the faces of the men he'd brought back with him. Perhaps hoping to see the head of MacDonell on a spike. But instead, they were presented with the frowning, fiery-tongued Lady Éabha who looked ready to take the warrior she rode with down to his knees.

Several gasps filled the air as his clan took her in.

"Our prisoner," Torsten announced, before anyone could make their own conclusions. "Laird MacDonnell was too much of a coward to speak with me. I have taken his wife, and he must come here to retrieve her. When he does, he will wish he'd never set foot on Mackenzie lands." Torsten studied his people and then nodded for his man to bring the lady to him. "Reinforcements have been stationed at all of our villages. The Mackenzies will not be taken by surprise again."

The people cheered, a resounding, booming sound that made his ears vibrate. Good, he'd not failed them completely.

Lady Éabha was thrust toward him, and he grabbed hold of her elbow, taking note of her escort's relieved expression.

"Ye've been tormenting my men." Torsten spoke under his breath.

"No more so than they've been tormenting me."

Torsten grunted. "Inside now."

"Have I any other choice?" she said haughtily.

He rolled his eyes. "If ye prefer me to put ye in the stocks, or tie ye to a post, I can. But I dinna think ye'd like what my people would do to ye in such a vulnerable state."

"Is your dungeon so much better?"

Again he grunted. Did she truly think he'd toss her in the dungeon? Hell, as much as a nuisance as she was proving to make herself, he still couldn't toss her into the dank dark with only rats to keep her company as they nibbled at her toes.

Torsten led her through the main door and up a set of stairs, entering into the small garrison chamber.

"My laird." His housekeeper, Mary, rushed from the cellar. "Oh." She stopped mid-stride, assessing the woman beside Torsten.

He could not blame Mary for her shock. Torsten had not brought home a woman since the death of his wife, nor had he planned to. But this was different. He wasn't bringing home a woman. Lady Éabha was his prisoner.

"A room for our *special* guest. One that can be locked. No one is to disturb her without my permission."

Mary nodded, her gaze roving over Lady Éabha's fine gown. Curiosity crinkled her brow, but Torsten did not give her any further information.

"Come with me then," Mary said.

Éabha scooted closer to Torsten. He wasn't sure if she was aware of her movements, but he was. He was aware of so many things when it came to her—and he couldn't get the sound of her soft sigh as she sank against him when they rode out of his mind.

He nudged her forward. Partly because he wanted her to go with Mary, but also because he needed to put some distance between them. Every time he was near her, his insides started to hum with an unwelcome hunger he wouldn't be able to satisfy on his own.

The lass was married, and his prisoner. Two very good reasons why he should not be attracted to her. And if he needed a third, being a MacDonell she was his enemy. Three strikes against her.

"Go," he said gruffly.

She looked up at him, a plea flashing in her eyes before she looked away. Chin rising with strength, she held out both of her wrists to Mary. "Take me away then, to whatever cell the brute wishes me to reside in."

Mary raised her brow, a wondering look at Torsten.

"Take her to the tower chamber. No need to bind her as, Lady Éabha suggests. She will not attempt to escape."

Mary's brows raised another octave, nearly touching her hairline and she didn't move.

"The tower, Mary."

His housekeeper did not argue the point as he thought she might. Why did it seem that every female in his company today wanted to dispute him?

Mary pursed her lips. "Aye, my laird."

"Dinna give Mary a hard time, Lady Éabha," Torsten warned.

"A hard time? I would never."

How was it possible she could sound so sarcastic and outraged at the same time? A good actress, she was.

"I'm not an imbecile, as ye might wish. I know what games ye play," he said.

Lady Éabha pouted, though he could tell it was forced. "I play no games. I am but myself."

"Then it's no wonder no one rushed after ye." The moment the words were out of his mouth he regretted having said them.

She flicked her gaze to the ground, the first he'd seen her shy away, and he'd not missed the subtle glisten of tears or the flush of hurt upon her cheeks.

Lord, he was a cad. Not in his care for more than a few hours and he'd already reduced her to tears. Well, she'd reduced many of his men to simpering lads, too. It would be a week before Little Rob felt as though he wasn't a stupid arse as she'd been so kind to label him. Perhaps she'd needed a scolding to take the chip off her shoulder. Even still, that wasn't his way. Torsten wasn't deliberately cruel, and though she might have warranted a good tongue lashing, he didn't want to crush her soul.

Yet, why did he feel the need to apologize? Torsten stepped forward, the words *I'm sorry* on the tip of his tongue, but he held on to them too long, for it had given her enough time to raise her gaze.

Venom filled her features.

He waited, expecting the worst. But she said nothing, simply stared with all the defiance she had inside her. Not a single comment meant to make his ballocks shrivel. And he didn't know what was worse, having her say something, or deducing every thought that went through her mind but failed to fall from her lips.

Her silence was deafeningly loud, pounding through his skull. Her stare, 'twas unnerving. Torsten had not felt this way from someone's glower—ever. Not even as a lad when his governess had rebuked him for tramping mud through their nursery after the floors had just been scrubbed.

"Take her up, Mary."

Mary tugged gently on Éabha's arm but his prisoner didn't budge.

Here it comes. This is when she shouts and rails at me.

But there was silence.

"My laird…" Mary looked utterly confused as she gazed from one to the other.

Torsten let out a low growl of frustration, and took Éabha by the arm himself.

"The keys." He held out his hand impatiently to his housekeeper.

Mary unhooked her set of keys from her belt and handed them to Torsten. He didn't have time to fetch his set from his chamber—left there when he'd gone to battle. And truly, he didn't want to take Éabha there in case the temptation he felt grew and his bed presented itself as the perfect place to see his need slaked.

"See that a meal is brought up," he ordered, annoyed. With himself. With Mary. But with Éabha most of all.

She didn't resist when he tugged her up to the very top of the stairs. She didn't try to slow his pace. If anything she ran beside him as he marched all the way up.

Torsten tugged her down to the end of the hall and thrust a key into a lock, shoving open the tower chamber door. A blast of air swirled around them as though it had been waiting for them to enter all along.

"This is where ye'll stay." He took a chance and glanced at her, wanting to see her shock at not being thrown in the dungeon.

But, he shouldn't have.

Her golden hair had tumbled loose of its tight plait, falling in soft waves around her face, drawing his attention to her creamy, high cheek bones, strong chin and graceful neck. The light from outside shone in stripes of gold and pink on her silky skin, reflected in the shimmer of her emerald green eyes, and the wetness of her lips where she'd licked them.

Mo chreach, but he wanted to keep her in that frame forever. He wanted to haul her up against him and kiss her. Tame the wild hellion that she was, only to have her fight back and—

And what? What in bloody hell had come over him? He couldn't be thinking of kissing her, bedding her. That was bad on so many levels.

She was a temptress. A wicked witch.

Nay, but he knew the truth. She wasn't either of those things. She was a sassy, feisty woman in need of a good—

Lashing. Tupping. Loving…

The harder he tried to rid himself of such lustful thoughts, the more forcefully they barged into his mind. Torsten wanted to bang his head against a wall—or through it.

So, instead, he put his hand to the small of her back—a mistake because he could feel the gentle curve of where her spine led to her buttocks—and prodded her into the room.

"Mary will bring ye something to eat."

Éabha planted her feet, hands fisted and whirled on him. "Put me in the dungeon, Mackenzie," she demanded through clenched teeth.

"What?" She'd taken him by surprise, and when he looked at her now, no longer was she that mystical glowing creature that had his blood pounding with need, but an angry woman bent on his destruction.

The stern look she launched at him was again one that had him questioning just how much power she wielded inside that willowy body. "I'll not have ye give me such a nice chamber if I'm to be your prisoner."

"Ye will remain here. With the door locked."

"Put me in the dungeon." Her hands, fisted at her sides, seemed ready to launch an attack at him. If he handed her a sword, he had no doubt she'd try to take his head.

"My lady, forgive me for saying so, but ye are not right up here." He tapped the side of his skull.

Her mouth fell open, a gasp of anger, but he didn't wait for her to speak.

"I have given ye a nice chamber. Dinna spoil it with your wayward tongue."

Torsten started to back out of the room, feeling the keen need to put distance between them. Lady Éabha was the exact opposite of his wife, whom he'd cared for greatly. His wife had been quiet, gentle. When they'd made love, he'd been afraid he would hurt her. He'd never let his desire overpower him. And then just like that, she'd been taken from this world, her delicate frame unable to overcome the strength needed to bring their child into this world.

Lady Éabha on the other hand was a force to be reckoned with.

"Ye overgrown sack of rotten turnips, ye *will* put me in the dungeon. I am a prisoner and expect to be treated as such. I want no special treatment for which your people can use against me."

"Use against ye?" Torsten glanced around the room at the comfortable bed, the set of chairs flanking a small rounded table, the carved wardrobe against the far wall, the chest at the foot of the bed, the two narrow windows overlooking the lochs and the Isle of Skye beyond. She was mad. Utterly mad. "Ye think the people will use your accommodations against ye? After all that's happened ye are worried about that?"

Éabha looked taken aback, the center of her throat bobbing as she swallowed, and again there was that dreadful silence as her eyes launched one vicious dagger after another.

A silence that screamed to be let out. The woman was hiding much, he could tell, but he could never hope to see it spoken. Nor was he certain he could handle it. In her presence for a mere few hours, he was ready to let her run.

"I dinna think ye understand the situation in the least," Torsten said. "Ye are my prisoner, aye, but in name only."

"In name only?" She shook her head. "Nay, ye said—"

"I said I was holding ye hostage until your husband comes to fetch ye. Until he presents himself to me."

She looked relieved, and then said the same thing she'd been repeating for hours. "He will not be coming."

"Ye keep saying that. But he is duty bound to do so."

"He cannot."

Torsten narrowed his gaze on her. The lady's jaw was set, her spine rigid and she met his regard with an unwavering strength that he'd not seen in most men.

"Why not?" he asked.

"Because, 'tis not possible." She straightened her spine and shook here head at him as though he'd asked to have a sweet cake before supper.

"It is verra possible, as we have just done the trip ourselves," Torsten said with a raised brow.

She looked away, but he noted the irritation in her expression.

44

"Are ye not Lady MacDonnell?" What other explanation could there be?

"I am."

"Then he will come."

Footsteps sounded in the corridor behind him as Mary approached with a platter of food and a jug of wine.

Torsten stepped aside as his housekeeper set the fare on the table, and then ushered in a servant to stoke the fire.

Éabha crossed her arms in front of herself, a protective stance, and watched everyone's movements, slashing glances at Torsten that had him more curious than ever about what could possibly be going through her mind.

"Eat," Torsten said as the servants left. "Rest."

"I will not eat."

"'Tis not poisoned." He walked over to the table, poured a cup of watered wine, sipped it, then, bit into a piece of chicken. "Ye see? Perfectly safe."

She rolled her eyes. "I will not eat, because I am not hungry."

Torsten gritted his teeth and headed toward the exit, not wanting to get into another sparring match. The woman was all over the place and taking him with her. He needed to veer off from whatever wagon path she'd launched him on.

He walked through the door, grabbed the handle and was pulling it closed when she grabbed hold of the edge and said, "Wait."

CHAPTER FOUR

Éabha cursed herself for speaking before thinking.

Wait for what?

Why would she want him to stay?

Torsten's expression was a mystery. The blue of eyes darkened, his gaze piercing, yet there were so many shadows surrounding his face she wasn't certain what to make of him. His entire being took up the space between the doorframe, and while she probably should have been intimidated by the sheer size of him, let alone his position in her life, strangely, she was not.

She'd never been away from Strome, at least not that she could remember, so being in a place that was unfamiliar, facing a fate that she couldn't possibly begin to imagine, left her feeling more than a little unnerved.

Escape was on her mind, but she couldn't stop thinking about what would happen to her when Mackenzie found out that her husband was not only dead, but she'd been the one who set the raid in motion. The very one he wanted to wage a war over. That was a contemplation she'd not yet let ruminate in her mind, for he would surely exact his revenge with haste.

"What?" he said, his tone more brusque than his appearance allowed.

She'd goaded him, and his men. Tormenting them to make herself feel better. But it couldn't last, and now, the prospect of being alone was... Oh, dear heavens... What did she expect him to do about it? Allow her to simply leave and roam free?

Éabha let out a sigh, disgusted with herself, with him, and the entire situation, so she loosened her grip on the door. "'Tis nothing. Never ye mind."

She walked toward the table, her stomach growling. She'd lied. She was starving and thirsty. But Mackenzie had yet to shut the door and she didn't want him to see that she'd backed down, so she turned her path toward the window, leaning against the stone wall as she gazed out over the loch and waited for him to leave.

The rising sun sent pretty colors shimmering on the surface of the water and a gentle, cool breeze, scented of mist and spring growth, blew in the window. The sight, the smells, all of it was beautiful, refreshing, and if she wasn't currently a prisoner, she might have appreciated it more.

"Lass, I know—" Abruptly Mackenzie stopped and cleared his throat. "If ye should need anything, then dinna hesitate to ask."

Éabha grimaced, a bitter laugh on the cusp of escaping. Why was he still there? "I need nothing from ye." Another lie.

His booted footfalls echoed on the wood planked floors and then she felt his heat beside her.

"If I might put your mind at ease," he said. "I would have ye know that ye are safe here."

"Safe?" She raised a brow and crossed her arms. Safe was not the word she'd use. Comfortable. Aye. He'd made certain she was the most comfortable prisoner in all of Scotland. She hoped this didn't mean he would… take liberties with her.

That thought sent an unwanted shiver over her. She straightened, held herself stiffer. Never.

"Aye. Ye're our guest for the interim. Take comfort that ye'll not be harmed."

She didn't want to be a guest. There was too much gray area between guest and companion, and no way did guest lead to prisoner. "I am no guest."

"Aye, not of your choice."

"Definitely not." She bit her lip, not wanting to sound so bitter, but unable to help it. The sight of him, his touch, it all might cause frissons of some strange need to light inside her, but that didn't mean it was her choice. Only that her body didn't seem to mind the close proximity of his.

"Well, in any case, if ye should need something—"

"I'll be certain to shout it from the tower window. If ye would leave me, now?"

Mackenzie pressed a hand to her shoulder, a gesture often meant to impart comfort. What the bloody hell? She stared at his long fingers curled over her delicate shoulder. He, too, looked to where he touched her, and there seemed to be an infinite amount of time where they were silent, standing there with his hand on her, their eyes locked on his fingers. But then, just as suddenly, he removed it, and retreated. At the door, he paused once more. "I am not an abductor of women. That is the dirty work of my late brother. That is why ye must understand ye are a guest here at Eilean Donan. I'd not have done it if your husband had not forced my hand. Something had to be done. And ye presented yourself."

Leaning a hip against the wall beneath the window she looked at him, not in the scathing way she'd been glancing at him since he'd taken her, but as more of a challenge. Challenging the good she sensed was inside him. No man without honor and goodness in his heart would try to explain to a woman why he'd abducted her—nor insist she was a guest. "No one can force us to do anything we dinna want to do."

Laird Mackenzie let out a short, bitter sounding laugh. "A truth well spoken, but not always achieved."

She knew that truth well, and was about to tell him so, but he was shutting the door, the key scraping in the lock—a reminder of just how much of a *guest* she truly was.

A good thing she'd not believed him.

As soon as she heard his footsteps echoing down the hall, she rushed to the table laden with food and ate with gusto, barely tasting the flavors, choking down large chunks of bread with massive swallows of watered wine. When she was done, she drank another full glass of wine as she gazed out over the loch. Though it was watered, she'd imbibed enough to feel slightly warm in her belly, and daring enough to formulate the many ways in which she could escape.

Mary was older, and more feeble-looking. Éabha could shove the housekeeper to the ground, knock her unconscious with the now empty jug of wine. She'd steal the keys and then she could escape and hide if she needed to. She was a good swimmer, she could leap into the loch and swim to the other side. If she could get ahold of a weapon that would be even better.

A soft, slow knock sounded at the door. Or rather from the lower part of the door. Éabha stared into her empty cup. Just how much had she drunk?

"Come in," she said sarcastically.

"I canna."

Éabha's head whipped toward the door. The voice had been that of a child. A very young child from the sounds of it.

"Who is there?" She set down her empty cup on the table.

"Me."

Éabha couldn't help a little laugh. "Me, who?" She tiptoed toward the door, got down on all fours and peeked beneath the crack.

"Me, Nessa."

A pair of tiny brown boots, and the hem of a blue and green plaid gown was just beyond the door. No one was with her. Then there came a tiny yap. Well, perhaps there was someone with her, a puppy.

Éabha sat back on her heels and touched the door, wishing she could open it. "What are ye doing up here by yourself, Nessa?"

"I wanted to see ye."

"Me? Why?"

"Because ye're pretty."

The child had seen her? Oh, Éabha prayed the child didn't know she'd been taken prisoner. The idea of such a thing could scare her. "Thank ye."

"Ye look like my mama."

"Where is your mama now?"

"She's with the angels."

Éabha's heart skipped a beat. "So is mine."

There was a little thump and scrape on the other side, and Éabha peeked beneath the door once more to see that Nessa had sat down, placing a black, furry puppy beside her. The little scamp yawned, and stretched out its paws scratching at the crack. Éabha tickled the puppy's paw pads and laughed when it crouched low and pounced on her wiggling fingers, nibbling.

"Who is that with ye?" Éabha asked.

"Oh, this is Bad Lassie."

"Bad Lassie?" Éabha laughed.

"Aye, that's what Cook calls her."

Éabha laughed. "Is she so verra naughty?"

"Mhmm. Can ye come out now?"

"I canna." She hated to deny the child—and herself. She'd much rather be out playing with the little lass and the naughty puppy.

"Why not?"

How could she answer such a question? Éabha guessed the child to be around three or four. Would she understand what a prisoner was? Well, it didn't matter. Éabha didn't want the lass to know she was a prisoner, if she didn't already. Children had an innate ability to include everyone, and Éabha wanted to be included. Aye, such a desire was irrational, but given that everyone else thought she was their enemy it was nice to have someone on her side, even if that someone was less than three feet tall.

"I am stuck." Éabha settled for that as an explanation.

"I'll go find someone to help." The child started to stand.

"Wait, ye canna. They—" She paused and changed her wording. "I want to stay here."

"But that's not fun. I canna braid your hair from behind the door."

Éabha could imagine the little pout the lass must be exhibiting.

"Ye want to braid my hair?"

"Aye."

"That would be fun." Éabha sighed. She'd been so thankful to the Lord above for not letting her conceive a child with her late husband, and yet she'd secretly yearned for one all along. "Mayhap when Mary brings me my supper, she'll let ye tag along."

'Twas risky, but if there was anyone else in this castle who didn't treat her like a prisoner it was Mary. The older woman hesitated to lock her in the tower when Mackenzie ordered it. Perhaps she'd indulge a child's wish.

"I will ask her," Nessa said in a singsong voice.

"Ye'd best run along now afore they find ye missing."

Nessa giggled. "I'm always missing. Papa says I'll be the death of him. Do ye think that's true?"

Éabha was glad the door between them hid her smile, else the child might think she was laughing at her. She peeked again beneath the door, wanting to get a last look at the lass before she hurried away. Her hair was dark and wild, a little frown creasing her brow. Bright blue eyes that reminded her of someone she couldn't quite place. "I think he only means ye scare the wits out of him."

Nessa made a little noise, then climbed to her feet and reached her chubby hands for the puppy. "I think ye're right.

He always presses his hands to his chest like I do when I see a spider. Maybe he thinks I'm a spider."

Éabha pressed her hands into the floor, laughing softly. "Ye'd be the biggest spider I've ever seen."

"Old Angus tells a story of a spider as big as a man."

"Does he now?"

"Aye. I'll tell ye about it when I come back."

"Where is your papa now?"

"Likely doing his duties. I snuck into the kitchens to see Cook and when she wasn't looking I snuck a bun and ran away."

A servant's child then. She seemed happy enough, and spoiled. If Cook cared too much about her pilfering buns and running away, she'd have tanned the child's hide long ago.

"Good bye, lady." And then Nessa ran down the hall, the puppy's yapping echoed off the walls in sync with the sound of her tiny feet skipping over the wood.

What a sweet child. Éabha sincerely hoped that Nessa would come back later with Mary, but she didn't expect her to. Once they found out that she'd been to visit her they'd put a stop to it, and send her home to her croft wherever that might be.

Her visitor gone, Éabha went back to the window to contemplate her escape. Though they weren't truly plans as of yet, just fantasies. And she couldn't very well whack Mary with a wine jug if the child was with her. She'd just have to wait until she was alone. Maybe in the morning. Though now that she'd thought about it, her plan sounded cruel. Mary had been kind to her and didn't deserve a beating.

But escape was the only way she was going to survive this. Though she'd instructed the MacDonnell men not to divulge the news of their laird's death just yet, word would soon leak out. With Éabha gone, they needed a leader, but since she'd failed to provide an heir and Donald's only child was dead, the clan would vote in the next chief—a title that would probably go to her hated cousin, George.

Éabha chewed her lip. If they voted in the new laird before she returned, then what would she be returning to? Nothing really. As her guardian, she expected the new laird would force her to remarry. She was still young and of childbearing age. Or worse, they could want her dead thinking to break the curse her ill-fated marriage had cast over their clan.

Éabha shuddered. Maybe she wouldn't return.

Aye, she needed to escape, but now she wondered if she would be better off going somewhere else. To seek asylum at an abbey, or even with the king himself. She was a lady. Her parents were of noble birth, though neither of them had been first in line.

She could be a lady's maid to the king's wife.

That would be preferable to a nunnery. With her life of sin, she'd probably be ridiculed and tormented. Her penance severe. Not that she didn't think she should be punished, but she didn't truly want to spend the rest of her days in constant torture.

Éabha left the window for the warmth of the fire. She held out her hands, rubbing them near the heat. Spring had begun, but the chill was still biting, and the tower chamber drafty.

She pulled one of the chairs from the table toward the hearth, settling onto the embroidered cushion and reaching her booted feet toward the flames.

A significant amount of time must have passed, as the room had grown dark with the setting sun.

Éabha startled when the chamber door opened, not realizing she'd fallen asleep.

"Your supper." Mackenzie strode into the room, holding a tray.

Éabha looked behind him for Mary, but there was no one else.

"Ye brought it?" she asked bluntly.

"Aye."

Had he gotten wind of the child's visit? Was everyone being punished for allowing the lass to sneak away?

He set down the tray and cleared away the remains of her earlier meal. "Come eat."

Éabha stood, still sleepy from her nap and lacking the energy to argue. She approached the table where he'd lit a candelabra, and sat heavily in a chair.

Mackenzie poured her a glass of wine and then stoked the fire, bringing the other chair back with him. He sat down, legs spread out before him, contemplative expression on his ruggedly handsome face.

"What are ye doing?" she asked.

"Am I not allowed to sit?"

"It is not my place to say."

He shrugged, then poured himself a glass of watered wine. She'd not realized the meal was set out for two—not just herself.

"Ye're eating with me?" Her tone was incredulous.

"Aye." He speared a piece of stewed lamb and took a bite. Candlelight flickered on his features. His blue eyes shined with the light, and a shadow of stubble-growth lined his jaw.

What fortune—or misfortune—it was to have a man so well-made be her captor. And why in blazes did he keep trying to act as though she wasn't exactly what she was? A prisoner. A captive. A woman held against her will.

Éabha didn't know what to think. Why would he eat with her? She glanced around her comfortable lodgings and at the meal laid out on the table. A table set for a woman befitting her station at Strome, not at Eilean Donan.

"I had an odd conversation with one of my men today," he said.

Éabha set down her cup of wine, feeling uncomfortable with how domestic this setting felt. And even more so with the way he was looking at her—curious, probing. An odd conversation… News couldn't have traveled so fast already, could it?

"How marvelous for ye." She picked up her cup again and took a long sip of the watered wine, wishing for once that she had a taste for whisky.

"He told me something I'd have thought to know by now."

"And what was that?" Oh dear heavens, this was when he'd tell her he knew of Donald's death.

Éabha bit the inside of her cheek, pressing her feet so flat to the floor, she was afraid she'd push right through it.

CHAPTER FIVE

Torsten studied Éabha a moment longer. She was nervous. On edge. Her fingers twitched around the stem of her goblet and she had a death grip on her eating knife, but she didn't sip or take a bite.

He wanted to broach a delicate topic with her, but was afraid to push too hard. She needed to trust him He wanted her to talk, not to clam up. "He told me that your husband… is of a relation to ye."

The lady paled, as he thought she might. When he found out that she'd been forced to marry her uncle at such a young age it filled him with rage. How could anyone have allowed such a thing to happen? Aye, Donald MacDonell was laird, but even lairds had to answer to their people. They were still held accountable, and yet no one had said a thing. Lady Éabha had no one on her side. At least, it appeared that way. And yet, somehow, despite the odds, she seemed like a strong woman. Unless all that bluster was a defense mechanism. Her way of protecting herself and warding off those who would attempt to abuse her. A skill she'd honed well.

Éabha sat back in her chair, eyelids lowering as she took a turn at assessing him. Her fingers clasped the arms of her seat. Rather than continuing to observe her, Torsten kept his gaze steady on her sparkling green eyes.

"Are ye asking for confirmation or because ye wish to add fodder for slandering me?" Her words were coolly spoken.

She was preparing to defend herself, and he had the distinct feeling she'd done so many times over the years. He didn't know why, but that knowledge made his chest ache and brought out the protector in him. What was it about her that drew him to her like a moth to a beacon of light?

"Neither." He tore off a hunk of bread and dipped it into the sauce on his plate, then took a large enough bite to keep him chewing for a few moments.

Éabha followed his movements with her eyes and then picked a small piece from the crust of her bread and brought it to her lips. "Then why does it matter?"

"I but wondered at your relationship with him. Ye continue to say he's not coming, and I canna help but try to figure out why." Torsten took a swallow of wine, wishing he'd brought a better vintage and not the watered down stuff he normally drank with meals to keep his wits about him.

His brother, Cathal, had been a drunkard, and Torsten didn't want his clan to think the same of him, so he suffered through the watery drink.

She didn't speak, but became increasingly interested in the rim of her goblet.

"Lass, how old are ye?"

"Twenty-one summers." She paused for a moment, took a sip of the wine and wrinkled her nose. "Your wine tastes terrible."

He ignored her barb. "And how long were ye married?"

"Six years."

"So ye were married at fifteen?"

She blew out an annoyed breath. "Aye. What difference does it make? I was of marriageable age. Plenty of lassies marry young."

"Aye, some do. Others wait a little longer." His own wife had been twenty when they wed, God bless her soul. "And your parents?"

Éabha pushed back in her chair, and shoved her plate forward. "Why are ye asking so many questions? 'Tis none of your concern, and has nothing to do with why ye stole me away. The only reason I can think ye'd bother yourself with eating your meal here and digging into my personal business is because ye're looking to make a sport of it." She leapt from her chair, the sheer force of her anger causing it to wobble on its back legs. "Well, I won't be made a fool of for your entertainment. Ye want to toss me into the ring, do it! But I won't allow ye to laugh at me. Nor will I share a meal with ye." She swiped her hand wide and hard, knocking her plate to the ground, her wine splattering over the surface of the table.

Torsten had not expected such an angry outburst. He leapt from his seat storming around the table toward her, forcing himself to stop just a foot away. Hands clenched at her sides, she breathed hard and fast, her cheeks filled with color. She was beautiful and terrifying.

"What in bloody hell has gotten into ye? I asked out of curiosity, because when I heard the news I could hardly believe it. 'Twas not your fault they married ye off to your uncle, and ye shouldn't blame yourself. Never would I dare to make a sport out of another's pain."

"My parents—they had nothing to with it. They died long ago. I dinna blame myself." Her hands flew to her hips and she glowered at him. "I was barely a woman."

"Exactly." He thrust a finger toward the ground as if trying to prove a point. His own chest rising and falling just a forcefully as hers. "But ye're verra much a woman now."

"What's that supposed to mean?"

"Only that ye shouldn't have swiped the table clear of your dinner. I've not seen a tantrum like that since I was in the nursery with my brother." Och, but he knew to say such was only inviting another storm of rage, but he had to point it out. He could not have her wasting good food and causing a mess every time she didn't like what she heard.

"A tantrum?" Her mouth opened in fury. "I am angry!"

"I can see that."

She stabbed a finger toward him. "Ye are the cause of my anger."

Torsten crossed his arms. "Am I now? Or are ye more angry that ye keep defending a bastard that would take advantage of ye when ye were just a lass?"

Her mouth fell open, and for a split second he thought she was speechless.

"Dinna presume ye know anything about me."

He shrugged. "I know a little."

"Ye know nothing other than rumors, some of which happen to be true. Ye're no better than a gossiping wench."

Torsten gritted his teeth, forcing his anger down. He couldn't react to every insult she flung his way. Like a filly... He had to rein her in. "I know ye're a spitfire and that ye use all this bluster to protect yourself."

She perched her hands on her hips and glowered fiercely. For a split second, he thought smoke might come billowing out of her ears.

"I know that ye've a temper as unpredictable as flames and oil."

"Ye insult me, and yet ye call me dangerous. If I'm so dangerous then best ye leave this chamber afore I harm ye."

Torsten grinned, suppressing the chuckle that itched to come out. He shook his head. "Ye dinna scare me."

"I should." She leapt toward the table grabbing hold of her eating knife before he could stop her.

The little wench brandished the blade toward him, one leg back, her knees bent, the hand without the weapon pulled back to balance herself and fisted as though she'd attack. She actually looked like she knew what she was doing. Very intriguing.

"Put it down afore ye hurt yourself," he said.

"I'll not hurt myself, ye bloody whoreson. I'm going to stab ye."

Torsten raised a brow. "Ye will not. I will not let ye."

"Ye have no choice. I've made up my mind."

Torsten smiled. He kind of liked the sound of that. A challenge. He was starting to have a little fun, even if it was at her expense. 'Haps it was best to let her rage it out. He'd trained plenty of lads who'd needed to do the same.

"I've never met a woman like ye," he said.

"And ye never will again, for ye'll not be leaving this room as anything other than a spirit."

"Ye wish to spar then?" Torsten pulled his *sgian dubh* from his hose. "I'll play this game, lass."

Éabha's lips peeled back in a snarl. "This is no game, ye imbecile."

"Now that's one name I have to say I'm not a fan of, for I am much smarter than most."

She rolled her eyes. "Enough talking. If I win, ye'll let me leave."

"If ye win, its because I'm dead, or unconscious."

She grunted. "Any last words?"

"Ye're a beautiful vixen."

That made her falter, her body swaying an inch or two back. "What?"

Torsten pressed his blade over his heart and looked her in the eyes. "I'm enchanted by ye."

Lady Éabha's eyes narrowed to slits. "Ye are trying to seduce me."

He winked. "Is it working?"

"Nay," she said, nearly choking. And with that, she leapt forward, swiping her tiny blade toward his hands in an effort to disarm him.

She was quick, but not quick enough. Torsten leapt back, out of her reach, but did not retaliate. He was going to let her fight him, but he didn't plan to lay a hand on her. She was like a child, or a puppy, that needed to be worn out, her anger satisfied, until she fell to a heap and slept the whole night through.

Her footwork was dainty, quick and well practiced, her thrusts just as skilled. Torsten was impressed.

"Someone has trained ye well, lass."

Éabha dipped low, swiping toward his shins, not responding to his praise.

"And they've taught ye to play dirty." Torsten dodged left. "Did I fail to mention I'm a skilled warrior as well? Seems only fair I should divulge such information."

"Pompous arse," she growled.

Torsten laughed. "What a mouth ye have. Did they teach ye that in training, too?"

"I hate ye!" she shrieked, her movements turning wild and reckless.

Tears sparked her eyes, and he realized that this fight, this anger, wasn't all about him. 'Twas as if she were releasing every emotion she'd ever felt. Years of pent up frustration.

Once he realized that, Torsten knew he had to let her blow off steam. Had to let her win a little. He'd seen men like this before, had acted the same way himself when he found out that his brother was a traitor, and planned to kill a mother and son in order to gain control of their lands for English access. He'd gone into a blind rage, wanted to murder anything that moved, because when he found out the truth, it was as if he'd discovered his whole life, most of his existence had been a lie.

Éabha came at him like a wild thing, arms flailing, feet kicking. He dodged, ducked and leapt back, until they were both covered in a film of sweat, their breathing labored. Acting on instinct, he grabbed hold of her wrist when she came close to swiping the blade across his cheek. He tugged her up against him, her body lithe, her height perhaps a hand shorter than his own. Torsten pressed her blade to his neck, holding her hand there.

"Is this what ye want, Lady Éabha? Ye want to kill me?"

Teeth bared, chest rising and falling in erratic breaths, she glowered at him, but said not a word.

"Killing me will not solve anything."

Her arm twitched, the blade nicking his skin ever so slightly. He could feel a tiny trickle of blood rolling down his throat.

She wriggled against him, horror showing on her face at what she'd done, but he held her tight. Every curve of her pressed against him. He stared at her mouth which had gone from a fearsome growl to open shock. Lord, but she was a beauty. Everything he'd ever wanted in a woman, and everything he couldn't have.

Her eyes dipped just enough to stare at his mouth. Without thinking, Torsten lowered his lips to hers. At first it was a soft brush, a simple slide of his lips over her warm, rage-filled mouth.

But then she dropped the knife, gripped onto him tight, her body shuddering in a sigh that seemed filled with surrender.

Torsten deepened the kiss, claiming her with one, then two, then three swipes of his tongue between the seam of her lips. Tasting her. Delving inside her delicious mouth. Dining on the thunder and fire of her nature.

Éabha clung to him, kissing him back with frantic need. Her fingers curled into his shirt, and he fisted his hand in her hair. Torsten walked her back to the wall, pressing her body up against it. Pinning her there, though he allowed her free reign with her hands.

He kissed her until he couldn't breath. Until all the blood in his body rushed to his center, filling his cock. But it wasn't until he grabbed hold of her gown, and was ready to wrench it up, that he realized what he was doing. This was unwise.

She was married. She was the enemy. She was his prisoner.

He couldn't take advantage of her like this, and yet, he'd wanted so badly to sink into the depths of her luscious body, to let out his own frustration. To drive into her, forcing them both away from the present and their own pain.

Torsten tore himself away from her. Staring into her wild gaze, her mouth red and swollen from his demanding kiss. Cheeks flushed from the fight and now from desire.

She half-heartedly slapped his cheek. The sound echoed in the room keeping time with their heavy breathing. He barely felt the sting, knew she could have done better. 'Twas a move meant to show she still had self-respect, and yet, she didn't really want to hurt him anymore than he wanted to hurt her.

"How dare ye?" she said, her voice strong but not full of conviction.

That didn't keep him from retorting, "I dared as much as ye did."

The flames he'd gotten used to, ignited once more in her gaze. "Ye're a bastard."

"Ye can lie to me and say ye didna enjoy it, but I know ye did as much as I." He stroked a thumb over her cheek and she batted him away. "I only regret that kissing ye was immoral. I've never dallied with a married woman."

Torsten raked his gaze over her form, taking in the way her breasts rose and fell, two points jutted from the fabric of her gown. The narrowness of her waist, the flair of her hips. Long legs, hidden beneath flowing skirts. "And trust me, 'tis painful for me to leave without having bedded ye. I want ye, dinna mistake it. But I'll respect your bond of marriage, even if it is inappropriate, dispensation or no."

Torsten backed way, his engorged cock throbbing, feeling awful for the words he'd spoken so harshly. Not a moment ago, he'd told her it wasn't her fault she'd been forced to marry her uncle, and now here he was acting like the bastard she accused him of being and thrusting her misfortune back in her face.

"Well, ye're wrong," she seethed, shoving away from the door, from him. "I did not like it. And I'd not allow ye to bed me if ye were the last bloody man in all the Highlands."

CHAPTER SIX

Éabha was a liar.

She lied to him. She lied to herself.

As a matter of disappointing fact, she had very much enjoyed his kiss. And the feel of his strong body against hers. Enjoyed the heat that coursed through her veins. And the tingling of her skin. The way her heart raced, and breathing grew erratic. The pulsing between her thighs. The optimistic thought that everything was going to change, that there was hope for the future and happiness within her grasp.

How could a single kiss make her feel all those things?

What was all of that?

Never had she responded to a man that way, and with good reason. Before she'd been married, one of the lads she'd been practicing swords with had stolen a kiss inside the stables. She'd felt light-headed and giddy, but none of these other things.

She'd forced herself not to vomit whenever her husband came near her. And she'd made certain to drink a concoction her maid brought whenever he mentioned visiting her room. It had kept her sufficiently numb and had prevented her from conceiving.

But there was no concoction here with Laird Mackenzie. And she'd been anything but numb.

Éabha stood at her full height and stared at the center of his forehead, unable to make eye contact in fear he'd see the truth in her gaze. The truth of how very much she wanted him to kiss her again.

Mackenzie studied her face, expressionless as he did so.

She didn't know what she feared more, the heat slowly filling her cheeks, or what thoughts could be going through his mind. Oh, she wanted to know but didn't want to know all at once.

"What are ye looking at?" she snapped, biting the inside of her cheek after the words escaped. She couldn't help but act this way, it had been her defense mechanism for so long. Attack before she was attacked. She did the same thing with her weapons as her tongue. Hurt before she could be hurt.

Torsten didn't even flinch. "Ye."

Éabha swallowed around the hot lump forming in her throat. *Do not cry.* "Why?"

He didn't move either. Didn't seem at all concerned with her biting words. "Ye intrigue me."

She titled her chin up, wanting to cross her arms over herself, but knowing at the same time it was a telling move—

showing him how much he disturbed her. "I am not a specimen meant to intrigue."

"But ye do all the same." He ran a hand through his hair, a flash of emotion flickering in his eyes before fading.

He, too, was equally disturbed.

Éabha blinked as though something were stuck in her eye, but there was nothing there, only the innate realization of how much this man affected her. She had to get away from him. But the only way to do that was for him to go. "Leave me, Laird Mackenzie."

"Torsten."

She squinted her eyes. "What?"

"My name is Torsten. Ye might as well know it if ye're going to kiss me like that."

Éabha sucked in a shocked breath, her hand fluttering to her chest. "*Me*, kiss *ye*? That is not what happened at all."

He cocked his head and regarded her intently. "Oh, come now, was our little play fight not a dance of seduction?" His lips twitched as he tried to suppress a smile, eyes sliding over her breasts and taut nipples.

Searing heat burned her cheeks all the more, despite knowing that he was teasing her, goading her into a response. Well, she wasn't going to give him what he wanted.

"Go to the devil." She crossed her arms over her chest, hiding the evidence of her desire.

"Well, lass, 'tis a place I might verra well end up. But at least I've enjoyed my evening."

Éabha gritted her teeth feeling so many emotions well up inside her all at once. How could he move her to such feelings? This was unlike her. He unnerved her, upset her delicate balance. "I hate ye."

His grin widened, and she found herself staring at his teeth, wondering how in all of Scotland he'd been born with such an even set. "Nay, ye dinna. Ye want to hate me. There is a difference."

"I want to hate ye, and I do. Now leave afore I decide to gut ye once more." Her knees started to shake. Not from fear, but from the thrilling rush brought on by fighting and then kissing and fighting some more.

Torsten stepped closer to her, reaching toward her face, but she slapped his hand away.

"Are ye daft?" she asked. "I told ye to leave."

"Ye did." He shook his head, as if confused by his own actions. "I'll send a maid to collect your tray, but if I were ye, I'd clean up the mess ye made, else they decide to add spittle to your porridge for your kindness."

Éabha blew out a huff. Of course she would clean up her mess, she wasn't cruel, or harsh to those who served. She'd never abused a servant before and wasn't about to start now. Even if she was a prisoner.

Torsten stared at her a moment longer. A little too long. So much so, that she started to feel warm all over again, and something inside her tugged. A need. A hunger.

Denying what she really wanted, she surmised the hunger must be for her dinner which was now spread all over the floor. She'd be starving tonight. Éabha glanced forlornly at the ground. Ravenous. Trying to battle the warrior, she'd expended a lot of energy, and now had no way to replenish it.

"Please go away," she said, her voice coming out quiet, almost helpless.

But she wasn't helpless. Nay, she was embarrassed. She'd lost her temper in the worst way, acting like a child throwing a fit over a stolen cookie or a gift not received. Then she'd allowed him to practically ravish her and she'd enjoyed every moment.

Éabha turned her back on Torsten, something she wouldn't normally do. She liked to have her enemies in front of her at all times, but the humiliation of her current situation sank in so deep, she could no longer face him.

His boots echoed softly on the wooden planks and then the door clicked closed.

Éabha whirled to find herself alone, and the sting of that stabbed her deep in the gut. But she would rather be alone than at home with her dead husband, pretending to mourn a man she despised and with the people who blamed her for all their misfortunes.

She supposed that, in a twisted way, Torsten had been her savior.

Sinking to the floor, she scraped the food into a pile, placing it on top of her metal trencher. Then she glanced around the room looking for a spare linen to mop up the spilled wine. Nothing. Out of options, she ripped a piece of linen from her chemise, then wiped the floor until the only thing left was a dark wet stain.

She added the broken trencher to the tray on the table, then moved back to her position at the window. The sun had set, and clouds covered the sky overhead. All was dark beyond a few lit torches on the walls and in the bailey. Shadows moved beyond the light. Guards on duty. Servants returning home.

Overhead there was a rumble of thunder. The air smelled wet, felt moist and humid. A moment later the first few droplets of rain pinged on the ground.

Éabha held her hand out the window, rain plopping onto her palm, cold to the touch. She brought her wet hand back inside and wiped it on the back of her neck, still feeling heated from her exchange with Torsten.

Lightning streaked across the sky, lighting up the area for a brief second. The loch tranquil and dark, glittered with the streaks of light. The mountains stood tall in the background. The stone wall that separated her from the landscape.

And a man, tall and thick with muscle. She could have sworn it was Torsten marching across the bailey.

She leaned out the window, trying to get a better view. But her only light was the torches, so she could barely tell if the people were men or women.

Another rumble of thunder was followed by a jagged glowing line of light. Aye, it was him. He stormed toward the stables, opening the massive door just as the sky returned to dark.

Was he going for a ride? In this weather? Where could he possibly go? 'Twas dangerous to ride in a storm. Lightning could strike a man down, or a tree could upend and crush him. A horse could be spooked by thunder and toss his rider. There were so many scenarios. None of them good.

Éabha smacked her hand on the windowsill, perhaps a reminder to slap some sense into herself. Why should she care where he was going? Who cared if it was dangerous?

There'd be no one from her clan coming to save her.

They were likely dancing a jig now that she was gone.

A soft knock sounded at the door. Éabha didn't bother telling whoever it was to enter, she was the one without the keys.

The door handle creaked and then a soft whisper of footsteps crept forward.

"Miss?"

Éabha didn't look, but did say, "Aye?"

"I've brought ye your supper."

Éabha did turn around then to see Cook, as old and gray as Mary, standing there with a new tray of food, a jug of wine, and peeking from behind her food-stained skirts was the tiny child who'd come to visit her earlier that day. She had dark hair pulled into a braid down her back, tiny curls tugging free around her cheeks and the nape of her neck. She was a teeny thing, short, with chubby cheeks and bright blue eyes.

"Well, hello there," Éabha said coming forward and then crouching down to tap the little lass on her nose. She glanced up at Cook. "Thank ye."

"The laird said ye accidently spilled your last tray." Cook assessed the mess on the table but didn't offer any further opinion on it.

Éabha grunted.

"I spill a lot, too," Nessa said.

"She insisted on joining me, though she should be in bed," Cook said, moving forward to set the tray on the table, and picking up the other tray to discard it.

Éabha smiled at the little girl. "I'm glad she insisted. I like visitors and she's a fierce one like me."

Nessa grinned, showing a row of even, tiny baby teeth.

"Well, if ye wouldn't mind keeping it between the two of us. I'm not certain the laird would like it." Cook's eyes pleaded.

He'd not said anything about whether or not she could have visitors, but she guessed it would be a nay, especially with a servant's child. "It'll be our little secret."

"I know we've no bond and ye've no loyalty to me, especially given your current situation, but Nessa, she's a sweet child and I couldn't resist when she asked," Cook said.

"I'm glad ye brought her, and bond or no, I'd not tell, for I hope she comes back to visit me again."

"Me, too," Nessa said. "I brought ye something." She pulled a scraggly-looking purple flower from her sleeve.

"A thistle. Why thank ye." Éabha took the flower from the child's outstretched hand, and held it to her heart, pretending it wasn't crushed. "It is beautiful."

"I found it outside."

"Well, that is a perfect place to find it."

"I'll get ye another in the morning."

"And then I'll have a whole collection."

Nessa beamed. "I love collections. I have a collection of rocks in my nursery."

"All shapes and sizes?"

"Aye, lady, all kinds. Come on, I'll show ye." Nessa started for the door and Cook braced as though she'd have to fight Éabha to stay put.

Éabha shook her head, not moving an inch. "I canna come with ye just now, Nessa." She gestured toward the window. "'Tis dark out and likely time for me to go to bed."

Nessa's shoulders slumped.

Éabha glanced at Cook. "Tell ye what. The next time ye're able to sneak up here, why dinna ye bring your collection and show it to me?"

"All right." Nessa's face brightened. "I will bring it tomorrow."

"Good, I shall be glad to see it."

"Come along now, Nessa, else your papa starts to wonder where ye've run off to."

Éabha smiled and waved goodbye to the little imp. "See you soon."

"Aye, verra soon," Nessa replied.

Cook grabbed up the discarded tray and shuffled toward the door. Balancing the tray she worked to shut the door, but looked on the verge of spilling Éabha's mess all over again.

With a sigh filled with irony, Éabha approached the door and took hold of the handle. "I'll shut it, but I'm afraid I will not be able to lock it."

Cook frowned. "'Twas not locked when I arrived."

"Oh." The word barely escaped her mouth.

Not locked? Torsten had left without locking her in? He'd ordered Cook to bring her more dinner but did not leave express orders to lock the door. And there were no guards standing watch either. What did that mean? That she was free to go? Was he testing her? Did he want her to try to escape?

Judging from the guards she'd seen outside her window, escape would be a tricky endeavor. He was taunting her, that was it. A prison door that was not locked, free to roam and yet no way to leave.

Éabha's stomach growled, and she returned to the table to see what fare Cook had brought her. A stew and another hunk of bread. Wrapped in a linen was a delicious smelling honey cake. A treat.

How odd.

But she thought nothing more of it, dipping a hunk of bread in the stew and scooping out a generous bite with the spoon provided. She ate her dinner with gusto and then savored the sweet honey cake. The wine in her jug was not watered, but rich and smooth.

A meal fit for a lady. Not a prisoner.

What did it mean? What game did Torsten play with her now?

CHAPTER SEVEN

"A word, my laird?"

Torsten glanced up from where he brushed down Lucifer to find his second-in-command, Little Rob, standing outside the stall. The man's brow was furrowed and he looked deep in thought.

Little Rob was probably the only man he trusted explicitly. He was definitely the only one that felt comfortable enough to speak freely, a fact that made Torsten trust him all the more.

"What is it?" Torsten gave Lucifer a carrot and a pat on his rump as he moved out of the stables, securing the door behind him. Though Torsten had sent his warhorse off with a stable hand, at the end of the day he always liked to give his mount a good rub down. It helped with the bonding process. Lucifer worked hard every day, and this was one way Torsten could show his appreciation.

Little Rob glanced around the stables. A few hands were mucking out stalls, filling feed buckets and sweeping floors.

"Perhaps in your library, my laird?"

Torsten narrowed his gaze, but didn't ask his man to explain. If Little Rob thought it was important enough to ask for privacy, then Torsten wasn't going to question him about it.

With a nod, Torsten led the way back to the castle and into his library. One of the servants had lit a fire in the hearth, and several of the wall sconces, knowing Torsten's schedule. After tending to his horse, he typically worked late into the night on ledgers, records, and missives, before catching a few hours of sleep and starting all over again.

Torsten headed for the sideboard, pouring Little Rob a dram of whisky but taking none for himself, even though he wanted to.

"Have a glass, my laird, ye've earned it." Little Rob nodded toward the sideboard.

Torsten shook his head, walking toward his massive carved oak desk, the same one that had been passed down by the lairds of his clan decade after decade. "I'll be fine without it."

Little Rob looked ready to say something but held his tongue.

"Out with it," Torsten said.

"Ye forget," Little Rob said, pointing to him. "I've known ye since we were lads. Ye're not Cathal. I know it. The clan knows it. Hell, all of Scotland knows it. None of us fear ye'll turn into him. Ye couldn't if ye tried."

This wasn't the first time his friend had tried to tell him thus, but it didn't matter. Torsten didn't want anyone to think he was anything like his brother—and if that meant not drinking whisky, then so be it.

"Well, if ye won't, then I won't." Little Rob put his cup down on the sideboard and crossed his arms. "Though, I think the two of us should have good cheer given we've both survived the day."

"I'll make ye a deal. I'll toast to Laird MacDonnell's death when the day comes, but I'll not have a drop before."

Little Rob picked up the jug of whisky and poured a second cup with Torsten staring at him in question.

"I said when he's dead. Did ye not hear me?"

Little Rob handed him the cup. "That's what I came to tell ye. A messenger arrived while ye were supping with the lady. Seems ye've good reason to toast."

Torsten took the offered cup but did not drink. "Are ye saying he's dead? Why did ye not find me immediately?"

Little Rob shrugged. "Ye asked not to be disturbed. I waited until ye made your trip to the stables."

Torsten frowned. "In the future, if the news is urgent, or as important as this, come find me, no matter what I've said."

"Aye, my laird." Little Rob raised his cup, but still Torsten refrained with a shake of his head.

"Where is the messenger now?"

"He's in the kitchen. I had Cook make him a meal, but I bid him to give me the message afore sending him there. He was to wait for ye after finishing."

"Tell me exactly what he said."

"He said that Laird MacDonnell was dead."

Torsten couldn't believe it. Was it true? Was MacDonell really dead? Could he even believe such news without proof? "Who sent him?"

"I didna ask. As soon as I'd word ye were done with the lady, I came to find ye."

"Bring him up."

Little Rob nodded and went to fetch the messenger.

Torsten stared down into the cup of whisky, the sent divine. He set down the cup on the sideboard. When he was certain MacDonnell was dead, that was when he'd celebrate.

Little Rob returned a few moments later, the dusty messenger in tow, still wiping crumbs from his face.

"Your name," Torsten demanded.

"Barnard from Clan MacDonnell."

"Who sent ye?" Torsten's questions were clipped. He'd no time to waste.

"George MacDonell. He's the master of the gate at Strome."

"Why did he send ye?"

Barnard glanced to Little Rob and then back at Torsten. "Our laird's passed on and the lady should be returned to our clan."

Ignoring the latter part of the message, Torsten asked, "How did he die and how do I know this is the truth and not a lie?"

Barnard paled. "'Tis the truth. I swear it. I saw his body with my own eyes."

"Pardon me for sounding harsh, but I do not know ye, nor do I find your clan to be trustworthy in the least." Torsten took a step closer. "Were ye among the men who raided my village?"

Barnard visibly shook, sinking a few inches as his knees knocked. "Nay, my laird, I've not been on any raids. I'm a mere messenger, I pray ye dinna kill me for doing my duty."

Torsten grimaced. "I'll not kill ye for delivering a message, but neither will I heed your message without proof of MacDonnell's death."

"Ye have his wife as prisoner, do ye not?"

"Ye must know I do." Torsten thought back to his conversations with Éabha, how she'd said her husband would not come for her, that she knew it for a fact. But she'd not once said he was dead. She'd never referred to him in the past tense and she never let on that he wasn't still alive.

Torsten glowered at the messenger. Who was lying and who was telling the truth?

"Then ye must ask her, my laird. She knows it to be true. She sat beside him when he breathed his last. Not a moment later ye came riding to our gates and she demanded that Master George raise the portcullis."

Torsten crossed his arms, assessing the lad standing before him. Barnard seemed to be telling the truth, but weren't messengers trained to look so? To have their words believed no matter how false?

"Why were ye sent here?" Torsten asked.

"To relay the news of my laird's death... and to escort the lady home."

Again, Torsten ignored what he said about Éabha. He didn't know why, but he simply couldn't acknowledge that she should be released. Sent away. Gone from him. He'd only just started getting to know her. "Why wasn't I told this when I was at Strome, if it happened as ye say, before I took the lady?"

"She ordered the men to remain quiet."

"Why would she do such a thing? Why would she allow herself to be taken?"

Barnard shrugged. "I canna presume to know the mind of a lady, my laird."

Neither could Torsten. Nothing Éabha did made sense, and yet at the same time, it appeared everything she did must have been carefully thought out. She was rash, aye, but methodical, too. When she'd been fighting with him in the tower room, every move had been calculated until her emotions got in the way.

Had her emotions gotten in the way upon seeing her husband die?

What would she have felt? Relief? Sadness? Fear?

Or had her willingness to go with him been just as calculated as her attack in the tower?

"What else did Master George tell ye to relay?" Torsten asked.

"Nothing, my laird. Only that our laird is dead, and I should escort Lady Éabha back to Strome."

"What could Master George hope to accomplish with such news?" Torsten mused. "If the lady already knew, who's to say she hasn't told me already?"

Barnard shifted nervously on his feet and shrugged. "I only do as I am instructed, sir."

"Then I shall instruct ye to return to your clan. Tell him we need proof of the laird's death and I demand to know the terms in which they wish to surrender to me."

"Surrender?" Barnard had the wit to look alarmed.

"Aye. Tell Master George that since their laird is dead and I hold their lady prisoner that I am declaring myself Laird of MacDonnell."

Barnard started to shake and turned a sickly shade of green and Torsten thought the poor lad might just vomit. He knew there was something the lad was aware of but hadn't yet told him. He was definitely hiding something. Torsten had a pretty good idea of what that might be and he hoped to scare it out of him.

Torsten took a step closer, and Little Rob followed until the lad was fairly sandwiched between them. He glanced up in fear as sweat beaded on his temples.

Torsten made a tsking sound. "Has Master George declared himself laird?"

Barnard shook his head so hard, Torsten feared he'd snap it right off.

Torsten leaned closer, smelling the stench of fear coming off him in waves. "Then who has?"

The lad held his hands up as if to pray. "No one yet, sir."

"I dinna believe ye. Some cock is crowing that he'll rule the roost. Who is it?"

Sweat trickled over Barnard's temple, down the line of his jaw and dripped onto his shirt. He continued to shake his head, eyes weary, lips as pale as his face.

"Ye might as well tell me, lad, or mayhap I'll have Little Rob take ye out to the bailey and put ye in the stocks, let the people deal with a traitorous MacDonnell."

Barnard raised his hands in surrender. "Nay, nay, that will not be necessary, please. Have mercy on me, my laird. Anything but the stocks. I'll tell ye. 'Tis Master George."

"And why should he proclaim himself laird? What right does he have?"

"He was the nephew of our laird. The clan elders thought him best."

Torsten gritted his teeth. "What relation is he to the lady?"

"Cousin. His mother was sister to the late laird. Aunt to Lady Éabha."

"What has been said about Lady Éabha, and her future within your clan?"

Barnard shook his head, but quickly started talking when Little Rob pressed a hand to his shoulder, squeezing none too gently. "That he will wed her."

Torsten grimaced. "What is it with your clan and intermarriage?"

Barnard made a choking sound. "Whatever do ye mean, my laird?"

Torsten stared at the lad incredulously. Did he truly not see it? He shoved away from the poor whelp. "Never mind. Deliver my message and return with his reply."

"Pray for me," Barnard said.

Torsten cocked his head. "Now why would I need to do a thing like that?"

Barnard was literally shaking, his knees knocking into one another. "Master George is a bit heavy handed when he doesna see things going his way. He's not likely to agree with your terms, and well... He does not abide by the typical courtesy given to messengers."

Torsten detested George MacDonell already, now he loathed him even more. "Well then, if ye do this task, and ye return in one piece, I'll allow ye to remain at Eilean Donan."

Barnard fell to his knees. "My laird." He shook his head, tears in his eyes. "I am honored ye would think of me, but I could not accept as I would be considered an enemy of my clan for defecting."

Torsten shrugged. He'd made a generous offer. It was the lad's choice to take it. "The offer stands. Ye need only take it.

And be brave. A predator can sense a man's fear a mile away."

The lad nodded, jutting his jaw and having enough gumption to cease the knocking of his knees. "I will remember your kindness, my laird."

"Go now, back to the kitchen with ye. Ye can finish your meal and sleep by the fire. With the dawn, ye go and deliver my message."

"Aye, my laird." Barnard scrabbled toward the door.

Little Rob followed. "I'll see him back to the kitchen."

Torsten nodded, walking toward his hearth to stare into the flames, the light beckoning him, and helping him work through the web weaving in his mind.

If MacDonnell was dead, why had Éabha not told him? What sense did it make to go with him if her husband was already dead and her leverage gone?

There was only one way to find out, and that was to ask her himself. But if she'd not told him before, why would she bother to tell him now?

The time was late, but not enough to keep him from knocking on her door. Torsten left his library and traversed the darkened corridors, up the stairwell to the top of the tower.

He'd not posted a guard at her door, nor had he locked it. She wouldn't be able to escape the castle grounds even if she did leave her room. No one would let her pass. Besides, he'd been trying to prove that she was no more a prisoner here than he was, just a guest under his protection. Her position was not voluntary, nay, but neither was his. They'd both been thrust into positions that neither of them necessarily wanted.

But who was he to pass judgment on her character? He didn't truly know her. And he had a sneaking suspicion she lied to him already, though he couldn't see what the advantage was.

He desperately hoped that MacDonnell was dead so he'd be absolved of the sin of lusting after another man's wife. But he also wished it were not true, for he wanted to be the one who issued the man's death sentence. Hadn't that been his plan all along?

The corridor was quiet and there was barely any light peeking from beneath her doorway.

Torsten's heart skipped a beat. Annoying as it was, he had a momentary flash of panic. Was she still inside? Did she already try to escape?

He approached the door, pressed his hand to the handle but thought better of turning it. He listened for sounds on the other side, but all was silent.

Just when he was about to burst inside, having convinced himself that she was no longer within, her muffled voice sounded on the other side.

"Who is it? Why are ye creeping outside my door?"

Her door.

Already she was taking ownership. Torsten wasn't sure why, but that made him smile.

"May I come in?" he asked, keeping his voice mild, and praying she didn't attack him when he opened the door.

"'Tis your castle." Her voice was filled with scorn.

Torsten chuckled. It was refreshing to have someone speak their mind to him.

Little Rob always had, but that was different being they'd been as close as brother's growing up. Torsten wasn't raised

86

to be laird, and so he'd not demanded the same sort of respect an heir would have. One minute he'd been in charge of training Cathal's army and the next he was being declared the laird of Clan Mackenzie. It had been a big adjustment for him, and for Little Rob, too.

Torsten pushed open the door to see the lass sitting in her chair under the window. A single candle sat on the windowsill, shining golden shadows on her lovely features. Her brow arched at him, haughty and begging for a fight.

"What do ye want now?" In the dim light he could make out her frown. "Another kiss? Perhaps a punch to the ribs?"

Heaven help him, he adored that sort of greeting. And if he had to take a punch to get a kiss, he'd welcome the blow.

CHAPTER EIGHT

Though she pretended to be relaxed, Éabha was strung tauter than a bow. She kept her back pressed to the chair, hands folded in her lap. In the dim light, Torsten wouldn't be able to see that her knuckles were white from the pressure of squeezing them.

Why was he here? What could he want?

The fact that her curiosity was piqued was most annoying.

She kept her face as even as she could, though she ground her teeth, and if he so much as gave her any indication he intended to kiss her, she'd make good on her intent to punch him in his solid ribs.

Och, but why did she have to think about kissing him? Or notice just how muscled his ribs were? His entire body? The man was all corded sinew and strength, and when he'd pressed his body to hers—

Nay, she wasn't going to reminisce about that.

Éabha forced her gaze back to the dark sky, covered in hazy clouds. The rain had stopped, but the clouds still hovered. Judging from the wetness in the air, she guessed it would rain once more before the sun rose. She imagined a great rain, enough to flood the loch so the water level rose up to the tower window and she could simply swim away.

"Well," she muttered, squeezing her hands even tighter. "What do ye want? Can a prisoner not get a moment's respite from her warden?"

"Warden?" He grunted and shuffled forward.

Oh, it was hard not to look to see what he was doing. To catch a glimpse of his expression. She almost needed to hold her own head steady so as not to face him. Her ears were piqued, keen for any sounds he made.

There was a subtle scrape of wood, and then his boots again on the floor. She sensed him getting closer and then he placed his chair down beside her, and lowered himself onto the seat. She watched from the corner of her eye, devouring the way his body unfolded beside her. The length and power of his legs.

He cleared his throat.

Éabha ignored him.

Well, ignored him with her words. Every part of her was aware of him, and she glanced at him subtly from the sides of her eyes. He lifted his legs, propped a booted heel on the windowsill and crossed one ankle over the other.

"What are ye looking at?" he asked.

For a moment she was startled, thinking for certain he'd caught her staring at him, but then she realized he was looking out the window. With a sigh of relief that she hadn't been caught, she eased up on her grip on her hands. "Nothing."

Torsten put his hands behind his head, only accentuating the width and breadth of his chest. "Do ye find it entertaining to look at nothing?"

A small grin touched her lips. He was trying to goad her, but she wasn't going to fall for it this time. She sank a little further into her chair. "Aye."

"Huh," he grunted. "That's interesting."

"Have ye never contemplated nothing?"

"Perhaps when I was young, but as of late, I've not the time nor the energy to contemplate nothing."

"I know that feeling. Well, I did know that feeling back at Strome. Now I have nothing *but* nothing."

Torsten laughed, and Éabha bit her lip to keep from smiling. His laugh was contagious, but she refused to catch his humor. He was having a laugh at her expense.

"But even in here ye will not only have nothing, for did ye not have quite a bit of something earlier?"

Éabha rolled her eyes, her fingers squeezing tighter together. "If ye're referring to my"—*tantrum*—"irritation, I'd prefer ye forget it."

"But how could I? I've never had a woman fight me afore now. And what if I was referring to more than your little fit?"

"Hmm," Éabha mused because she didn't know what else to say.

"Hmm?"

So he would force her to answer. Fine. But she wasn't going to acknowledge his kiss.

She clenched the arms of her chair, clicking her nails on the wood. "I find it sad no woman has challenged ye before now."

She watched from the corner of her eye as his head shot toward her. "Is that so?"

"Did I not just say it?" she snapped.

"The question was rhetorical."

She jutted her chin. "I prefer to be literal."

"Then ye truly do wish to either kiss me or punch me."

Éabha groaned and moved with exaggeration away from him, scooting her chair along the wood a good foot's length. "I do wish to strike ye. I wish to escape this place and never see ye again."

Torsten laughed again, a low scraping sound that slid over her nerves in a way that was not unpleasant—which only irritated her more. Why did part of her have to like him?

"Why are ye here, Laird Mackenzie? What could ye possibly want other than to torment me? I do not want your company. I do not want to talk to ye. If anything, I want to slit your throat and watch ye bleed." Yet, she really was finding talking with him to be entertaining, at least more so than the silence of her chamber. And she'd be lying if she didn't keep sneaking glances at his mouth and reminiscing about their kiss.

"If ye truly wish me to leave I will. But only after ye answer one question for me."

She sighed deeply, hoping to impart that she felt put out, even if she was curious about what he wanted to know. "What question?"

"Where is MacDonnell?"

A chill snaked over her skin. She stilled her movements when she really wanted to rub away the chill. "He is at Strome. Where else?" She spoke the truth. Donald was at Strome.

"Ah, ye speak literally."

"How else would I speak?"

"Tell me the truth."

"I did."

Torsten let out a low growl, and planted his boots firmly on the floor with a loud clunk. He pressed his hands to his knees and slowly turned toward her.

Éabha glanced at him warily, working to keep some measure of control. She wasn't afraid of Torsten, but she was afraid of revealing the truth. She had to work so hard to keep all comments on Donald MacDonell in the present rather than referring to him in past tense. What would happen when Torsten found out? She'd be no more use to him. To anyone.

And then what would her future hold?

"We've had a messenger," Torsten said. She could feel his eyes probing her, but she refused to meet his gaze. "Look at me," he demanded.

And she hated that. Because if she didn't look at him he would guess that she was lying and if she did look at him, he would know, too, for certainly the truth was written all over her face. A double-edged sword. Which would hurt worse?

Well, she'd have to risk him seeing the truth in her eyes. Working to keep her face void of emotion, her eyes blank, Éabha raised her head and met his gaze.

Deep blue eyes regarded her. Beautiful in color, deep and full of life. Almost fascinating enough to make her forget where she was and what he was asking. Captivating enough that she was willing to forget her past, and dream of a happier future.

Almost.

Éabha slowly drew in a breath, pushing away any and all odd thoughts.

Torsten cleared his throat, breaking whatever spell had held them both captive. "As I said, we've had a messenger," Torsten continued. "Do ye want to change your answer?"

Her answer... Her answer to what? Oh, aye, about Donald. She never wanted to talk about Donald again. Didn't he understand that? Well, she supposed he didn't. He was obsessed with her late husband.

Éabha frowned, but didn't break eye contact. "There is nothing for me to change. I know not what ye want from me, Laird Mackenzie, but Donald MacDonnell is at Strome, or at least he was when ye stole me away."

The muscle in the side of Torsten's jaw clenched. "I'm going to ask ye another question."

"Ye said ye'd leave me after I answered *one* question. I answered. Now leave."

Torsten shook his head and sat back, getting comfortable once more. "I've changed my mind. I want ye to answer another."

"We dinna always get everything we want." Éabha raised her hands, indicating her surroundings. "As evidenced by my current situation."

A strange look came over Torsten's face. "Then do me the honor of answering another question, and mayhap on the morrow, I'll allow ye outside."

"Ye didna lock the door, remember? I can go out whenever I want."

"Ye are right."

"Then ye admit to leveraging nothing as I already had the ability to walk outside?"

Torsten stroked a hand over his chin. "Aye. Ye're right. I took ye away from Strome. I brought ye here against your will, but I dinna want ye to be my prisoner. I'm not the kind of man to treat a woman so foul."

Éabha frowned, not wanting to hear his confessions, or his admissions, whatever they were. She preferred not to think of him as human or with decency. "What is your next question? I find myself growing tired." That was a lie. She was anything but tired. Torsten's interest in her had her feeling alive and wide awake, and she hated it.

"What do ye want, Éabha?"

She raised a brow, slightly confused by his question. "What do ye mean? What do I want with… what?"

"What do ye want from life?"

That was not a question she'd been expecting at all. Especially from a man who'd captured her but allegedly not taken her prisoner. Why did he have to be so… so… so charismatic? Why did she have to find herself liking him? If they met at a feast she'd have been drawn to him immediately. And would have flirted with him when Donald wasn't looking, if only to feel those nice warm feelings a woman got when a man showed interest. But this was no feast, and she had no right to feel those things, and he had no right to elicit them. "I am a woman, my wants are of no consequence."

Torsten raised a brow. "Ye are more than a mere woman."

Éabha jutted her chin, looking down her nose at him. "I did not say I was *mere.*"

Torsten leaned forward, elbows on his knees, eyes locked on hers, and a throaty chuckled pushed past his lips. "Ye know talking with ye is like sparring empty handed with a gifted swordsman. Your tongue has wicked edges, and I find my own counter measures to be dull."

Éabha couldn't help laughing at that, and the tone in which he said it. He wasn't angry or irritated. In fact, he sounded enthralled. Her heartbeat kicked up a notch as it did every time she spoke to him.

She wanted to hate him, but she could not. He fascinated her. And no matter how hard she tried to push him away he only scooted closer—literally and figuratively.

"Then I suppose, if per your analogy, I am the gifted swordsman I need a bigger blade than the eating knife ye provided me with."

Torsten laughed, and tapped the back of her hand before sitting back. "If that is what ye want, then on the morrow that is what ye shall receive."

"I dinna understand." Éabha shook her head, turned her gaze fully on Torsten. What in blazes could he mean?

Torsten sighed and stood up, towering above her, his scent that of horses and leather mingled with something spicier and pleasant. "I want the truth from ye Lady Éabha, and if it means I have to prove myself trustworthy, then so be it."

"But ye do not know if I will try to kill ye. How can ye trust me?" She touched her hand to her chest. "Seems to me ye are a fool to give your enemy a weapon."

Torsten leaned against the wall, partially blocking the window from her view. She was forced to crane her neck to look up at him, and suddenly wished she, too, were standing.

95

Again he tucked his hands behind his head, casual and even vulnerable to an attack. He was completely at ease. "I am no fool and *ye* are not my enemy."

"I am a MacDonnell. We are all your enemy, are we not?"

He shook his head, keeping his gaze intently on her. "Did ye attend the raids on my lands?"

"Nay."

"Did ye kill my people."

Éabha chewed her lip. "Not directly."

"Not directly?"

Éabha pinched the armchair tight. How could she have been so foolish as to confess such? She did stand then, running her palms down the front of her gown, needing to feel the ability to run should she need to, though where she'd go was another matter.

"I've never been one to shy away from blame when it is fairly placed," she said. "I may not have been on those raids, but I am just as responsible as the men who did go, including Laird MacDonnell."

"But as ye said, ye are a woman, your wants are of no consequence. How could ye be responsible?"

Éabha shrugged. "My personal wants are not, but when my people are starving because of me…"

Stop talking!

Did she need to gag herself to keep quiet?

Irritation pulsed from Torsten. She could feel it radiating in the air around her. His hands came down from behind his head, thumbs hooking into his belt, within closer reach of his weapons.

She couldn't do this. She couldn't stand here, couldn't wait in the tower until he decided to put an end to her. Until he found out the truth, which he must have if a messenger had arrived. She knew what he'd been asking before. Torsten wanted confirmation of Donald's death. But she wasn't going to give him that much. And now she'd as good as told him the raids were her idea.

"Why not put me in the stocks? Have your people abuse me until I breathe my last. I do not want to waste away in this chamber. Enough talk of trust and weapons. Do with me as ye intended all along."

"I have no intention of seeing ye harmed." His voice was low, soft, the same way he'd spoke to her before as though he expected her to turn rabid, and sought to soothe her.

That made her even angrier. Why must he be so kind to her? So understanding? So sympathetic? She needed him to be harsh. Needed him to punish her.

"And I have no intention of remaining your prisoner. Dead *or* alive. This must end."

Torsten's gaze raked over her. Even in the dim light she could see the fire in his eyes, the desire wound tautly in his sculpted body.

She swallowed around the lump that had formed in her throat, held her head high, straightened her shoulders, defying him outwardly even if inside her veins thrummed, thighs quivered, and her nipples hardened.

"Take a good look, Laird Mackenzie. Memorize it if ye have to. Come morning, I will no longer be your concern."

Torsten's eyes widened, and there was a flicker of some emotion she couldn't be certain of. Respect?

She had no idea what she would do before morning came, but she had to do something. And perhaps, on second thought, she shouldn't have mentioned that small bit of her plan—of no longer being his concern—to her captor, for suddenly he shifted forward. Before she could retreat, he'd picked her up and tossed her over his shoulder. Her stomach crushed against his rounded shoulder, knocking the wind from her. He started for the door.

When she caught her breath, she shouted, "Put me down, ye brute!"

"I've no intention of seeing ye harmed, my lady. And if I have to keep an eye on ye all the day and night, then so be it. Wouldn't want ye to do anything rash."

He trudged toward the door, ducking down so as not to bump her head on the frame. Considerate of him. But it only made her more angry. Why did he insist on treating her with kid gloves?

"Put me down, ye mangled, rotten sot!" She banged on his back with her fists, tried to kick him where her legs dangled, but he held her tight around the backs of her knees.

"Och, Lady Éabha, no need for all the fuss." He patted her behind, making her growl with irritation.

"Cease this at once!"

Torsten chuckled.

"I changed my mind. I'll remain your prisoner. Put me down."

"Nay." His tone was entirely too jovial.

"Where are ye taking me?"

"The only place I can be certain ye dinna escape—my bed."

CHAPTER NINE

Torsten had not gone to Lady Éabha's chamber with the intent of carrying her off to his own. Not in the least. But here he was, the warmth and weight of her on his shoulders. The fire of her anger lighting sparks in his veins.

Of course, he had fantasized about carrying her off ever since bringing her to Eilean Donan, but he never anticipated seeing those fancies through. Well, he supposed, he wasn't seeing *those* through as much as he wanted to. Simply seeing to her safety. She had after all threatened to disappear.

The way she wriggled against him, her breasts, pert and round, on his shoulder blade, had him gritting his teeth and all the blood from his body pooling at his groin. Aye, he wanted her. Immensely, in fact. But he wasn't one to dabble with a married lady—even though he'd already crossed the line when he kissed her. Lord, he prayed she was a widow.

But, even if she was, he was making the vow, here and now—he might tuck her into his bed, but that was it. No touching. No fantasizing. No looking.

Not a damned thing.

Torsten picked up his pace, eager to have her behind his closed door, and to get some sleep. The quicker he closed his eyes, the better.

"How dare ye?" the lady seethed. She still pounded against his back and tried to kick him.

He held her tight around her lithe thighs, unable to keep from noticing there was more muscle to her body than he'd originally thought. She was not a waif, but a woman as trim as a warrior, but still soft enough to make him groan.

Torsten was practically jogging now. "I do dare, madam, for ye've made it clear ye need to be guarded at all times."

"Ye are not guarding me."

"Oh, aye, lass, *I am*." Torsten shoved open his chamber door, carried her all the way inside and tossed her onto his massive four-poster bed before walking backwards to close the door so he could keep an eye on her. He wasn't about to let his guard down even for a minute so she could exact revenge on him.

Just as he'd thought, Éabha bounded from the bed and raced toward him, her intent to either maim him or dodge past him through the quickly closing door. But he wasn't about to let her go.

And then she screamed—a sound so loud, his ears actually rang. Torsten winced.

"Cease that!" he bellowed, fearful his guards and any servant nearby would come running.

The woman screamed again. Mouth wide, eyes wild. A banshee she was. She was doing it on purpose.

"Och, but ye'll be the verra death of me," he shouted, reaching for her, his sanity close to the edge. Maybe if he just wrapped her up tight in his arms he could silence her.

When she reached for the sword hilt at his hip, Torsten had enough. He grabbed hold of her, whipped her around so her back was to his chest and crossed her arms in front of her, trapping her in his grasp.

For the moment, she stopped screaming, and that was a blessing. He let out a silent breath of relief, eyes momentarily closing as the ringing in his head slowly ebbed, and thanking the saints none of the servants or guards had come crashing through the door.

"Have ye lost your mind? Are ye mad?" he whispered into her ear. Then thought, oh, dear heavens, maybe she *was* mad…

Maybe that was why her uncle had married her. Taken pity on the poor lass. They'd not had any children, so it could be assumed they'd never consummated their marriage. Made sense. It also made sense that her clan would not come for her, that she wouldn't expect them to. *Hmm…*

But, up until now, he had respect for her calculated tongue and intelligent eyes. Not at all what he'd expect from a person gone mad. Then again, madness did not take away from intelligence or the ability to manipulate a situation.

Perhaps he'd bitten off more than he could chew.

"Mad? Ye canna be accusing me of losing my mind when I've been taken prisoner and now forced to bed my captor." Her voice was shrill, limbs shaking.

Torsten stiffened. Well, that explained it. "I never said anything about bedding."

"Ye did so! Ye said ye were taking me to your bed, and now ye've tossed me on your massive mattress and locked me in your chamber."

This was all making sense now. The poor lass thought he was going to rape her. He might have screamed, too. "Tsk tsk. For a lass who claims to speak literally, ye certainly have the wrong of it." Torsten leaned closer, his mouth only an inch from her ear. "I said I was taking ye to my bed, where I can guard ye. I never said I was going to touch ye."

She shivered, and it took a force of will not to do so himself. Desire coursed a potent path through his body. He was fairly positive that if she turned in his arms and claimed she wanted him to strip her bare and pleasure her for hours that he would oblige. Married or a widow, Éabha was an enticement he was finding hard to push away.

"Well," she said, her voice shaky. "Then let me go." She gently arched her back—her buttocks pressing enticingly against his groin—as she worked to free herself from his grasp.

He did let her go—begrudgingly.

"If 'tis all the same, then I'd like to get this over with. I'm verra tired." Lady Éabha didn't turn around. She didn't say another word, simply walked toward his bed, sat on the edge and kicked off her shoes.

She refused to look at him, and he couldn't stop staring.

Without bothering to set them neatly aside, she left her riding boots in a heap and then laid back on the bed. She closed her eyes tight, placed her hands over her waist, fingers clasped. Stiff as a board. If he hadn't known she was alive—

and oh, how well he knew that hot blood flowed in her veins—he would have thought her dead.

"Ye can get beneath the blanket," he said. "My chamber is not the warmest in the castle." In fact, it was the coldest with the most draft. He'd chosen it for that fact since he was always hot.

"I'll live," she said without moving or opening her eyes.

Torsten grunted. "I'm actually not certain of that, lass." He opened the trunk at the foot of his bed and pulled out an extra thick plaid blanket. "If ye dinna want to share the covers with me, I can understand that, but no sense in torturing yourself. I'll not be finding ye frozen to death come morning."

He gently laid the blanket over her, resisted the urge to stroke his fingers over her cheek or to tuck it around her body.

"Good night," he said.

She opened one eye to glare at him. "I dinna wish *ye* a good night. I wish ye night terrors," she responded.

Torsten chuckled and tapped the tip of her nose. She tried to bite his finger.

"Charming," he teased.

"Hmm. Thank ye for the blanket." She frowned, and watched him as he walked around the side of the bed. "Won't ye be sleeping on the floor?"

He locked eyes with her. "Nay."

Her eyes widened. "But—"

"I've already told ye, I have no intention of raping ye. Go to sleep." Torsten walked to the far side of the bed and sat on the edge, his back to her for the first time, though he kept his ears keen for anything she might be doing behind him. He tugged off his boots, unable to leave them haphazardly on the floor as she had. If in the middle of the night he was summoned, the last thing he needed was to trip over his discarded shoes. And thinking better of it, he stood up and moved hers neatly to the edge of the bed so she didn't trip either. He shouldn't care, but he did.

Returning to his side, he unbelted his plaid, setting it folded neatly on the trunk with his sporran. He leaned his sword against the wall beside his pillow and left his *sgian dubh* strapped to his arm beneath his linen shirt, another strapped to his ankle. Torsten did not like to be caught off guard or without a weapon on his person—even when he was sleeping.

Normally one to doze in the nude, for the lady's sake, he'd keep on his long shirt, though in all honesty he wouldn't have minded being naked and shocking the hell out of her.

Torsten extinguished the single torch on his wall, then laid down on top of the covers, not one to use them either. He supposed he could have told her that, but he kind of liked the act of putting the blanket on her. It felt... warm. Endearing.

Och... Mo chreach...

He tossed an arm over his eyes. What the bloody hell was he thinking? *Warm? Endearing?* He sounded like a damned woman, not the fierce warrior, proud laird, he was.

What had she done to him? She was changing him. Set a spell on him.

She breathed so softly beside him. Her body slight beneath the blanket, and yet he'd felt all her delicious length and curves. Long legs. Long arms. Graceful hands. What he wanted to do with those lengthy limbs, those delicate hands...

Oh, for the love of all that was holy, would he get a damned wink of sleep with her lying in bed beside him?

Likely not.

Éabha laid as still as possible, hands over her middle, eyes squeezed shut. She might appear to be calm, even asleep, but she was nowhere near that state.

Everything inside her vibrated. Her skin, her heart, her lungs, her brain. She couldn't stop thinking, feeling, sensing. Every shift of Torsten's weight on the bed had her nearly leaping from the mattress—and she didn't know what she would do when she landed on her feet. Would she flee from him? Would she fight him? Would she sink into his arms and demand a kiss? Surrender to desire?

She wasn't entirely sure. And perhaps that was most frightening of all.

Her status as prisoner of Laird Mackenzie had not been long, and yet she found herself already more intrigued by him than was appropriate given her situation and who she was.

It was sad really, pathetic, even.

Éabha blew out a silent sigh. She was his prisoner, abducted for only one reason—to gain access to her husband. A husband who was deceased. A husband whom she wished she'd never been married to at all. Nothing but hardship and heartache had come to her since her parents death. First she'd been tormented by her cousin George as a child, the loss of her cousin Dugal, whom she had actually liked, and then her marriage to her uncle, the downward spiral of her clan's fortune, and now this.

But *this*—Eilean Donan, Torsten, Nessa, Mary—all of it, them, were the most pleasant things to happen to her in so long. As far back as she could remember. She could be herself. Not what someone else wanted or expected. There was so much freedom in that.

And yet, she was just a captive. A hostage.

Then why did it appear as though Torsten felt more for her than he would a mere prisoner? Was it because he was trying to trick her into letting down her guard? So he could, what? Gain information? Bed her?

Well, her guard was up quite high given that she was sleeping in his bed. Éabha almost reached up to rub her temples before she remembered she was supposed to be asleep. She pinched the blanket instead.

Oh, dear heavens… Another thought occurred to her which made her want to leap from his bed and kick down the chamber door. On the morrow when the servants saw her here, she would be labeled a whore. Once more the place between her legs giving others cause for disrespect and resentment.

That made her want to rage at society. She was not a whore. She was not a woman of loose morals. She respected the sanctity of marriage, all moral codes and the edicts of God and the church. She was a good person.

Though her eyes were closed, Éabha could feel the sting of tears.

Thank goodness for the dark. With Torsten unable to see her, she let her tears fall. It took a lot of energy to always be strong, but in the dark, when no one could see her weakness, she allowed herself a moment of self pity.

"What is wrong?"

Éabha stilled.

Torsten shifted on the bed. She refused to open her eyes, but could feel his gaze on her. He must have rolled to his side.

She feigned sleep. Pinched her lips together, squeezed her eyes shut, to try and cease her crying.

"I know ye've no reason to confide in me, but if ye want to, I can listen," he said.

Did the man not understand how ridiculous he was? He was part of the reason she was crying. She was a prisoner, a commodity, nothing more, and he'd forced her down here into his chamber—

Éabha drew in a deep steadying breath. No more ranting. No more endless questions in her mind. She was clearing herself of everything. Quiet. Solitude. Sleep.

"Lass?"

"I am sleeping," she said softly.

"Do ye often cry when ye sleep?"

"Have ye ever heard of giving someone a bit of privacy?"

The bed shifted again under his weight, and for a moment she breathed out a sigh of relief, hoping that he had rolled away from her, but then his warm fingertips stroked her cheeks, wiping away her tears.

"Stop," she whispered, gently pushing his hands away, eyes opening to see his darkened shadow. "Why are ye being so nice to me?"

Torsten did stop touching her, though he stayed close. "When I went to Strome, I was intent on seeing damage done. But I gave explicit orders that no women, children or elderly were to be harmed."

Éabha stared at his silhouette leaning on his elbow closer to her than he should be. He didn't say anything else, so she waited patiently, studying him in the dark.

Several moments later, he spoke. "When ye came through the gate, and ye stood there, tall and proud, taking ye was the last thing on my mind. But then…" Torsten flopped back on the bed, a whoosh of air blanketing her with his masculine pine scent. "'Tis funny how the dark can make us both anonymous and expose us at the same time."

"What do ye mean?" she asked tentatively.

"I can hide my face from ye. I cannot see what ye think of me, and yet, because of that, I feel I can say more than I normally would."

"To a prisoner?"

"To anyone, and Éabha, ye are not my prisoner."

Éabha bit her lip, squeezed her fingers tighter together, but even those visceral reactions didn't still the beating of her heart. Did Torsten just confess that he was confiding more to her, a virtual stranger, than anyone else?

"Why did ye take me?" she asked, risking him shutting down completely.

"I confess it was spur of the moment. And I do regret it."

Why did that sting? She wanted him to regret it, and yet, knowing he did made her feel… sad.

"Not because I haven't enjoyed meeting ye," Torsten continued. "In fact, and I shouldn't say this, but, in truth, ye are the single most interesting person I've ever met."

"Thank ye," she said, feeling herself grow warm. Och, but she was a ninny, allowing the pretty words of a warrior to affect her. She'd not tell him she felt the same way.

"Have ye ever heard of my brother, Cathal Mackenzie?"

Éabha searched her mind, the name familiar, but she wasn't able to recall his face. "Not much. There was a rumor he was in league with the English."

"Aye," Torsten let out a sigh filled with pain. "He was. He was also trying to abduct his betrothed and her son, some say to kill them so he could take over their land. Cathal was impulsive. He imbibed too much in drink, women and war. He's gone now, but the taint of his actions, it still covers me and this land."

"Ye're afraid that ye'll end up like him." She stared off into the darkness, and silence enveloped them for several heartbeats. "Or that others will think ye are like him."

"Aye. 'Tis the reason behind so many of my own actions, and the reason I deprive myself of certain things."

Éabha saw a chance to free herself, using the only weapons she had at her disposal—her intellect and his weakness. "Do ye intend to kill me, Torsten? Do ye intend to steal the MacDonell lands as your brother tried to do to his woman?"

The deep sigh that escaped him was powerful enough to ruffle her hair. She'd struck a chord.

"Nay, I dinna intend to kill ye."

"And MacDonell lands?" She squeezed her hands together so hard, the tips of her fingers went numb. Though she was the late wife of the laird, because she was the eldest surviving kin—her cousin George was younger—the lairdship could theoretically fall to her. Torsten might not know her uncle was dead, but she still needed to know.

"Do ye want them?"

Had she heard him right? Éabha's breath escaped her in a whoosh. She couldn't have. Why would he ask, or even care, if she wanted Strome and the MacDonell lands for herself? She was a woman. She had no choices. No ownership. "What?"

"Do ye want them for yourself?"

She'd not heard wrong. He'd truly asked her. Éabha was completely baffled. "Does it matter?" She shook her head. Nothing she'd ever wanted had mattered before. "They will never be mine."

"That is not what I asked."

"I canna answer."

"Has no one ever asked ye what ye want?"

"Only ye. And why do ye keep asking? Ye didna ask me afore ye took me."

"I know. As I said. I do regret it." Torsten reached between them, fingers lightly trailing her hand. "I want to know. Ye dinna have to tell me, but I'm asking all the same. What do ye want?"

Éabha's throat swelled with emotion. What had Torsten said before? Darkness lent an anonymity, a power to confess things a person wouldn't in the light.

"I dinna know what I want, honestly. But I do know I dinna want to be beholden to another man."

"And what about united, Lady Éabha?"

"Is there a difference?"

CHAPTER TEN

"Aye. There's a vast difference between being united and beholden." Torsten studied her in the dark. She was rolled toward him, he could tell that much. An improvement. Better than her feigning sleep while she cried.

Hearing the subtle shift in her breath, the almost imperceptible shake of the bed, he'd recognized it for what it was. When he was a lad, he'd crawled into bed with his mother on more than one occasion as she sobbed. She'd been quiet, just like Éabha, but he'd felt it and when he touched her face it had been just as wet as the woman's lying beside him. He'd never found out why his mother cried so often, but he'd never forgotten it either. She must have been terribly unhappy, and he surmised it to the fact that she'd never been able to make one choice on her own. Even as a young lad, knowing most of the ways in which the world worked, he'd vowed to give his own woman a choice. He'd done that for Anna, as much as he could.

He wanted to do it for Éabha, too.

"I do not believe there is." Lady Éabha's voice was resolute. "For a woman. I dinna want to talk anymore. I'm tired."

There was no arguing with her, or disagreeing. Her tone lacked her usual swath of sarcasm, so resolute was she, it caused Torsten to feel a tinge of sadness, for she was right. As much as he wanted to believe there was a difference, because for a man there was, for a woman, the truth was opposite.

"I'm sorry for that," he whispered, rolling onto his back and tossing his arm over his eyes. "Good night."

Lady Éabha didn't respond. She turned on her side, away from him, a deep sigh escaping her. Soon her breathing turned rhythmic. Enough to lull him into sleep.

As the night wore on, and the chamber grew more chilly, Torsten woke with the subtle shifting of his bed partner. She wasn't crying this time, thank goodness. Éabha was inching closer to him. In the light of the moon shining through the cracks of the shutters, he could see the very delicate shake of her shoulders as she shivered.

She was trying to hide how cold she was. He watched her move slow as a snail, lifting the covers from beneath her and sliding under them, layering the other blanket he'd give her on top. But, she still shivered.

Torsten let the minutes pass, watching to see if she'd grow warm, but even the added blankets didn't seem to help. The fire in the hearth was banked emitting little warmth.

Having pity on her, he started to get out of bed to boost the blaze in the hearth, but thought better of it. Rolling onto his side, he wrapped his arm around her waist and tugged her close, giving her his body's heat.

Éabha did not protest. She didn't make a sound, in fact. She snuggled close, her bottom wiggling against his groin. Torsten clenched his teeth, holding in a groan as he stared up at the ceiling, willing the rafters to be more intriguing than the soft swells of her arse, and the arc of her hip to her waist.

Her shivers abated, and soon she was softly breathing, the sound once more lulling him into a deep sleep.

But his restful state didn't last long. Dawn broke before he felt restored—odd in itself since he'd been able to function without sleep for many years. With the rising sun came a shocked gasp and a shout of outrage.

Torsten leapt from the bed, dagger wrenched from his wristband and sword held aloft in the other hand before he could even register what had happened.

Mary, his housekeeper, stood in the doorway with a bucket in her hand. Éabha flew out of the bed, and wrapped the blanket around her like a shield—hiding her fully dressed body making an innocent situation look completely indecent.

Éabha glanced blurry eyed from Mary to Torsten, confused at first and then reality dawning.

Lord, how he wished he'd not been holding his weapons and instead had sought to comfort her. Startled from sleep she most likely had forgotten where she was. Torsten slipped his dagger back into his sheath, and placed his sword on the bed.

"Apologies, my laird, I didna realize ye were still in bed." Mary started to back from the room, but not before giving

Éabha a pointed stare. "Normally, ye're up a bit earlier than this."

Éabha's face flamed red. This was going from bad to worse.

When Mary reached the doorway, Torsten stopped her, if only to ease Éabha's embarrassment. Mary had been their housekeeper since he was a lad, though it had been a few years since she'd seen another woman in his room, this wouldn't be the first time. And how he wished it was exactly as it looked. "There is nothing untoward happening here."

"As ye say, my laird. 'Tis not my place to judge." But she was judging, it was written all over her face.

Mary disapproved. Did she disapprove of Éabha or the idea of him bedding her? Either way he was irritated. Why should she disapprove.

"Ye dinna understand. I merely brought Lady Éabha to my chamber to keep her from flinging herself out the window."

Mary's free hand flew to her mouth and she stared wide-eyed at Éabha. "Oh, dear heavens, ye wouldn't child, would ye?"

Éabha shook her head. "Nay. I wouldn't." She glared at Torsten and so did Mary, making him feel like a little boy about to be punished. "I told Laird Mackenzie such but he didna want to listen."

"Ye make it sound as though—" He stopped himself from saying that he forced her, when in fact she'd been the one to force his hand, because he had indeed tossed her over his shoulder but only because she was going to do something rash. He'd had to stop her. Torsten let out a frustrated growl. "Mary, would ye see the lass back to her chamber. Have a bath brought up for her, and see if there are any clean clothes she might borrow."

"From…" Mary trailed off, and he knew she was asking about his late wife, Anna. Anna had been about Éabha's shape, though Éabha was easily half a foot taller.

"Aye, from Anna." Much of Anna's wardrobe had come from his own mother, as the gowns were made with Mackenzie colors and wool.

Mary nodded in approval, which he found odd. Since when did he need approval from his own servants, and her blatant disapproval of finding Éabha in his chamber had been glaring.

"I dinna want new clothes," Éabha stated, tossing the blanket onto the bed. "The ones I have are perfectly fine."

"They are filthy," Torsten said, taking in the dirt around the hem, the streaks on the skirt. Lord he was a cad not to have given her something else to wear sooner. "Let one of the laundresses wash it for ye. Then ye can have it back."

She pouted at him, trying to look offended, but then she glanced down at her clothes, her forced pout turning to a frown.

"I may be holding ye here, but as I've said many times, ye are not a prisoner. I'd not be giving my guest proper attention if I allowed her to walk around in rags."

"Rags… Ye contradict yourself," she muttered.

Mary looked from one to the other, a gleam growing in her eyes that made him weary. For heaven's sake what was his housekeeper thinking? Her not so subtle shift in moods was starting to grate on him.

"Go, Mary, for goodness's sake, and bring Lady Éabha a hearty meal. She looks ready to blow away."

Éabha let out a disgruntled huff and marched toward the door after Mary.

"My lady, wait," Torsten called, walking toward her. "Mary, she'll meet ye upstairs."

Mary nodded and left the chamber.

As he approached, Éabha glanced down at his legs with widened eyes and he remembered that he only wore a shirt. Well, he didn't care. She'd rubbed her saucy little arse all over him last night. Perhaps not to be seductive, but all the same, it wasn't as if he were completely nude.

"What?" she asked, an attempt at being abrupt.

Torsten held out his arms to the side. Saints, but he was going to have a little fun teasing her. "I but wanted to point out that I did not attempt to rape ye last night, even if ye did entice me."

Éabha winged a brow, pursing her lips. "Entice ye?"

He crossed his arms, and gazed down at her. "Ye rubbed all over me."

Her regard was scathing, incredulous. "I did no such thing."

Torsten grinned. "Och, but ye did, when ye were shivering."

"I never shiver." She fisted her hands rigidly at her side to hide a very obvious shudder.

Torsten took a few more steps, closing the distance between them. "That sounds like a challenge."

"A challenge? Now ye're the one who is mad." But she backed up a step, her body language telling him she wasn't so certain.

"Mayhap." All thoughts of teasing left. He wanted to feel her shiver in his arms.

Éabha bit her lip, her eyes sliding over his face toward his mouth. "Can I leave now?"

"To have your bath and break your fast?" He imagined her lounging in the water, one long leg draped over the side, steam rising and an enticing smile on her lips. That was not good. Blood pooled toward his middle.

"Where else? Likely ye'll not allow me to leave the castle."

"Not yet."

He'd kept his voice low, not menacing, but still her throat bobbed wildly in response.

Éabha cleared her throat, crossing her arms over her middle as though to protect herself. "What does that mean— not yet?"

She backed away until her rear hit the wall just beside the doorway. Torsten followed.

He pressed a hand beside her head, caging her in, liking the way her body leaned toward him even when she tried to back away.

"It means exactly what it sounds like."

"Ye will set me free."

Torsten shrugged. "I would set ye free much sooner if ye were honest with me."

"I have been honest." But when she said it, she glanced away for a fraction of a second.

Liar.

"As I said, when ye're honest with me, and perhaps with yourself."

She inched closer to the door, and Torsten let her.

Lord, even in the morning she was an enticing specimen. He wanted to scoop her up and carry her back to his bed, press her into the mattress and show her just how much he enjoyed her company.

Ballocks… Enjoyed her company?

He barely knew the chit, and already he was thinking like a romantic sot. Nay, it wasn't his mind thinking, but the other part. His cock, swollen and filled with craving. Except, it wasn't just lusting for her body. He liked the chase, too. And the quiet in the middle of the night.

Not since his wife had he wanted a woman more. Did that make him a cad? Was he sullying Anna's memory?

"Go take your bath," Torsten croaked, his gaze raking hotly over her frame. "Leave me. Now."

If she didn't walk out that door in the next ten seconds he was going to shut and bar it, keeping her in his chamber the rest of the day.

Éabha must have seen the desire in his eyes, for she gasped and ducked beneath his arm, hurrying from the room.

Torsten slammed the door shut behind her, and let out a growl of frustration.

What the bloody hell was he doing? Toying with her. *And himself.* The messenger said Laird MacDonell was dead. If he was, then Torsten had nothing else to hold against the MacDonell clan. He should return her to Strome with a stern message. That any more disturbances on his land would mean all out war, and this time he wouldn't hesitate to burn their walls to the ground.

That would be the right thing to do.

So why did he keep hesitating?

Why did he not simply open the door, shout for Little Rob and tell him to take her away?

Torsten grabbed hold of the handle, yanked open the door, prepared to do just that, but Éabha stood right outside, her hand raised, poised to knock, stopping him in his tracks.

"My laird," she started, and stopped.

Torsten grabbed her wrist and yanked her back into his room. He shut the door and pressed her up against it, his body colliding with hers. Heat to heat.

"I told ye to leave," he said, searching her face, her eyes, looking for permission.

Desire flared, her pupils dilating. "I know, but—"

"Do ye not realize what ye're doing to me?" He slid his hand over her hip, pressed his erection against her belly, and drank in her gasp.

"I… I am not doing anything," she said.

Torsten pressed his forehead to hers, twirled one of her golden locks around his finger. "I'll give ye one more chance. One more chance to escape me, else I'm going to kiss ye, Éabha."

"Kiss me?" She didn't leave, in fact, her hips pressed a little closer to his.

Mo chreach. How was he supposed to handle this?

"Leave, Éabha. Go now, for I canna help myself. The moment I saw ye standing so tall and proud… I wanted ye. And last night, pressed against me, it was all I could do not to take ye then and there. Go. Before it's too late."

His mouth was only an inch from hers. One slight shift forward and he'd press his lips against her softness. Torsten breathed in her scent, delighting in the faintly floral fragrance that clung to her wild hair.

Still, she didn't move.

"Are ye testing me, lass? Do ye think I will not kiss ye again?"

She shook her head. Did she not test him or did she not think he'd kiss her? Torsten didn't care. He could barely think beyond her sweet mouth and emerald eyes that looked just as hungry as he felt.

Keeping his gaze locked on hers, he closed the distance between them, brushing his mouth gently back and forth over her soft lips. Éabha sighed, didn't try to escape, but tilted her chin, pressing her mouth closer to his.

She didn't close her eyes either, but challenged him with her gaze as she kissed him back. Kissed him back eagerly. Exploring, testing.

Sweet Jesu, who was this woman?

Torsten held one of her hips tighter, slid his free hand along her jaw, threading it into her hair. He glided his tongue along the seam of her lips, thrusting inside when she gasped in pleasure. And then she covered his hand with her own, wrapped her other arm around his back. Her touch was tentative at first, searching, and then as their kiss deepened, her fingers pressed urgently to the muscles along his spine.

He tasted her sweetness, drank of her, all while they kept their eyes locked on one another.

Never had he kissed someone this way. Never had he wanted to, but he found the way she intently stared back at him, the way her pupils dilated, all too intriguing. All too enchanting. All caution tossed to the wind. They challenged each other. Who would be the first to surrender? God help him, he didn't want it to end.

She held him captivated, and he could have stayed right here, like this, for hours. Tasting. Exploring. Claiming.

Claiming?

Aye, he was claiming her. For his own. For this moment, she was his and his alone.

Torsten growled low in his throat, anchoring her to the door with his body, feeling the softness of her breasts, the firmness of her thighs, the curves of her hips, and cursing himself for every move, word and touch.

CHAPTER ELEVEN

Pinned to the door by hard muscle and raw passion, Éabha could have been dreaming. A very wicked, sensual dream. But she wasn't. This was real.

And she was most certainly going to be labeled a hussy, but she couldn't help it. Couldn't stop the way her hips pushed forward, seeking the heat and hardness of his body, the way her hands explored, and her tongue—

Sweet heavens, she was winding her tongue wildly with his.

And she shouldn't. She should push him away, but…

Oh, her body—

Every inch of her vibrated, pulsed, sang with delight and madness.

Aye, utter, decadent insanity.

There was no thinking. There was no reasoning. There was no right or wrong. Only the need for him to never stop.

That was the only way to explain why this was happening and why she wasn't pulling away. She'd fought Torsten—literally—since the moment he'd captured her and now, here she was indulging in a purely carnal whim.

A whim she shouldn't have the luxury of acting upon. One in which she'd never indulged before. And probably would never get to indulge in again. Except this wasn't the first time he'd kissed her and the way their bodies collided promised it wouldn't be the last.

Did she want that sort of promise? The sort of tangible responsibility that came with kissing a man with such passion?

Oh, be gone with ye, reason and logic! This felt too good to stop. Just a little longer. A memory to savor on those long, lonely nights that were certain to be her future.

She'd never felt this way before. Never had cause to feel this way. This good. She never realized that a man's touch could elicit such a response from her body, or such impulsive, instinctual reactions. She didn't know how she knew what to do. She mimicked him. But most of it was natural curiosity.

"Éabha," Torsten was murmuring against her mouth, then he was sliding his lips along the line of her jaw, down her neck and nibbling on her collarbone. "Why, Éabha?" he asked.

She didn't know the answer, for she wasn't aware of the question.

"I shouldn't," he said, tugging on the fabric at her shoulder with his teeth, his hands skimming her waist.

Heat seared where his mouth touched her, flaming down her arms to her breasts. Her nipples hardened, aching, swollen, needing.

Éabha's eyes rolled back into her head as pleasure radiated all over, then pummeled her at her core.

"Why, indeed?" she gasped. "Nay we shouldn't..." But neither of them stopped.

He kissed the side of her neck, gently nibbling on her jaw, then spread his hands wide over her ribs, and brushed his thumbs on the undersides of her breasts.

"Ye are married. I dinna dally with married women." But the way he was pressing his arousal, hard and thick, against her hip said otherwise.

She should tell him she was no longer married, put him out of his misery, but then why would he keep her here?

But still... She should tell him. Leaving was probably best, now that he was cupping her breasts, rubbing her hardened nipples and making her want to strip out of her clothes and lay herself out for him like an offering to the ancient gods.

"I am..." She was about to tell him the truth, about to utter the words she'd kept locked up since meeting him, but stopped herself.

Torsten backed away from her, thrusting his hands into his hair, leaving her cold and hot all at once. He glanced at her with trepidation, irritation and flaming desire. The man was just as much at war with himself as he was with her.

"I'm sorry. I dinna know what came over me," he said.

Éabha straightened on unsteady legs, working to fix her hair which was certainly a fright. Her lips felt swollen, and the skin of her jaw was raw from where his stubble had scraped against her. She wanted to tell him to throw caution to the wind, apologies be damned. But this was probably for the best.

"The same thing that came over me," she whispered, softly yet full of confidence. Éabha straightened her shoulders. "I will not apologize for it."

She spoke the truth. Why should she be sorry for how she felt, for her longing to experience a kiss so heated her toes curled into the floor—still curled.

Torsten looked surprised. The corner of his lip twitched, and she could see just a twinge of satisfaction in his eyes. She hoped her own gaze mirrored the same approval.

Well, if she couldn't be completely honest with him about Donald, then at least she could be honest about this. "I've never been kissed like that. I shan't deny that I liked it."

Torsten grinned, his lips curling upward in a wicked, roguish sort of way. "Ye told me ye didna like my kiss afore."

Éabha pursed her lips. "That is what a lass is supposed to say. But as ye know, I never say what I'm supposed to. I did like it. Too much." She smoothed the skirts of her gown. "And now I'm leaving to go take my bath and I will not think about this moment ever again." Now, that was a lie. 'Twas more likely that the Highlands would never see a winter again than she'd not think of his kiss.

"Nay?"

"Nay."

"I confess, my lady, I'm going to have a hard time not thinking about this moment for the rest of the week, possibly the year. Most likely I'll never get it cleared from my mind." He swiped his hands over his face before settling them back on his hips. "Ye're a delicious and high-spirited lass."

Éabha worked to clear her throat. She'd never received such praise, nor been told she was delicious. She lifted her chin, and put her hands on her hips to steady herself, but mostly to keep from reaching for him and begging him to kiss her once more. "I'm certain ye've got a fair number of lasses willing to slip between your sheets."

"Aye." He nodded, his gaze raking hotly over her form. "But there are none I'd allow, save ye."

Éabha tilted her head, studying his well formed body, and the casual way in which he stood. There was a connection between them. She'd felt it from the start, and the more time they spent together the stronger it became. But she didn't want to acknowledge it.

"Why only me?" she asked. Did she really want to know the answer? Why didn't she keep her mouth shut and leave? She had no business being so brazen.

Her eyes slid to the very bed he spoke of, but she forced them back to his face.

Having seen her roving look, he raised a brow, drawing her attention to his eyes, filled with mystery, danger and desire. The color of bluebells, shaped like almonds and fringed with long, dark lashes, they drew her in. Eyes that she could have stared into all day long—and would have if he'd kept kissing her.

"There are many reasons, all of which will likely bore ye." But he spoke with a lilt in his voice that begged her to explore his answer.

Éabha tossed her hair, feeling more and more confident, a glow from the inside spreading outward. How was it possible for him to make her feel this way? She felt... Beautiful. Desirable. Intriguing. "I am not easily bored, Mackenzie, and if I didna truly want to know, I'd not have asked."

He cocked his head at her, grabbed up his plaid and slung it around his hips, haphazardly attaching his belt. She bit her lip, trying to force the heat burning her face to abate. It was obvious why he'd felt the need to cover up. The front of his shirt had been jutting out unnaturally—or perhaps what was very natural given his state of... desire. She swallowed hard around the knot forming in her throat and forced herself not to think about his erection, or the way it had felt pressed to her hip.

"I've mentioned it to ye afore now. I dinna want to gain the same reputation as my brother. He was a whoremonger, a rapist—not a man I want to emulate. On top of that, I lost my wife some years ago."

The desire and heat that had been battling in her nether regions took a dive somewhere near her feet, leaving her feeling cold and uncomfortable. She'd not realized he'd been married before. A widower. "I'm verra sorry for your loss, and for... for taking advantage of that, though I didn't know it. I should have asked. As for your brother, I'm certain people know the difference."

"Och, lass, I was the one taking advantage. It's been many years since Anna passed, and she was ill to begin with. A weak disposition from birth. And, my brother, Cathal, well, there is a saying that often the apple does not fall far from the tree."

"Are ye a rapist?"

Torsten frowned, offended that she would suggest it. "Nay."

"Was your father a rapist?"

He crossed his arms over his chest, even more offended. "Nay."

127

"Was he a promiscuous man?"

"Nay. Not that I know of. What sort of questions are these?" His tone was filled with warning.

Éabha held out her hands in surrender, a soft smile touching her lips. "I but wanted to point out that there was one bad apple in the barrel and as ye said, he is gone now."

Torsten quirked a smile, his stiff stance easing. "Aye, a good point to have made."

"And certainly in the time that he's been gone ye've proven yourself worthy have ye not?"

"I have tried. But your husband has been the bane of my existence. Yet another reason why I should not have…" He waved his arm in the direction of the wall where she'd been very passionately pressed.

A slight twinge of desire passed through her, but she worked to tamp it down. There was more than just passion sparking between them. Torsten had told her much of what went on in his mind, and she had, too. They'd breached a level she would have rather they held back from, but which they seemed incapable of fighting off.

"I have something to confess." Éabha's hands started to shake. What was she doing? She'd spoken before thinking, caught up in the moment.

She knew at this point Torsten would not harm her, so it was better to tell him the truth than for him to find out from someone else. To show him she trusted him with her secrets just as he seemed to trust her.

"Donald, he is—"

"Papa!" The chamber door flew open and a child ran into the room.

A tiny black-haired imp ran straight for Torsten, and leapt into his arms. A rambunctious tug at Éabha's skirt had her looking down to find the same black puppy that had been with the child who'd visited her outside her tower door. The puppy had a mouthful of her hem and was growling and yanking it in a one-sided game of tug-of-war.

"Stop that," Éabha said, with a stunned laugh.

Torsten was a father?

He'd just told her he had been married… But he didn't say he was a father.

Éabha bent to remove her gown from the puppy's mouth and it rolled over onto its back, wiggling and waiting for a belly rub.

"Lady!" the child yelled, and scrambled from Torsten's grip.

"Nessa, dinna," Torsten said, but it was too late.

Nessa had thrown herself into Éabha's arms and since she was squatted down petting the puppy, she was thrown off balance tumbling backward with the child on top of her.

Nessa placed small, warm and sort of sticky, hands on either side of Éabha's face. "Now I can braid your hair."

Éabha was tongue-tied, so she simply nodded.

Nessa was Torsten's daughter. The little pixie she'd thought belonged to a servant was in fact the daughter of the laird.

"Where is your nursemaid?" Torsten asked.

Nessa leapt to her feet and put her hands on her hips. "She fell asleep again, Papa. I found Cook and she fed me a roll."

"Where is she sleeping?" Éabha couldn't help but ask.

Nessa shrugged. "We were outside for a walk."

Torsten rolled his eyes and let out an irritated growl. He scooped up Nessa and yelped when the puppy bit his ankle.

"Ye'd best get back to Mary," he said to Éabha. "Your bath will be cold."

Nessa wrinkled her nose and made a disgusted noise. "I hate baths. A cold one would be verra bad."

Torsten sniffed her and pretended to smell something foul. "Oh, dear heavens, I can tell."

Nessa giggled and pressed her forehead to his. "Dinna tell my nurse."

Éabha could have melted into the floor at witnessing such a tender moment between father and daughter. The man was powerful, a skilled warrior, a good leader, a protector, an excellent kisser, respected women's rights and now he was a good father, too? Why couldn't Torsten have a horrid temperament and pockmarks all over his face? It would make leaving that much easier. And she knew he wouldn't let her stay. No matter how strong the connection between them was, it didn't erase the fact that she was his enemy.

"Good to see ye again, Nessa," Éabha said, then scooted out of the room, realizing too late she'd let it slip that this was not her first time meeting the little girl.

"Again?" Torsten called after her.

But Éabha didn't stop walking. In fact, she picked up the pace, hurrying down the corridor toward the stairwell. She could hear Torsten come out of his chamber, perhaps wanting to follow, but then he growled, "Ow," and she was certain the puppy had nipped him again.

She laughed behind her hand and hurried up the stairs to her tower room, confident that he'd have to deal with his two surprise visitors before coming after her, and by then, Éabha could come up with some reason as to why she'd met his daughter before. One that wouldn't get everyone in trouble.

Mayhap she could tell him she'd seen the child outside, and called a greeting to her.

She'd also have to find another chance to tell him about Donald, since she'd been interrupted. Perhaps it was a good thing. It bought her some time to come up with an alternate plan. She wasn't going to try to escape, not yet. In fact, she was growing more and more confident that Torsten just may just let her go. He was a good man. He wouldn't hold her prisoner if there was no reason to, and though before she thought confessing Donald's death would seal her fate, perhaps now it was actually the key to setting her free.

In her chamber, Mary had set up a thick wooden tub, lined it with linen and steaming water filled its depths.

"I worried ye'd not come and all this would go to waste," Mary murmured. "We've kept it hot with hearth warmed rocks."

"I'd not waste it, Mary. My thanks for having it arranged."

"Shall I stay to help ye?"

"Nay. I can manage."

Mary eyed her funny. "I think I'd better stay. Ye made mention of offing yourself, and drowning is a way in which ye could see to it."

"Are ye offering me another option?" Éabha said, a teasing glint in her eyes.

Mary looked horrified. "Nay, nay, that was not what I meant at all."

"I'm jesting with ye. I promise not to off myself." Éabha untied the ribbon in her hair and worked the braid from its weave.

131

"I think his lairdship would want me to stay."

Éabha rolled here eyes. "Fine, if ye must, but I can handle washing myself. We both know I'm not a guest."

"His lairdship says ye're a guest."

Éabha grunted, then started to remove her gown, but found it difficult given it was tied in the back. Mary moved to help her, and when she was finally divested of it, she sank into the steaming water with a sigh. Oh, how it felt wonderful to scrub herself clean. Almost as though she were scrubbing away not only several day's worth of grime, but also her past.

Leaning back into the tub to soak, she stared up at the rafters and listened to Mary chatter on about something that happened in the kitchens earlier. Éabha realized that for the first time in a long time, she wasn't afraid. She didn't feel heavy with burden. Aye, there were still several things on her mind, but so much weight had been lifted, simply by leaving Strome.

Perhaps this was an opportunity to start over. To build a new life for herself. She just didn't know how to go about it.

But there was one thing she was certain of: she was never going back to Strome Castle again.

That place held too many deep, dark secrets and sins.

Éabha was not herself there. There was one thing she'd learned since meeting Torsten, she *liked* herself, a realization she'd never had before.

And Torsten, bless his wicked heart, brought out the best in her.

CHAPTER TWELVE

Torsten carried his daughter to her nursery though what he really wanted to do was march straight up to the tower chamber to find out exactly what Éabha meant when she said it was good meeting his little imp again. Nessa obviously knew who Éabha was and he wanted to know everything. Wanted to douse his burning curiosity.

He glanced at his daughter's dark curls and immediately dismissed the idea of interrogating her about his *guest*. She smiled up at him, a sweet little cherub, and he kissed her on the forehead.

Most people said Nessa looked just like him but he thought she was the spitting image of his late wife. She was a troublemaker of the first order, raining havoc on the castle since the day she was born.

And today was no different. There was smudge of dirt across her chin, and a twinkle in her eye that made him want to search every fold of her gown to see what she was hiding.

"What have ye been up to today?" he asked.

Nessa shrugged. "Nothing."

A candid response that meant she'd been up to *everything*.

He'd been almost certain that Éabha was going to confess about her husband's death. Torsten had seen a flicker in her eyes when he mentioned that it was immoral for him to kiss a married woman. Aye, it was, but not if was indeed a widow. They made quite a pair, he begrudgingly admitted to himself.

He shouldn't like her. But he did. He actually liked her a lot.

'Twas a fact his blood burned for her with a lust he'd not felt since he'd first discovered women as a lad. But this was hotter, deeper. And then, as he'd just discovered, there was the weird realization that he actually enjoyed her company, sparring and all. He couldn't say that about most men, much less women, as they were another story altogether. *A mystery.* But there was something about Éabha... He could have bantered back and forth with her all day and night.

Torsten liked how she challenged him. He admired her spirit, but also her ability to get him to open up.

He'd confessed more to her than he had to anyone in years, even his wife who'd been so weak, and often ill, that he'd been hesitant to share anything more than a proper *good morn* in case it worried her overmuch. He'd loved her, aye, as a husband should love his wife. He offered her protection, a home, and she'd willingly gone about her duties, even insisted they have a child when he wasn't certain it was a good idea. There's had been a marriage of convenience to strengthen an alliance arranged by his brother Cathal. And it turned out to be the only decent thing his brother had ever done for him.

Torsten held Nessa a little closer. He was glad Anna had forced his hand, else he'd not have this perfect little troublemaker who made his life worth living. His biggest concern had been whether she'd end up with the same weak heart her mother had, but so far she'd proven to be hardy.

"Now where did ye say ye left your nurse?" Torsten asked.

Nessa giggled. "By the goats."

He rolled his eyes. This was the fifth nurse he'd hired in the past three years for his darling daughter. No one seemed to understand her spirit. They wanted to rein her in, break her down. He would never allow that. So when he stepped in, they quit, saying she was spoiled, unruly and would turn out rotten to the core. Torsten knew in his heart that wasn't true. He didn't believe a child's spirit had to be broken in order for them to grow to be a good person. Nessa was a sweet girl, and intelligent, too. Full of love, excitement and expression, they were all things that went along with raising a child—his child. Even if she was as ornery as the day was long.

This latest nurse, however, was taking his guidance too literally, because when he said he wanted Nessa to have the freedom to make choices, the nurse simply fell asleep and let his daughter scamper off. That wasn't exactly what he'd meant. So, Nessa spent more time getting into Cook's hair than anyone else. Thank goodness Cook had been with his family since he was a boy and found Nessa to be something like a grandchild, else he might have to worry about her getting whacked by a spoon instead of stuffed full of sweet rolls.

"Tell me, little lass, where did ye see Lady Éabha before now?"

"In the tower, like a princess."

"Oh, really? In the tower?" He tickled her belly. "Did she call ye up to save her from the dragon?"

Nessa laughed. "I'm not a knight! But I am like a princess, right, Papa?"

Torsten tweaked her nose. "Aye. The fairest of them all."

"Nay, Lady Éabha is the fairest. I saw ye bring her in, and she reminded me of Mama."

Torsten's face fell. "Ye were a wee bairn when your mama went to the angels, love, ye remember her still?"

Nessa shook her head. "The lady, she looks like what I think my mama would look like."

That tore at Torsten's gut. Éabha looked nothing like Anna. They were exact opposites in coloring and build. But when Nessa had imagined a mother, she saw Éabha in her mind's eye. Perhaps it was more than simply what Éabha looked like, but that Nessa could relate to her fiery nature. In her, she saw a like spirit.

Torsten hugged his daughter close and kissed her cheek. How would he ever be able to tell his child that the woman that reminded her of her mother was the blood of his enemy—her enemy. Of course, he wouldn't. Only a cruel father would do such a thing, and he wasn't cruel. He'd simply have to hope that when it was time for Lady Éabha to depart that Nessa soon forgot about her, even though he knew he never would.

"Ye are the sweetest thing," he said.

"Nay, not the sweetest. Cook makes verra good cake."

"That is true. Would ye like to see if Cook has any cake for ye?"

"Aye." Nessa wiggled in his arms and he set her down, chasing after her through the corridors and down another set of winding stairs, his heart skipping a beat every time her little feet hit the stones, afraid she'd tumble head over heels.

"Not so fast, Nessa," he called.

That only made her laugh. She found it quite hilarious whenever he worried about her.

At least she wasn't born with her mother's weak constitution, God rest her soul, or else he was certain to have lost her already.

Torsten rounded the last stair and chased his daughter to the kitchen where it just so happened a frantic nursemaid was peeking under the work tables and into the cupboards.

"Did ye lose something?" Torsten said.

The woman jolted and whirled to face him, her eyes locking on Nessa who happened to have the intelligence to look contrite, hands folded and head bowed.

"There she is." The nursemaid pointed at Nessa. "That child is wild, unruly—"

Torsten held up his hand, refusing to hear another word. Nessa inched closer to him, holding onto the plaid at his thigh. "I'll not hear another word. I trust ye've gotten more sleep employed by me than with any other."

The nurse's mouth fell open, her cheeks growing red as cherries.

"I dinna pay ye to nap. I dinna pay ye to endanger my child."

Everyone in the kitchen worked hard to pretend the three of them weren't there. Chopping, kneading, cleaning, stirring. Their movements were fast and their eyes locked on their tasks. All except one. Cook raised her brows—a look he'd seen a thousand times before. Especially in his youth. Torsten took the cue, understanding this was hardly the place to reprimand her.

"Come to my library at once."

He whirled on his heel, little Nessa still clinging to him.

"I want the lady, Papa. Let me go to her with Bad Lassie. She likes Bad Lassie."

"She would," he murmured.

Glancing at Cook he tossed her a hopeful look and Cook smiled, calling Nessa to her.

Torsten led the way to his office, semi dragging his heels. He'd have to sack another nurse, or have her quit on him. Didn't matter which as the outcome was still the same. He'd be without a nurse for Nessa. Again. Without someone to help mold her and shape her.

I want the lady…

Interesting. Maybe Nessa was onto something with that line of thought. He could offer the position of nursemaid to Éabha and then she could stay—but more importantly, she would understand his want for Nessa. She would honor it.

Wouldn't she?

Torsten frowned.

This had nothing to do with his child's request. He was grasping onto anything that would keep Éabha here, for once she told him the truth about her husband being dead he'd have no reason to hold her, and if he did decide to keep her, his clan would begin to question his motives.

His morals.

His ability to rule.

They might think that he'd turned into his brother. He couldn't allow that. No matter how much he wanted Éabha. His reputation, the respect of his people meant more to him than any woman ever could. At least that's what he kept telling himself.

Inside his office, the nurse looked just as contrite as Nessa had in the kitchen. Actually, she looked terrified. It seemed, more and more, he had that affect on women. Was he really such an ogre?

"Apologies, my laird," the nurse whispered. "I should not have spoken that way. The child is sweet. I dinna want to lose my position here."

Torsten nodded wondering if she didn't want to lose her position or her ability to nap.

"I'll give ye another chance since ye seem truly remorseful. Please have a care. She is young and though she is wild and fearless, she is still vulnerable. I dinna want her to get hurt, and ye are here to teach her and protect her."

"Aye, my laird."

"Go now, see that she is cleaned up. She's a mess."

"Aye, my laird. Thank ye." The nurse ran from the room.

At least she'd not quit. That was a first.

It was time he and Éabha had a serious discussion, one in which his lips did not end up on hers. It would be a struggle.

As he topped the stairs, he could already hear little Nessa's voice carrying through the door, followed by Éabha's. They were singing. Nessa must have run up there as soon as he left her in the kitchen. Seems the child wasn't going to be getting a bath anytime soon since it was unlikely her nurse would search the tower for her. Torsten rolled his eyes, and shook his head with a slight chuckle. There was never a dull moment when it came to being a father, and he rather liked it that way.

Their voices carried lower, and then there was the sound of laughter. A sweet tinkling sound. Again he felt that strange beat in his chest, as though his heart were fluttering. But his heart didn't flutter. He was a man. A warrior. They didn't feel such things.

And yet, there it went again.

Torsten gritted his teeth.

He was intruding. He should just let them enjoy the moment and be on his way. He had so many other things to attend to. He needed to check on the repair of the village in the north that had suffered at the hands of the MacDonells. There were other villages he needed to reinforce. There were provisions to record, and weapons to sharpen. Armor to shine. Horses to break. Squires to train. Ledgers to be revised.

But no matter how many reasons he had for turning around, his feet continued to move forward, closer and closer until he was touching the door handle.

Torsten stilled. Listening.

They continued to sing, their voices filled with a happiness he'd not expected to hear from either of them. Why did it seem like he was spying on an intimate moment?

Because he was.

His precious daughter had bonded with the woman he'd taken captive. And he'd allowed it to happen. Perhaps not initially. Nessa had a mind of her own and sought Éabha out, but he could have put a stop to it. Right then and there. He could have made certain that his daughter didn't go near the tower again. Instead, he'd not said a word either way and concocted some harebrained idea that Éabha would be the perfect woman to help raise his child.

She would be.

It would work out perfectly for Nessa. She'd have someone there to guide her who possessed a spirit close to her own, one that Torsten could actually respect.

But on the other hand, he didn't want to force Éabha. That was something he refused to do. She'd have to want it. It would have to be her idea. Because he would never force her into something she didn't want. He'd already done that once. And hadn't she said the last six years of her life were miserable? He wouldn't add to her pain. So, if he asked her to stay and care for his daughter, she would think it was the only way to get out of being held prisoner. That was no good. And then, there was also the niggling fact that Nessa's nurse didn't seem of a mind to quit just yet.

Nay, Torsten couldn't suggest she stay on to help with Nessa.

Éabha had to make the suggestion.

He just needed to find a way to plant the idea in her head without her knowing what he was up to. And then of course, he'd have to dismiss the nurse, which shouldn't be too hard. Hell, the woman just might quit sooner than later anyway.

Slowly, he backed away from the chamber, satisfied that the two of them were getting along and no longer feeling the need to intrude. Was he being tricky? Letting the two of them bond? Should he intervene before someone got hurt?

Mayhap he should. Then again, Éabha and Nessa had met on their own. He'd not had anything to do with it. In fact, if they'd kept it a secret he'd not even know at this very moment. With that thought in mind, and his guilt pushed aside, Torsten continued on his way.

A few minutes later, he was growling at himself in disgust—because he'd whistled all the way down the spiral staircase like a lovesick lad who'd drunk an entire jug of whisky and then stolen a barrel more. What in bloody hell was wrong with him?

There was only one way to crush this feeling rushing through his veins—sword fighting, and not with the woman who was the cause of so much conflict within him.

And that was where he remained for the next eight days and nights. Battling his demons, and praying whatever had gotten into him would stray. Tiring his men. Pushing his body to the limit. And when he'd exhausted from training, he went over ledger after ledger. Riding the perimeter of his lands. But even exhausting his body did nothing to sway his subconscious. For whenever he returned to the castle, his feet seemed to have a mind of their own, taking him up those spiral stairs, all the way to the very top, where he could hear Éabha inside. Sometimes alone, sometimes talking with Mary, other times singing sweetly to his daughter.

He was going mad. Mad with… Nay, he dared not even think it. Simply mad.

CHAPTER THIRTEEN

Éabha woke to a room that was slightly frigid. The fire in her hearth had banked during the night, and the temperatures outside had cooled enough to create a frost that glistened like diamonds on the stone by her window. Thank goodness she'd had the forethought to close the shutters before going to bed.

Éabha slid a finger over the frost, watching it melt from the heat of her skin. She drew a swirl, and then several more, creating a silhouette of the landscape beyond the castle that faded as the sun warmed the stone.

Drawing and painting had been a talent she'd possessed as a little girl. She'd drawn everywhere, dirt, mud, stones, carved into trees and when she was lucky, on parchment or even an occasional canvas. She'd grown quite good at making egg tempura paint in shades of browns, reds and black. And even dabbled in oils using flowers, roots and minerals to create colors.

143

Creative artistry was not a skill her husband had found useful, unless she were making a tapestry, or embroidering the hem of a shirt, and so she'd let that piece of herself slip into some locked part of her mind, waiting for the day it could be freed.

Was that today?

She stared down at the fading outline in the frost, desiring greatly to draw at that moment. Perhaps while she was here, to fill the time, she could simply ask Mary if there were any paints. If not, she'd ask for the ingredients she needed to make them herself. Or at the very least, a flat stone and some charcoal she could color and then clean off to color again.

There was a knock and then the door pushed open to reveal the very woman in question.

"Mary," Éabha said with an excited smile. "Just the woman I was thinking of."

"My lady." Mary nodded, her gray hair swept into a tight bun, and the stains on her gown from the day before washed clean. "I trust ye slept well."

"As well as could be expected." Éabha rocked on her toes, fingers laced in front of her, nervous about her request. Well, she might as well just get it over with before Mary rushed off to go about her other duties. Éabha didn't want to spend another day staring out into the bailey wondering if she'd see Torsten or not. It had been so long…

"Mary, I was wondering…"

"Aye, dear?"

"Has there ever been a painter at Eilean Donan?"

"A painter?" Mary tapped her chin. "Aye, mayhap some ten years ago. He was painting a portrait of our laird's father, the old laird. Did a right good job of it, too. The old laird was verra proud of it."

"Fascinating. I'd like to see the portrait."

Mary nodded, straightening Éabha's bed. "It hangs in the great hall over the hearth. Why do ye ask?"

Éabha shrugged, and sauntered to the table to examine the porridge and dried fruit Mary had brought her—the same meal she was given every morning. It was a long shot, but she might as well ask. "Did he leave any of his tools behind?"

Mary frowned, and dusted off the side table. "If he did, they'd be in the cellar. There's a shelf down there filled with a mess of things people have left behind. We've never gotten rid of them or given them away because of the time the old laird's sister left a shoe behind. Lord have mercy, the woman was right mad when she found out we'd repurposed the leather." Mary shook her head, her mind on the memory. "Right mad, indeed. Haven't gotten rid of a thing since."

Éabha chewed her lip. "I wonder if I might have a look?"

Mary's frown deepened and she put her hands on her hips. "What's this about? Ye're not getting anymore silly notions of offing yourself are ye? Hoping to find a hangman's noose?"

Éabha raised a brow in question "With painter's tools? I'd not get far."

"Ye want the painter's tools..." Mary's words drew out as she stared at the wall, again, her mind far off.

Éabha could practically see her thoughts working their way out, her hands itching to reach out and grasp onto whatever it was Mary searched for.

"Are ye a painter, then?" Mary asked.

Éabha shook her head vehemently. "Nothing so glamorous as that, nor as talented. I dabble, that is all."

Mary glanced around the tower chamber, taking note of how it lacked any kind of entertainment. "And ye're likely bored out of your mind up here all day. Ye've been helpful to those in the kitchens and gardens, but I suppose as a lady, there are other things ye'd like to put your mind to."

"Aye. It doesna mean I won't keep helping elsewhere, I promise."

"Eat your porridge and after the men have gone off to train, I'll take ye down to the cellar to see if we can find anything. But dinna get your hopes up too high. Ten years is a long while, and if he left anything, it's likely not to have stayed put all this time. Things have a way of walking off. Not everyone was here for Lady Winifred's outburst."

"I will not get my hopes up." But Éabha clapped her hands, showing her hopes were already high. She quickly sat down, and feigned interest in her breakfast. "I will be prepared for nothing more than disappointment."

"Sounds like a mantra ye've used often."

Éabha laughed, a sound that was hollow. "Perhaps it is my motto."

"Och, but dinna say such." Mary came forward, and patted her shoulder.

Éabha met her gaze. Mary had become a dear friend to her over the past couple of weeks. "I only speak the truth, Mary."

The housekeeper clucked her tongue, then made her way out of the room, leaving Éabha to draw designs in her porridge with her spoon and to pray with every ounce of her soul that there was at least one paint brush in the cellar. Just one. That was all she needed. She wouldn't be greedy.

She stared at the walls around the room, so bleak. They would be the first things she'd paint. Torsten would likely be angry that she'd dare to deface his walls, but she didn't care. He'd left her up here for over a sennight to twiddle her thumbs. She'd spent so many hours staring out the tower window that she knew exactly the precise moment the blacksmith would appear from his hut, and the exact position of the sun and moon when the men would change positions for guard duty.

She even watched as Torsten left the castle to trek across the bailey, heading toward the fields where he'd train with his men. Sometimes he returned and sometimes he didn't. And every night that he was here, after supper was served, he made his way to the stables. What did he do inside, she couldn't be sure, but she imagined him caring for his mount, Lucifer. Imagined that the lumps in his hands were carrots or apples—for she could never really get a good sight on them. Sometimes his second-in-command would join him, other times it was another warrior, and even once a young squire.

What she liked most about watching everyone out the window was that no one knew she was snooping. She could see all their interactions and was learning about each and every one of them, and they were none the wiser. She knew their schedules, their gaits, which laundress tried to avoid which stable hand, and who the scullery maids were secretly kissing when the sun set.

The door to her chamber was still unlocked. She could have traversed the castle and made her way outside for a close up of all the goings on, but she never quite found the courage to do so. It was only when Mary dragged her down to the kitchens or thrust her into the garden that she left the tower. Why? It just felt so much safer up here. Just as anonymous as it had been when she and Torsten had opened up to each other in the dark.

At Strome, she'd never been able to observe anyone this way. She'd always been too busy looking over her shoulder, or hiding. Trying to stay out of everyone's way. To be invisible in a world where she was very much in the public eye.

She hated to admit it, but being here, taken against her will, had finally given her the opportunity to examine herself. To remember the things she liked and disliked. To bring to mind that she did want a child, and so what if she pretended that Nessa was hers? No one knew. She longed to pick up the sword again. She'd been mightily impressed that the skills she'd learned as a girl, though they'd laid dormant, had been like reflexes when she fought with Torsten. Having time to reflect had helped her recall her joy of creating. And thank goodness for Mary who was going to help her do it.

Éabha hurried to finish her porridge, for when Mary returned, she did not want to waste another minute in the tower. Not when she could be searching the shelves looking for a paintbrush.

She didn't have to wait long. Mary returned quickly, a beaming smile on her already creased face.

"I have spoken with Cook." The older woman rocked on her heels as though she held some exciting secret.

Éabha pushed back her bowl, filling the tray so Mary didn't have to. "That's lovely. What is she going to make that's got ye so excited?"

Mary rushed forward. "Nay, dear. Ye dinna understand. Cook was here when the painter was."

"Oh?"

"And she recalls the painter did leave many things behind, including a canvas."

"A canvas?" Éabha's heart fluttered.

"Aye. They are in the cellar. Come. She's even agreed to help ye mix a few paints. She helped the painter do so and she's fairly certain she remembers how." Mary grabbed her hand and started to pull her toward the door. "I'll send someone up later to get your tray."

"I am so grateful to the both of ye for your help. But I have to ask—why, Mary?"

Mary stopped walking and gave Éabha a quizzical look. "What do ye mean why?"

"Ye've been more than kind to me since your laird brought me here. This is going above and beyond that kindness."

Mary shrugged. "Aye, what of it?"

"Tell me why? Please?"

Mary drew in a deep breath. "Truth be told, my lady, none of us think of ye as a prisoner. In fact, a few of us are hoping ye'll stay on."

"Stay on?"

"Well, the lass, she loves ye, and our laird... he seems, well never mind about him. 'Tis our sweet Nessa. She's never taken to anyone quite like she has ye. Oh, dear." Mary covered her mouth with her hand. "I've over spoken. 'Tis a problem I have. Forgive me."

Éabha patted Mary on the back, glad that the housekeeper had confided in her. She was going to miss Nessa immensely when the time came for her to leave, and it was good to know that so many weren't against her being at the castle. "Dinna worry over it. There is nothing to forgive."

"Suffice it to say, my lady, we have agreed to help ye with your painting. We want to see what ye come up with."

"It's been many years since I picked up a brush. I hope ye are not too disappointed."

"None of us will be. We lack the skills to hold a brush ourselves, and so we respect ye for your courage to try."

Éabha laughed. "Ye make it sound as though I were going to pick up a sword."

Mary raised a challenging brow. "Is a painter's brush not like a warrior's sword?"

Éabha rolled her eyes. "Now ye're just trying to flatter me." If Mary had seen the way Éabha attacked Torsten in those first few hours she'd been here, she'd not think so highly of her.

To keep Mary from seeing the way her face reddened at the thought, Éabha placed her arm around Mary's elbow and urged her along. "Shall we? I'd love to paint a landscape of my view from the tower window."

"Oh, how lovely."

"Ye can hang it in your chamber as a thank ye."

"How about in the kitchen where we can all see it?"

"Perfect." Éabha would be more than proud to display her artwork. That was, if it turned out all right. She had a sudden twinge of panic. She'd not painted in so long, and so many people were counting on her. Well, never mind that. An artist never revealed their work until they were done, and she wouldn't either. They'd just have to wait until she was ready.

Mary led her down the stairs and across the castle before grabbing a torch and going down another set of stairs into a darkened cellar. Shelves lined the walls floor to ceiling filled with various tools, pots, jars, jugs, dried foods, jerky, oatcakes, textiles. She led her down the rows until they came to a line of shelves that looked to hold a host of diverse items.

"This is the place things end up that we know not where they belong," Mary said with a little laugh.

Without thinking, Éabha took the torch from Mary's grip and held it closer to the shelf so she could see better. There really was just about everything. Scraps of material that were cut into odd shapes, a stray boot, make that four, none of which had a match, a candelabra broken at the center, a chipped jar, an old doll, and a few carved wooden toys.

"Why aren't these up with Nessa?" Éabha asked.

"'Haps no one knew they were down here."

Éabha picked up a wooden dog. "I think she'll like this one."

"Most likely."

Éabha dug through the piles, her eyes lighting on a rolled up canvas. "Please be empty."

Mary took back the torch and Éabha slowly unrolled the canvas, praying it was clean. She didn't want to paint over another artist's work. Inch after inch revealed white—and what was this? A second canvas! And more! Several brushes fell to the earthen floor. Her heart skipped a beat. Could this truly be? Not one brush but three, *and* two canvases?

"Oh, my," Éabha said. "It is my lucky day!"

"I'll say," Mary replied. "Will ye look at that?" Then with her free hand she crossed herself. "'Tis a sign, dearie. Ye were meant to be here."

With the paintbrushes in her hand, Éabha straightened and cast Mary a weary glance. "I dinna believe in signs."

Mary's mouth dropped open as though Éabha had just confessed to worshipping the devil. But she didn't say a word.

"However, I also do not believe in wasting good fortune when it is presented to ye. So I will make good use of these tools. I am most grateful to ye, Mary for helping me find them."

They retreated from the cellar, Éabha following behind the elderly woman, her words creeping their way through her mind.

A sign.

Meant to be here.

How many times had she already thought that being here seemed more of a blessing than a curse?

That was another secret she'd have to keep to herself.

CHAPTER FOURTEEN

"What were ye doing with Lady Éabha in the cellar?" Torsten crossed his arms over his chest and stared his housekeeper down. He'd seen them both approach the cellar but he'd been distracted by the stable master who was having trouble with a shoe on one of the horses, and was unable to follow them to see for himself.

He'd avoided Éabha long enough now that knocking on her door and demanding to know what was happening seemed awkward. The fact that he'd taken her against her will from Strome didn't count anymore because after that first sword fight, she'd earned his respect and her freedom. Now, hours later, when he'd finally broken down, and decided to go up to the tower, awkwardness be damned, because he needed to see her, he ran into Mary on the stairwell.

Mary's fingers were stained with various odd colors, which given it was spring might not have caused him to pause, but he knew for a fact they were not yet dyeing any wool because shearing was late due to the raids.

Something was definitely off.

Mary fidgeted, not meeting Torsten's gaze, and not answering his question. His housekeeper had never been this disloyal before.

Torsten straightened, staring the older woman down. He tried to keep his voice steady as he spoke. "Mary, for the love of all that's holy, what is going on?"

Mary shook her head, glanced about, perhaps deciding if she should run up the stairs or scoot around him to go down. Thinking better of it, she looked down at her toes. "The lady paints," she said faintly.

"Paints?" Torsten cocked his head, staring at the top of Mary's bun, willing her to meet his gaze, but she did not.

She nodded, her bun bobbing, eyes still locked on the ground. "Aye."

"What does she paint?"

"Landscapes, portraits." Mary looked ready to bolt, her feet now shuffling back and forth. "Anything really."

Éabha was an artist. Fascinating. From the way she'd fought with a sword he'd not have guessed she was also skilled with paints, but her fiery nature, the vibrancy of her, that leant to a creative spirit. What was the big secret? "Why was it so hard to tell me that?"

"I was not certain if ye'd approve of me getting the supplies for her." She quickly hid her hands behind her back. "On account of her being your special guest. Apologies, my laird, for overstepping my bounds."

Torsten was ready to throttle his housekeeper and anyone else, for that matter, who tried his patience. Did no one believe she wasn't his prisoner? Well, he supposed he would have to prove it.

It had been hard enough to keep away from the lass the past week. He'd worked himself to the bone to keep from thinking about her, and every horse in the stables had been thoroughly groomed considering he ran in the opposite direction of the castle whenever he thought about her.

"I do not have any qualms or reservations regarding the entertainments of Lady Éabha."

Mary raised a brow, and he knew she was thinking about when she'd walked into his chamber to find Éabha in his bed, no matter how innocent it actually was. Hell, that fell right into the category of no reservations.

Torsten narrowed his gaze, giving her the same look he gave wayward squires, but Mary didn't seem fazed. She'd known him since he was a bairn and though she respected him and was loyal, she didn't always keep her opinions to herself when they were alone.

Mary tidied her neat bun which didn't need any straightening and again Torsten observed the stains on her hands.

"Why do your hands have different shades on them? Ye're not dyeing wool yet are ye?"

"Oh!" Mary gasped and stared at her fingers, their knuckles swollen with age and splashes of green and red surrounding the natural age spots. "I was helping Cook."

"What was Cook doing?"

"Helping Lady Éabha."

Torsten drew in an annoyed breath. "Will we go in circles again, Mary? Mayhap being a housekeeper at Eilean Donan is not your calling."

He'd made threats like that to her before, the first time when he was a wee lad of four. Mary knew he'd never sack her, but still it was a good reminder that her impertinence would not be tolerated. Torsten didn't like it when he had to resort to such tactics, but in this case, it seemed the only way to get the information he needed.

"Apologies, my laird." Mary straightened her shoulders, eyes glimmering with strength. She was protecting the lady. Torsten liked that. Seemed Lady Éabha was having an affect on more people than just him. "I was helping Cook who was helping Lady Éabha make paint."

"For her paintings."

"Aye."

"I want to see." Torsten stepped up, prepared to move around the housekeeper.

Mary flung out her arms, stopping him. "Wait!"

"For?" Torsten ground his teeth, working hard not to snap.

"She asked not to be disturbed. Something about needing peace in order to create."

What in the bloody—

Torsten cut himself off before he became too irritated. "Mary, this is my castle, these are my lands, and last time I checked, I was laird. Not to mention I am the one who brought the lady here to begin with."

"Ye are correct on all counts, but ye see…" Mary wrung her hands. "I think she was hoping to keep it a secret and I'm afraid I've gone and ruined it."

"Ruined her secret?" Torsten crossed his arms over his chest, uncertain how to feel about this. "A secret from me?"

"Aye. She thought ye'd be disagreeable about it."

"Why would I?"

Mary shrugged. "She might be all fierce bluster on the outside, but on the inside she is in need of tenderness and care."

His housekeeper's words caught him in the chest, making the muscle behind his ribs squeeze. Given how strong Éabha appeared at every moment, it was hard to remember that she might need some coddling, too. "All right, I will not go and look now." He'd respect the secret project for now. "But I want a report."

Mary's head bobbed emphatically, relief clouding her eyes. "Aye, my laird."

The sound of little feet clambering down the stairs caught Torsten's attention.

"Papa!" Nessa bounced against his leg. The front of her gown was smeared with green and red, a line of it down and across her face, just like when he painted himself with woad.

"What's this?" he asked, looking to Mary. "Is everyone in the castle helping but me?"

"Well," Mary smiled sheepishly. "When the lass saw what the lady was doing, she wanted to try and Lady Éabha is so verra patient with her."

"Och, I know it." Torsten lifted his daughter, hugging her to him. "Were ye painting?"

Nessa held her fingers to his lips and said, "Shh… We're not supposed to tell."

"What is Lady Éabha painting?" Torsten asked in a low whisper.

"Everything." His daughter's voice was filled with such whimsy it took Torsten's breath away.

"Everything?"

Nessa nodded. "Everything I can see."

He chuckled. Obviously he wasn't going to get a straight answer from his daughter, she was too much in awe.

"And what did ye paint?" he asked.

"I painted a picture of ye."

"Me?"

"And Lady Éabha."

"Can I see it?"

She shook her head. "Not right now."

"Where is it?"

"In the tower room."

"I see. Well, then, I suppose we should see ye up to your nursery for supper."

"I am verra hungry." Nessa rubbed her belly.

"Me too."

"Want to eat with me, Papa?"

"Aye, I would." He turned to Mary. "Have them send my supper up to the nursery tonight."

"Aye, my laird."

After tucking his daughter into bed, Torsten made his way back downstairs. 'Twas time for his nightly ritual. A trip to the stables to see about the horses. He passed through the kitchens grabbing a few carrots. Cook nodded at him with a secret smile that made him think her and Mary had been doing a lot of talking.

Once into the bailey, he glanced up at the castle, seeing a light in the tower window.

Éabha.

The moon was bright, the sky clear. The past few days had been overcast, leaving the night darker than it was now.

He could barely make out her silhouette, but she was definitely there beyond the window. And then she grew closer, as if sensing him. He raised his hand to wave, not certain if she could see him. Her silhouette grew and in the dark of the night, the shadows of the torches bounced up the walls illuminating her as she leaned out.

"My laird," she called down to him, her voice jovial.

"Lady Éabha."

"I must ask ye. What is it ye do each night when ye head to the stables?"

She'd watched him each night? He couldn't tell her that he headed there to get her out of his mind. To fight the demons of his desire…

So he answered banally, to keep her, and anyone else listening, from realizing just how eager he was to talk to her. "I care for the horses."

She swiped the hair from her face. There was a slight wind and he supposed high up in the tower, it would be swifter than down here on the ground.

"How many Mackenzie horses are there?" she asked.

"There's not enough for ye to escape with, if that's what ye're thinking," he teased.

Her glittering laugh tinkled in the air just above his head. Several of the villagers slowed and looked up, but others tried hard to be inconspicuous as they eavesdropped.

"I would not dare steal a warrior's horse."

"Whose horse would ye steal?"

"That's a good question. And one I'm not certain I can answer as I've never actually been put in the position to steal one."

Torsten chuckled. "Would ye care to see the horses, my lady? Come down and show me which one ye'd steal."

Silence followed his request. His heart thumped behind his ribs and the smile that had graced his face slowly ebbed. He blinked, trying to see if she was still there. The shadows and a wayward cloud covering the moon made it hard to tell. Then she moved, and he felt disappointed she was still there. He'd hoped she was on her way down.

"I'm not certain that's a good idea," she called.

"Aye, most likely not." The lie caused him to frown. He wanted her to come down. He'd not seen her in so long that he actually craved her nearness.

Just when he was about to turn away, her voice came to him again.

"After all, I may decide to steal your sword and make off with whatever mount I choose."

Torsten couldn't help his grin. No matter the time spent apart, or how much he'd tried to forget her, they seemed to pick up right where they'd left off. "Ye'd steal a warrior's sword but not his horse?"

"Aye."

"Why is that?"

"A horse bonds to his person, a warhorse especially. If I stole the horse, the warrior's life would be in danger. A sword on the other hand is easier to replace."

"Some would argue that a man's sword molds to his hand and one can never find the same weight or likeness again."

"A thought I will consider before I steal yours."

Torsten laughed. "Well, my lady, I will bid ye good night, unless ye wish to come down."

Again a moment of silence that had him questioning the bond they seemed to have formed. "I will be right there."

Torsten had not expected, though he'd hoped, that she would come down and he found himself feeling more on edge than he was comfortable with. Why did he have to feel this way? He hated it. It made him feel like a ninny. He was no weak, panting green lad. He was a man. A warrior, and it was high time he started acting like it.

A heartbeat later she was bursting through the doors of the castle, gliding toward him, tall and lithe and filled with energy. He'd never seen her so happy, and all thoughts of showing her his might, being the warrior, dissipated because truth be told, he just wanted to keep seeing her smile.

"My lady," he said, taking her hand and pulling her knuckles toward his lips.

She yanked away. "I'm a mess. Ye dinna want to kiss my hand."

Torsten grabbed her hand back, seeing the various colors in slashes of a rainbow. Paint.

"I dinna mind." He brushed his lips on her knuckles and let her hand go before she could protest. And he didn't ask about the paint. He wanted her to tell him all about it without prompting.

But Éabha didn't seem inclined to give him any information. So be it. He'd wait until she was ready. Prove to her that he was worthy of her secrets.

Torsten offered his arm and she took it, her long, paint-stained fingers gripping him.

"Have ye much experience with horses?" he asked.

"Aye. My mother and I used to ride together when I was young."

"That is a nice memory to have of her."

"Mhmm. I'm glad to have it. After she was gone, I rode with my cousin."

"Dugal?" Torsten fought a jealous sting of her riding with another man. It was in the past, and if he had any say in it, she'd be staying right here with him, and he'd be the only man she rode with from now on.

"Aye. He was a good friend. I do miss him."

Torsten knew too much about loss and grief, and so he stroked the back of her hand in comfort. "How did he die?"

Torsten held the stables door open and she slipped inside. They were greeted by warmth and the mingling scents of hay, leather and horse sweat. Luckily the lads had mucked the stalls enough that the smell of manure wasn't overpowering.

"'Tis a bit of a mystery. He became verra ill after a hunting trip. Seemed like a bout of dysentery at first, but there were other signs that had many questioning whether something else was the cause."

"I'm sorry. Did they ever figure it out?"

She tugged her hand from his arm to stroke a woman's saddle hanging with the other tackle. Perhaps on the morrow he'd ask her to go for a ride.

"Nay, they did not. It was a sad loss for his clan."

"Your clan."

"Aye." Éabha took quick steps toward the closest horse and he had a feeling she was trying to escape him, or at least escape the fact that she'd just insinuated the MacDonells were not her clan.

"Is this one yours?" She grabbed a handful of hay and held her hand forward allowing the horse to nibble from her palm.

Torsten puffed his chest. "They are all mine, lass."

Éabha rolled here eyes, ignoring his boast. "Well, which is the one we rode here on?"

"Lucifer. He is over here." Torsten headed toward the large stall in the center of them all.

Éabha chuckled. "Does your horse know the meaning of his name? I should not laugh."

"On the battlefield he shows all men the meaning of his name."

"Oh, he is even more impressive now that I am not filled with rage."

"Ye're not?" He watched her face, the way she tried to hide her reactions from him but found it hard to do so.

"I am not."

"Ye're lying," he teased.

She glanced at him with a sly grin. "I'll have ye know, warrior, that I have not had the slightest urge to steal your sword and run ye through. That's saying a lot."

"I suppose I should be flattered ye've not got murder on your mind."

"Ye should, for I find it very hard not to wrap my fingers around your neck most days." But her eyes moved to his lips, and he knew she must have been thinking about kissing him. His blood fired.

"Have ye any treats for Lucifer?" She was trying to change the subject.

Torsten cleared his throat. "I'd not have him go soft on me, lass."

"And yet ye come each night bearing gifts."

Torsten grinned and winked. "Ye're right. Ye've been watching me."

He reached into his sporran and pulled out a carrot.

"I knew it," Éabha's eyes lit up. She reached for the carrot, but Torsten closed his fingers around it. "I see. Ye dinna want me to feed your warhorse because I would be spoiling him. But 'tis all right if ye do it."

"There is probably some truth to that."

"Then what is the real reason?"

"We play a lot of games ye and I," Torsten said. "We confess things we'd not tell others, and yet, we still take steps backward."

Her gaze swept over him, studying him in a familiar way that made his blood heat all the more. "Ye are my jailer."

"I am not." Torsten stepped back and swept out his arm. "Go. Take Lucifer. I'll not stop ye, lass. I will not hold ye here against your will, but I will not force ye to go if ye want to stay."

Éabha shook her head, cheeks reddening as she realized what he'd said. He wanted her to stay.

"It's... It is not safe for me on the road alone," she said, licking her lips nervously.

"Did ye plan to have an army with ye when ye contemplated escaping last week, when ye told me ye would no longer be my concern?" Torsten inched closer, about to admit that she would always be his concern.

"Ye know I could not," she said softly. "That is not fair."

Torsten was near enough now to smell her floral scent mixed with something more tangy—the paint. "Tell me what ye were doing in your chamber just now. Let me in on your secret."

She raised a challenging brow, her lips quirking into a teasing lilt. "What a woman does in her chamber is not a man's business."

Torsten stroked one of her fingers that gripped the gate of the stall. "Have I told ye how much I enjoy bantering with ye?"

She didn't move her hand, even as she looked down and watched him touch her finger. "As a matter of fact, ye've told me quite the opposite."

Torsten smiled. "Tell me."

Éabha leaned her hip against the stall and then faced him. Slipping from his touch, she held out her hands, and then glanced down at her stained fingertips. "I've been painting."

"'Tis not a task one often sees a woman do."

"Aye. That is why I'd hoped to keep it a secret."

"I am in awe of ye and your many talents. I would not deny ye your desires." Torsten meant with regards to painting but the way she looked up at him, her eyes locking on his had him thinking of other cravings, yearnings. The very ones he'd been fighting the past few days and the reason he'd been avoiding her altogether. "I have to go," he mumbled.

"Already?" She sounded disappointed.

"Aye." He gritted his teeth. "Stay as long as ye like, and if ye do decide to steal a horse, please, dinna take Lucifer."

And then he was walking, long strides that were nearly a run. If he wasn't out of the stables in the next few seconds he was going to turn back around, grab her up in his arms and kiss her until they both melted into the pile of hay.

CHAPTER FIFTEEN

Éabha fingered the long line of knots down her hair that was meant to be a braid and smiled at Nessa. Loose in some places and tighter than steel in others, 'twas a good effort for a lass so young. Nessa had tucked herself into Éabha's side where they now lounged on the floor before the banked hearth. The puppy napped soundly in a tiny black ball near their feet.

The child had come to visit her every day for the last sennight, sometimes multiple times a day, especially when Cook or Mary seemed overly harried by her. They painted several of the blocks on the stone wall, and between projects, Nessa loved to play a game she called princesses in the tower, which always resulted in Éabha's hair being braided.

Torsten had been like a shadow since she'd visited with him in the stables. Avoiding her for just as long as he had before. It made her sad not to see him. Well, in the flesh. He haunted her dreams every night. It had been seven days since he'd last come to see her. And for seven nights she'd lain awake wondering if he would crash through her door and carry her to his chamber.

When they'd been in the stables together, his finger sliding over hers, she'd been certain he would kiss her again and certain she would not deny him. But then he'd hurried away leaving her feeling lost and embarrassed. What had she done to push him aside? What could she do to bring him back?

At night she'd avoided her window as much as possible, knowing that he knew she liked to watch him. She didn't want to be caught doing so, caught seeking him out when he'd been the one to turn away.

Éabha squeezed her eyes shut and rubbed her temples in an attempt to get him out of her mind, but it didn't work. She couldn't stop thinking about him. All this time she'd been begging him to let her go, but now that he had, she wanted him to claim her once more.

"Éabha…" Nessa drawled out, waving a pudgy hand in front of her face. "Do ye like it?"

"Wonderful job, lass," she said. "I've never felt more beautiful."

"Ye should show Papa. I want to show him mine." She touched the braided ring around her head that Éabha had constructed—she was getting rather good at this game.

Éabha simply smiled, not wanting to dash the wee one's hopes. If Torsten had anything to say about it, they wouldn't be showing him Éabha's hair. She'd have better luck convincing Little Rob that she didn't mean what she said about his small brain when they first met.

Doubts crept into her mind. Maybe she shouldn't have allowed Torsten to view her inner self. Her fears. Her insecurities. Would he use them against her? She couldn't make herself believe that. He couldn't possibly be manipulating her. Looking to exploit her weaknesses. She was pretty good at reading people. Or at least she thought she was. Could she truly be so wrong about him? She prayed not, and pushed those thoughts away. There was no changing the past, she of all people knew that. There was only the future to look forward to, and hers was filled with question.

With a long drawn out breath, Éabha stood up and straightened her skirts, plucking an almond from the bowl in the center of the table where they'd had their noon meal. Nessa yawned, accompanied by a loud sigh.

"Ye look sleepy." Éabha smiled and stroked the lass's cheek.

Nessa stuck out her lower lip and shook her head. "Not sleepy." But her mouth opened emitting another yawn, proving otherwise.

Mary swept through the door at that moment to clear away their dishes and nodded her agreement. "'Tis just about that time. I'll take her to the nursery."

"Where is her nursemaid?" Usually the harried young woman would be along around this time with a warm cup of milk for her charge.

Mary frowned. "I thought ye knew. She left."

"Left? To go where?"

"Someplace else. She was a cousin of one of the maids, suppose she found work that didna require as much... energy." Mary smirked.

"That's a shame for Nessa." Éabha glanced down at the little imp burrowing into the side of her gown, her thumb creeping toward her mouth. "How many others have there been?"

"At least five or six. I've lost count."

Éabha frowned. "A child needs more structure. More stability."

"Well, I tend to agree with ye. But his lairdship's not one for structure with the wee one, and so she tends to run amuck which causes those hired to care for her to run off."

"Structure doesna mean a child's spirit canna be free," Éabha said thoughtfully. "I was allowed quite a long leash, but I still knew the rules."

Mary raised a brow as if to say, *look where it got ye*.

Éabha forced herself not to stick her tongue out. "Well, it doesna matter, besides, I'm not going to be here long and it's none of my business."

Mary mumbled something that Éabha couldn't quite make out, and she wasn't certain she wanted to know what it was anyhow. The way the laird had been avoiding her, even *she* wondered why she stuck around. He'd told her she was free to go. So, was everyone wondering why she hadn't bolted through the gates?

Curiosity got the better of her. "What was that, Mary?"

"Nothing, my lady. I'll see Nessa to her chamber and then I'll return for the dishes." She set the tray back down on the table, and moved to scoop up the child, but Éabha stilled her hand.

"I still have the freedom to move about the castle, nay?" The words were out of her mouth before she had a chance to pull them back.

169

Mary cocked her head. "Aye."

"Then I'll take her. 'Tis the floor just below mine, aye?" If poor Nessa was going to have to deal with the loss of yet another caretaker, than the least Éabha could do was put her down for her nap.

"I suppose that would be all right," Mary said.

"If his lairdship thinks it's fine for her to visit me here every day, I'm certain he would allow me to help."

"Ye are likely right, but if he disapproves, I'll blame ye for it."

Éabha smiled. "I'm certain I can handle his bluster."

Again, Mary gave her one of those odd looks as though she were trying to work out some problem in her mind. Most likely trying to figure out why the laird kept avoiding her.

Éabha scooped up Nessa who nestled against her shoulder. Seeing her lass removed from the floor, Bad Lassie jumped to her feet, prepared to follow.

"And ye'll want to go outside, too," Éabha said, then looked at Mary. "Where does the pup normally walk?"

"In the back garden, mostly. His lairdship doesna want him causing a ruckus in the main yard or down by the loch. Come to the kitchens after putting the lass into her bed and I'll walk with ye. I could use a bit of fresh air."

"That would be nice."

Éabha looked forward to the fresh air herself. She'd been cooped up for the past several days with her paints, which she very much enjoyed, but she needed to feel the sun on her face.

"Go out this door here," Mary was saying. "Down the stairs to the next level and take the third door. That's her chamber."

Éabha followed Mary, walking carefully given her arms were heavily laden and the puppy weaved between both of their feet.

"For Heaven's sake, Bad Lassie, quit that," Mary said, irritated when she nearly tripped.

"Oh!" Éabha squealed when the puppy decided a game of tug-of-war was appropriate with the hem of her gown. "This pup has verra bad manners."

"Aye. Free rein and all," Mary chuckled.

Éabha furrowed her brow, concentrating on balancing Nessa in one arm while she tugged her gown out of the pup's mouth with the other. "One can still play within the boundaries set for them."

"Can ye?"

"Aye," Éabha said. "Ye see, I have painted, played with a puppy and a child today."

And dreamed of kissing the laird. Feeling his hard body pressed to mine…

"Then perhaps I shall reconsider my stance."

"Ye might think about that," Éabha said, a bit too much consternation in her tone. "I've seen what can happen when a person's spirit is broken. They are never quite the same again."

"There ye are," Mary said, nodding her head toward the third door. This floor did not have a long corridor, just a short vestibule and three doors. "And for what it's worth, I'd never try to break her spirit."

Éabha balanced Nessa again on one arm and then twisted the handle until the door popped open. Bad Lassie ran inside the large chamber, obviously knowing where her home was.

"See ye in the kitchen," Mary called as she disappeared down the spiral stairs.

Éabha stepped inside, gazing around at the bright whitewashed walls, the colorful tapestries, the wide hearth and rocker, and the beds. More than one, and two cradles as well. Three of the beds were neatly made up, but one was rumpled, and she bet it was Nessa's.

Bad Lassie ran right over to the rumpled bed and hopped onto it.

"Now, why hasn't anyone been up here?" She assumed the nurse was supposed to take care of it, and already had proven to be lax in her tasks, having taken her leave afore seeing the day's chores completed.

A bowl of uneaten porridge sat at a round table, set with four chairs. The chamber must have been on the corner of the tower, for it had windows on two sides, enough to let in plenty of light, and fresh air, perfect for a nursery.

Éabha carried Nessa to the rumpled bed and was going to tuck her in, but decided instead to put her in one of the clean beds. The sheets were in need of a good wash, not surprising given Nessa always looked as though she had rolled in a pile of mud before noon each day.

Nessa mumbled something, then snuggled her body beneath the blankets and was fast asleep.

Éabha smiled down at her, feeling that familiar ache of sadness creep through her. She wanted a child. But at this point, she wasn't certain she ever would. One needed a husband for that—or at the very least a bed partner—and she was without.

A convent was looking more and more like her only option. For a brief moment, she'd fantasized that a life here,

172

with Torsten was only a kiss away. But he avoided her like the plague now, and she wasn't going to embarrass herself further.

Aye, the convent it was. A life of servitude. She'd heard the servants make mention of Nèamh Abbey on the Isle of Skye. Something about a lady coming to the castle from there before. That was where she would go. For, in order to be placed within the king's household, she would have to get there first, and traveling on her own would be too dangerous. Aye, she could wield a sword, but she couldn't fight off a band of outlaws on her own. Second, she would need to be recommended as someone suitable enough to serve the queen or one of her children, and right now, Éabha didn't have anyone to recommend her. She was essentially without a clan. And her past wasn't particularly glowing considering she'd been married to a vile laird, who also happened to be her uncle.

Mayhap she'd been thinking a bit too highly of herself when she considered being a lady's maid, though her mother had descended from royalty, her father did not. He was a MacDonell, and her tinge of blue blood, her link to royalty, had not saved her fate so far.

But it just might help her gain access to a quiet nunnery.

With a sigh, Éabha gently clapped her hands and the pup eagerly leapt from the dirty bed to follow her from the room. She shut the door on her way out, and made her way down the stairs in search of the kitchen, much more practiced this time in keeping her balance on the narrow, winding steps with a furball weaving between her legs.

At the bottom of the stairs, two guards stood outside of a closed door. They glanced at her, recognition hitting before they returned to staring at the far wall.

What were they thinking?

Oh, stop that! she warned herself. Trying to figure out what they thought about her would do her no good.

"The kitchens?" she asked pointing in the direction she knew very well was the way to go. Why did she feel the need to gain their permission?

They both nodded for her to continue down the corridor, but offered her nothing more.

"Come, Bad Lassie."

The corridor was dark, because none of the sconces were lit. They must be saving their resources, which was fine for those who lived in the castle, and knew their way around. But for her, it was a little unnerving. Though she'd been at Eilean Donan for weeks, she wasn't confident enough to walk its corridors in the dark. She slid her fingers over the stone walls to keep her balance and guide her way.

The scents of roasting meat, simmering herbal stew, and baking bread grew stronger. Her mouth watered as though she hadn't just eaten the noon meal with Nessa. At least she knew she was going the right way.

Bad Lassie ran ahead, her barks echoing back to Éabha, and then fading.

"Wait!" she called, lifting the hem of her skirts, prepared to run. She didn't want the kitchen staff to be angry with her for letting the puppy loose in the middle of their preparations for the evening meal.

"Wait for what?"

Éabha stilled as a deep male voice sounded behind her. She had a moment of panic until she realized it was Torsten.

She turned around, seeing his dark shadow towering behind her. Her heart skipped a beat. She'd not expected to feel this way after not seeing or speaking to him since their moments in the stables. Her throat tightened and her belly flipped.

"I wasn't certain ye still lived here," she murmured sarcastically, unable to hide the hurt of his avoidance. "How long have ye been following me?"

"Since ye asked my men the way to the kitchens, though I'm certain ye already knew."

Traitors. They'd acted as if it was no big deal that she was walking around but they'd obviously interrupted whatever was happening behind the closed door to tell their laird all about it. Then again, she had brought the attention on herself. If she'd simply walked past them with her head held high, mayhap they would have ignored her.

And then Torsten wouldn't be standing before her.

She licked her lips nervously.

What did he want?

What did she want?

Éabha straightened, her nerves making her jumpy. "I suppose ye'll want me to go back to my chamber, but before I do there is something ye need to know."

"I dinna want ye to, unless ye want it. Tell me what's on your mind."

There he went, confusing her, acting as if he cared. How could he avoid her for so long and not say a thing about it?

"The nursery is filthy. Whoever was in charge of Nessa did a poor job. Her sheets are full of mud from whatever mischief she got into yesterday."

Torsten grunted, but said nothing.

"Mary told me the nurse has left, and I think that's a good thing as she wasn't properly caring for the child."

"My child."

"Aye, your child."

"And I suppose ye think ye could do a better job?"

Éabha placed her hands on her hips. Was that a challenge? "I already have."

"Well, I'm glad ye suggested it."

"Suggested what?" The conversation had taken a turn she'd not expected.

"That ye'd be her new nursemaid."

Éabha drew in a breath, excited at the prospect of having an excuse to stay, but not wanting him to know it. "I did not suggest that."

"Ah, I am mistaken."

Lord she wished she could see his expression. "A child needs structure and support they can count on."

"And ye know so much because…"

"I was once a child."

"And were ye a parent?"

Éabha swallowed hard, feeling a dagger twist in her gut. "Nay. But that does not mean I am ignorant."

"Hmm," Torsten said. "But ye've plenty of opinions."

"I have opinions about most things," she said begrudgingly. So he thought she was good enough to care for his daughter, but not good enough to speak her mind on the subject. "If ye'll excuse me."

She tried to skirt around him, to head back to her room confident Bad Lassie had made it to the kitchens and when she didn't arrive Mary would take the pup out for walk, but Torsten blocked her way.

"Where are ye going?" His voice was low, skating over her limbs like a caress. His fingers touched her elbow, but didn't grab hold.

"Back to my chamber."

"Where were ye going before that?"

"To the kitchens. Ye know that."

"But, why?"

"To take Bad Lassie out into the gardens."

"Then why would ye let me change your mind?"

She hated how her heart thudded in her ears and her throat went dry whenever she spoke to him. Would his presences always overwhelm her? Would she always lose her breath? "Because ye dinna want me to."

"I never said that."

Och, but she was more confused than ever. "What did ye say?"

"Only that if ye think ye could do a good job, I'd be honored if ye looked after my daughter."

Honored. Oh, what a dream it would be to stay. But... She couldn't. Not if she was going to be tormented by Torsten avoiding her one day and kissing her the next. As much as she loved the child, she needed to love herself more. Éabha shook her head. "I already told ye, I canna. I will not be here long, and she should have someone she can count on."

Torsten remained silent, and Éabha's limbs tingled. She wanted to run and stay put at the same time. To leap into his arms and shove him away. She was so confused.

"I shall escort ye to the gardens," he said softly. "The smells are quite heavenly at this time of year."

"I'd not think a warrior would care about such things." She couldn't deny him the escort, even if she wanted to. When it came to Torsten she was so weak.

"I dinna. But ye're a lady, and do not all ladies love flowers?"

Éabha shrugged, her tongue feeling swollen. "I dinna presume to know the workings of others' minds."

Torsten laughed, reached for her, his hands brushing her elbow again as he tucked it around his arm. Warmth emitted through his shirt, and she lightly placed her fingers on the muscles of his forearm.

"Why do ye laugh?" she asked.

"Because ye contradict yourself."

"How so?"

"Ye make plenty of assumptions about the workings of my mind, and yet, just now, ye said the opposite."

Éabha furrowed her brow. She could barely make out the workings of her own mind, let alone his. "I think ye goad me purposefully."

Torsten let out a mock gasp. "Me? I would never dare, my lady."

"Humph."

He led her down the hall, then opened a door which led to a garden with a high wall, and the sounds of the loch coming from the other side.

She was greeted with the sights and smells of a lovely lush garden. Drawing in a deep breath, she scanned the spring blooms with delight. Bluebells swayed in the breeze, interspersed with growing herbs. Yellow roses along the walkway matched the gown she wore, the one that had belonged to Torsten's wife.

"It really is beautiful," she murmured.

Torsten's blue gaze bored into hers. "And so are ye."

CHAPTER SIXTEEN

"Ye've shaved," Éabha said, here eyes focused on Torsten's smooth chin, avoiding the compliment he'd just paid her.

A subtle breeze freed a few golden curls to dangle by her ears. He itched to wrap them around his fingers.

He smiled and winked, feeling more pleased than he should at her observation. "Ye've noticed, eh?"

She flicked her green gaze back toward the flowers and shrugged. "'Twas obvious. Ye'd a good bit of stubble afore."

"I was training with my men while ye were singing nursery rhymes."

She glanced sharply back at him. "How did ye know I was singing?"

Torsten bit the side of his tongue. Dammit, he'd not wanted to let that out. Now she'd know he'd been spying on her.

"Nessa told me," he lied.

Éabha straightened, her eyes locking on his, challenging. "How long have ye had the skill?"

"Skill? I've many skills. To what do ye refer?"

Éabha grinned, and slid him a *got ye* glance. "Your choice, the skill of reading minds or the skill of telling a tale—ye're not so good at the latter."

Torsten narrowed his eyes feeling like he'd been thrust into a game in which he didn't know the rules. This feeling was odd for him, especially since he was the one normally in control. But whenever he was around her, he lost his good sense.

"What are ye accusing me of?" he asked.

Again that dainty shrug, and then she was sauntering away. There was something so mesmerizing in the gentle sway of her hips. The beauty of the garden around them, the sweet chirping of the birds making their spring nests, and the not so far off lapping of the loch at the water's edge. Och, but he wanted to lay her down right now. To make love to her beneath the spring sky.

"I did mention I took Nessa back to her chamber," Éabha was saying.

"Aye."

"Did I not mention it was directly before coming down the stairs? Unless of course, ye meant the singing we did yesterday, or the day before that, in which case, perhaps ye are telling the truth." She glanced at him over her shoulder, her gaze sliding over him. "But, I doubt it."

"Ah…" Torsten let out a short laugh. "So ye've caught me."

"Caught your little tale, aye, but what *aren't* ye telling?"

Torsten blew out a breath and took wide steps to catch up, needing to be close to her. To absorb her. "Must I confess?"

She tapped her lip, drawing his attention to the lush red line. "I am not your confessor, so nay."

"But are ye not curious?" Lord, why did he *want* her to be curious?

"A little."

That made him smile. Oh saints, but he was certainly acting the part of a young lad who'd just discovered flirtation.

"I came to find ye," he admitted. "But when I heard ye singing…"

She stopped walking, and tapped him in the chest. "Ye spied on us."

"Not exactly." He reached to catch her finger, but she danced away.

"Long enough, ye stood there, to spy."

"Not nearly." He wiggled his brows.

She stopped walking again, and he nearly ran into her, grabbed onto her hips to steady himself and her. "Not nearly?"

Ballocks… He ached to tug her back against him, but he had to let her go. She turned around to face him.

This part of the flirtation, the seduction part, Torsten was good at. His grin widened and he leaned down just enough that he was invading her space. Éabha's eyes flicked to his mouth and then back to his gaze. Oh, how he wanted to gloat, to say, *got ye*, but he didn't.

"I'd have stayed longer. I'd have come earlier," he said.

Pink edged up from the collar of her gown toward her chin. "I have a feeling ye're referring to something improper."

"Would I?"

She nodded slowly. "Ye would."

"And what would that be?"

She swallowed, her throat moving delicately. He needed his lips to be there, to feel the pulse of her heart beneath his kiss.

"Mayhap that ye would have liked to see me earlier, when I was having my bath."

Torsten leaned just an inch closer, breathing in her sweet, clean scent. He'd liked her essence before, but now… He'd pour it in a cup and drink it all day long.

"Have I rendered ye speechless?" Éabha said, placing her hand over her heart which only served to draw his attention to her breasts. He wanted to touch them, to peel away the layers of her gown and chemise and touch them, to watch her nipples harden beneath the sun's rays and his gaze. To press his lips to the place over her heart, then skim them over the soft mounds until his tongue flicked delicately over each rosy peak.

"I'm never speechless." His voice was low, throaty, quite obvious that he was in fact, going to be speechless momentarily if he couldn't stop thinking about all the things he wanted to do to her body.

Éabha laughed. "We both contradict ourselves."

"Perhaps we canna help it." He reached for her, his fingers grazing her elbow as he trailed a path down the length of her arm to her hand, and brought her fingertips to his lips.

She sucked in a breath, the pinkness of her neck having reached her cheeks.

"Ye confuse me," she whispered.

"I confess to confusing myself."

"Ye confess much this afternoon."

"Too much."

And then he was tugging her into his arms, sweeping her out of the view of the castle and beneath an arbor full of winding vines and red blossoms. His lips claimed hers, searing, hot, demanding. He needed her. Couldn't go another second without tasting her. Och, but it had been so long since his lips had touched hers.

"What is it about ye?" he asked as he savored her lips. "I canna leave ye alone. I tried. And I tried again. But I have failed."

"Ye must." Her hands slid over his chest, pressing into his muscles.

"I canna. Tell me, tell me what I need to know," he said. "Tell me the truth about Donald."

Éabha yanked away from him, her hands flying to her cheeks. "Ye kiss me to hear me confess?"

"Nay." Torsten shook his head and reached for her but she backed away. "Not at all." He raked his hands through his hair. "I need to know the truth." He gritted his teeth as she took another step back. "I need to know if I'm kissing a married woman or a woman who is free to return my…"

His what? He would not dare confess to anything more than his desire for her.

"Your what?" she asked, her eyes wide, hands still pressed to her face, demanding he confess a secret he was not yet willing to admit.

Torsten shook his head. "My desire." He was a coward, fully aware it was more than simple desire that heated his blood, though that was a big part of it.

And now she knew him for a fool, too.

Éabha shook her head. "Ye think to take advantage of me."

"Never." How could this moment have turned cold so quickly?

"Ye think because I married a man I abhorred, that I would willingly fall into bed with ye?"

"Ye used past tense."

"Past tense?"

"He is dead, is he not? Tell me and we need not worry about sin."

Éabha's hands fisted and she thrust them down at her sides. "Ye're incorrigible, only interested in two things—my body and my husband's death."

Torsten shook his head vehemently. "That is not true."

But she didn't let him finish, she marched forward, poked him in the chest and glared, the fiery side he knew so well rearing its head.

"Well, I'll tell ye the truth and then be done with ye! He is dead. Your men killed him. He died only moments afore ye arrived at the gates of Strome. Are ye happy now?"

Torsten nodded. There was more he wanted to say to her, to comfort her, to tell her she wasn't right about him, that he wasn't only interested in her body and her husband's breath, that he wanted her, all of her, but his brain was moving too slow, and his mouth felt as though it had been filled with sawdust.

Éabha let out a disgusted little squeal and whirled on her heel.

It seemed his feet were also moving too slow, his boots perhaps nailed to the garden path.

"Éabha, wait!" By the time he'd said the words and shifted his feet she'd already rounded the corner and gone through the garden gate.

He started to run, finding the garden empty around the side of the castle and the gate securely fastened. He wrenched it open, and took off at a run, seeing the flutter of fabric near the loch gate stairs.

His guards would never let her out of the gates. But when he reached the stairs they nodded to him and she was nowhere to be seen.

"Where is she?" he demanded.

"On the shore, just as ye instructed."

"What?" Exasperation tore through him.

"She said ye'd given her permission, that ye were just behind her and when we saw ye…" They trailed off realizing how she'd played them.

Torsten shoved past one guard. "We'll discuss this later." He ran through the gate, just in time to see her walking fully clothed into the loch.

"What the hell are ye doing?" he shouted. "Stop!"

But she continued into the water, using her arms to pull herself forward. The loch would be frigid, she'd freeze afore she reached the center, but perhaps that was her plan. To drown herself. Had she not hinted at offing herself before?

For the love of all that was holy, he couldn't lose her!

Torsten unbuckled his belt, his weapons falling in a heap with his plaid as he rushed toward her. He didn't bother removing his shirt or boots, but ran headlong into the water. She was two dozen paces ahead of him and moving fast, despite how much the water must be weighing her gown down.

Not once did she glance back at him as he shouted. Torsten ripped through the water, closing the distance, but it seemed to take forever to get to her. The bottom of the loch was no where near their feet and they both treaded water, her sinking before flailing above. Water splashed with her movements. The gown had to weigh as much as a man and sucked her down, but she tried with all her might to rise above. Every time she went under he felt his heart stop as he moved faster and faster. Then she'd appear again, sputtering and drawing breath before sinking.

Finally, he reached her, and when he did she fought him, swinging her delicate fists toward him, and slipping under the water in the process. The loch was cold enough that it turned her lips blue. Since his muscles were still warm from chasing after her, he didn't quite feel the chill yet, but his skin was prickly. He swam in the cold loch often, and knew he'd be fine, but she was already frozen to the core.

"Let me go!" She tried to wrench away from him, slipping under once more.

Torsten hauled her back to the surface, pinning her arms at her sides. "Nay! I won't let ye drown yourself."

"Drown myself? Ye fool! I would never do such a thing."

Her legs wiggled against his. She was trying to kick him but the weight of the gown combined with the power of the current kept her from being able to do so.

Torsten tightened his hold around her and shouted. "So ye simply thought a dip in the freezing loch was a good idea?"

She stared at him, wide-eyed and incredulous. "Nay! I sought to escape ye. To swim to the other side. I didna realize how far it was…" She trailed off, teeth chattering.

"*Mo chreach* ye little fool, ye'd have killed yourself afore arriving. Ye're drowning right now!"

"I know how to swim."

"But ye obviously dinna know enough to take off your gown."

"I dinna want to be naked."

"Too late." Torsten yanked at the back of her gown, finding the soaked fabric hard to tear. "Ye'll have us both drowning."

As he fought with her gown, the current picked up in the center of the loch, tugging at her. He had to get her out of this gown. He reached for the *sgian dubh* at his ankle and started to cut at the ties.

"What are ye doing?" she screeched. "Ye're ruining it."

"I'm saving your life, ye nitwit." The last of the ties were cut, and he struggled to yank the fabric from her flailing body.

When he finally had it off, he wrapped one arm around her waist, and used his other to start swimming.

"I dinna want to go back to your castle!" she called out, her teeth chattering.

"Ye've no choice, and this time I'm locking ye in, husband or nay."

"He's dead! Let me go! Ye've no further need of me."

"Ye're even more of a fool than I could have imagined."

For once, she did not respond, and he thought it might have been the cold taking over her, but she still held that haughty glower, so he warmed inside knowing that she still had enough gumption to be angry with him.

Torsten used her silence to continue propelling them toward the shore. Fighting her, fighting the current, the cold, it was exhausting.

By the time they got to the water's edge, he was spent. He hauled her onto the shore and laid down for a moment upon the reeds and water grasses to catch his breath. The sun felt good on his skin, but the gentle breeze only made him colder.

She sat beside him, in her soaked chemise, shivering and pouting. He tried not to look, knowing full well now was not a good time to observe the very perfection of her long legs and the swell of her breasts.

Several guards rushed toward the shore, calling out to him.

"We are all right," he answered.

He climbed to his feet, and gathered up his plaid, then wrapped it around Éabha's shoulders to hide her near nakedness. Even though she protested, he lifted her up, tucked her against his chest and carried her toward the shore stairs. She shivered in his arms, and lowered her eyelids, no longer glaring at him, but looking rather lethargic.

"Ye've made your point. But next time, just steal a horse," he muttered.

"My laird!" Little Rob was the first to reach them.

"Have the hearth stoked to blazing in my chamber. Send one of the men to find my belt and sword by the loch shore. And send for Mary to tend the lady." Then he turned his attention to Éabha. "I'll ready your horse myself, but first, warm yourself so ye dinna die of chill afore ye attempt to leave again."

CHAPTER SEVENTEEN

Éabha was too cold to really think, but Torsten's words echoed through her mind over and over and all she could think of was, why?

Why was he being so kind?

Was he truly going to let her go so easily?

And most of all, why had she been so impulsive as to jump into the loch? Clearly the other side was far away. How had she thought she could swim the length of it? She wasn't daft. She knew better than to think she wouldn't drown. Her emotions were running rampant, making her act illogically. She should have stolen a boat. Then, perhaps, she might have made it.

Shivers wracked her body. The fabric of her chemise was cold and clinging. A heaviness weighed inside her, too, as though her bones had turned to ice, and if Torsten dropped her, she'd crash through the earth, disappearing forever.

She was vaguely aware of voices. But only heard Torsten's replies in deep rumbles of his chest. She was too weak to hold onto him, and feeling too stupid to try. She kind of hoped he would drop her so she could vanish, be swallowed up in the dirt to keep from having to face the mortification that surely awaited her.

But no such luck.

Torsten carried her through the castle, and up the stairs, not showing any signs of exhaustion. But regardless of his demeanor, the weight of her drenched chemise, and the half-soaked plaid feeling like a dozen large stones, she was certain he must be getting tired. She was also certain that she'd not be able to walk if given the chance. She couldn't even feel her toes.

Not only were her feet numb with cold, her limbs were heavy and she felt as though someone had shoved ice beneath her skin and into her bones.

Teeth chattering fiercely, she still protested for Torsten to put her down, because she had pride after all, but he ignored her, and she knew that even if her words had been more audible, shouted from the very depths of her lungs, he still would have disregarded her demands.

Torsten carried her through the door of his chamber, his four poster bed and stark walls looming. She longed for the comfort of her tower chamber, with its stone walls covered in the paintings she and Nessa had made. Besides, being in his chamber was simply unacceptable.

She tried to wriggle free. Everyone was certain to talk. At least when he'd taken her to his room weeks ago no one but Mary had borne witness to it. Now the entire castle knew she was here. Practically naked. And without her wits.

Servants bustled about the room, stoking the fire and doing other things her blurry vision couldn't pick up on.

Torsten laid her on the bed, and brandished his dagger over her.

"Nay," she said, trying to get her words out more forcefully.

She didn't want to die. How could he trick her like this? That's why he'd said those pretty words about letting her ride off with one of his horses, because he didn't plan to actually let her.

Éabha drew in a deep breath and waited for the tip of his blade to pierce her skin. She stared him right in the eye. She might not be able to move, but she wasn't going down with her eyes closed.

Torsten brought the blade closer. "I'm sorry for this, lass, but it must be done."

Éabha wanted to cry, but her stubborn streak refused to show him she was beaten.

He touched the blade to her chemise and then wrenched it to the side. The fabric, which had grown unbearable tight, suddenly loosened.

"What…?" she asked.

"'Twas necessary, else ye freeze. Ye're already blue," he was saying, and then servants were yanking at the fabric, and Éabha tried to move her limbs to cover her nakedness.

She saw Mary, her face grim. No doubt Mary thought she'd tried to drown herself, too, having borne witness to her previous declarations that she'd off herself in order to get away from Torsten. But those had been empty threats. She didn't want to die.

Jumping into the loch had not been an attempt to end things, aye, but, she'd only wanted to leave the castle, to somehow get to the other side. To travel to Nèamh Abbey on the Isle of Skye. The servants had said it was an accepting place with a Mother Abbess who took in many women. When she'd thought that Torsten was only interested in her body, nothing more, she'd felt bereft, lost, useless. Escape from such wretched feelings had been the only thing on her mind. She'd not drown herself, ever. That was too painful a death. And killing one's self was a sin. She still hoped to atone for her past transgressions, she'd not be able to do that if she spent eternity walking Purgatory. Didn't they understand that?

A sudden cold burst of air touched her skin and she realized she was naked, the damp borrowed plaid gone, too. The servants looked away and a moment later, the bed dipped and she was filled in a cocoon of warmth.

"'Tis the fastest way," Torsten said, his naked arms coming around her waist from behind and tugging her back flush to his searing skin.

"Ye are... n-naked," she said through chattering teeth.

"And so are ye."

"L-Lord, help m-me," she said, whispering a prayer for forgiveness.

"Believe it or not, this is not a seduction," he said. "'Tis the fastest way to get your body temperature up, I swear it."

She still felt frozen to the core, but around the edges, it seemed warmth was trying to push its way in.

"Damn ye for scaring me like that," he was saying against her ear. "What in bloody hell, Éabha? Why would ye do that?"

"I t-told ye. I was tr-trying to get to the other s-side." She was so cold. She blinked her eyes closed, feeling too tired to hold them open.

"Dinna fall asleep," Torsten said, perhaps sensing a change in her breathing.

His hand rubbed at her hip, her thighs, her ribs, her arms. A large, muscular leg draped over hers, and instinctively she tucked herself into a ball, the bottoms of her feet pressing to his much larger calves.

"I'm t-tired."

"Whisky!" Torsten called, and a cup was pressed to her lips.

She took a sip, dribbling some on the sheet beneath her since her lips were numb, and then she took another sip, feeling the warmth of the fiery liquid burning a path down her throat.

"We're n-not alone in my shame," she whispered.

"There is no shame," Torsten said, his voice filled with conviction.

"They w-will all think I t-tried to k-kill myself."

"To all who bore witness, here me now," Torsten bellowed. "The lady did not try to drown herself. She simply wished to swim to the other side of the loch fully clothed."

There was a murmuring around the room and Éabha didn't know which grew more, her mortification or her desire to murder him.

"Ye dinna h-have to say everything I do."

Torsten grunted. "Ye wanted it known. I solved the problem."

"Not everything is so easily solved."

"Says the woman who thought it smart to swim in an icy loch fully dressed."

She could have told him about Nèamh Abbey, but she kept it to herself. "I'm sorry about your wife's gown."

"It is only fabric, Éabha. Things can be replaced. Lives canna."

She snuggled closer, somehow she was not as cold, not as numb, but feeling safe and warmer. "Ye risked your life for me."

"I would do so again."

His words warmed her more than his body. Her heart lurched.

Her eyes were closed, her nose pressed to his forearm. "Ye are better to me than any jailer ought to be. And I like ye more than a captive should like her captor."

"Ye've never been my captive," he whispered.

"Ye lie." She opened her eyes attempting to peer behind her.

"Och, for perhaps an hour or two, and then ye were forever known as my guest," he chuckled. "Ye know the door to your chamber was unlocked after the first night."

"But it *was* locked."

"For your protection."

"Mine?"

"My people are verra angry with your clan." He continued his vigorous stroking of her limbs.

Her toes were starting to tingle in pain, her fingertips, too, but at least her teeth seemed to cease their chattering.

"As were ye," she said.

"Aye."

"I am sorry, Torsten." She licked her cold lips.

"About?"

Éabha closed her eyes, and laid her head back down on the pillow. "The raid was my fault."

Torsten stiffened behind her. She expected him to slip from the bed, to leave her there in her frozen misery, but he didn't leave her.

"Our people were starving. My marriage, my sin, 'twas an abomination that brought ill-will to our clan. I suggested that Donald go and steal a few provisions." Hot tears spilled from her eyes. "I never expected he would do what he did." She openly sobbed now. "I am the reason your village was desecrated."

"Nay, nay, nay," Torsten said. "He would have done so anyway. MacDonell was always raiding our lands. 'Tis the reason I told him war was coming."

"He didna tell me." She'd always thought he left too eagerly to go and raid. Donald had liked it.

"Why would he? The man did not respect ye as a partner, or as a wife."

A hot tear spilled onto her cold cheek. "He respected no one but himself."

Torsten sighed, his stroking less vigorous and more comforting. "The two of us, we are letting dead men rule our lives."

"That seems unfair when ye say it."

"It is unfair. But it seems to be who we are. The two of us, taking on the burdens, the sins of others, and repenting for actions neither of us had a say in taking."

Éabha turned around again, her eyes lighting on his. "Do ye forgive me?"

"Ye've done nothing that needs forgiveness." He nuzzled her cheek, the both of them oblivious to the servants in the room.

"But I have," she whispered.

"Well…" He grinned. "'Haps, I might not have chosen to go for a swim today."

Éabha laughed, feeling as though some of the ice in her bones was thawing.

"Your body is warming."

"Thank ye, I am feeling better. Sleepy, but better."

The room filled with a delicious herbal aroma. "Broth, my laird."

"Do ye think ye can sit up?" Torsten asked her.

Éabha nodded. Did she want to, was another question. Lying in Torsten's arms was one of the most wonderful feelings in the world, and it wasn't simply a sensual thing. It was comfort and camaraderie he was providing her. But she was certain as soon as she could feel all of her limbs, being pressed against his hot, *naked,* body would be the most sensual thing she'd ever experienced. She didn't want to get up, and yet, she knew she must.

Torsten helped her to sit, wrapping her in several plaids, to protect her modesty. The fire was blazing, and two servants stood beside it, one feeding it wood, the other stirring the fiery embers.

Little Rob leaned against the doorframe and Mary was setting down a tray on the table. She brought a bowl of broth to her laird, who handed it to Éabha.

"Ye first."

Éabha tentatively took hold of the bowl, pulling it to her lips and taking a long sip. The broth was decadent. Warm, savory. It filled her belly, thawing her insides.

Mary returned with another bowl for Torsten, who drank his much quicker than she had. Éabha tried to give him the remaining half of hers but he insisted she finish. She did so slowly, her lips finally warm, though the tip of her nose was still pretty cold. Her hair was wet, and left a chill upon her shoulders.

"'Haps now I should sit by the fire to dry my hair," she said, handing the empty bowl back to Mary.

"Good idea." Torsten tugged on the shirt Mary had given him and climbed from the bed.

She started to unravel herself from the blankets to stand, but he shook his head and lifted her.

"Ye need to stay wrapped up. There is still a chance ye could get sick from the cold."

"But I am feeling much warmer."

Torsten gave her a stern look that rivaled some of her own and she clamped her mouth closed. This was a new feeling, being taken care of and being cherished. For most of her life she'd been left to her own devices. Even when her uncle had married her she'd been abandoned to the wind. No one was her champion. She had to be her own savior. And she'd accepted that. Excelled at it—or at least to the degree in which she was allowed.

No one had ever been as tender with her as Torsten.

It seemed so backward and unfair, that the man who had stolen her away could be her savior after all.

He settled her on a bearskin rug before the fire, then sat down beside her. Mary draped another plaid blanket around his shoulders, and started to brush her hair. Torsten flashed Éabha a smile that she couldn't read, because it was one she'd not seen before. He almost seemed shy, vulnerable, but only for a moment before the tough warrior returned.

"Have ye saved many women from drowning?" Éabha asked.

"Ye'd be my first."

"Ye seem so skilled at it."

"That doesna mean ye should do it again."

Éabha laughed, taking a goblet that was handed to her. It was more whisky. She took a long sip, feeling its potent effect starting to make her feel light and free. "I promise, I will not jump into another loch again."

"Unless of course it's the height of summer, and the water is warm, and ye're not wearing any clothes." Torsten flashed her a devilish wink.

Éabha's mouth fell open. "Ye're wicked, Laird Mackenzie."

He shrugged. "Mayhap another skill I possess."

"Hmm," Éabha said, taking another sip. She passed the goblet to Torsten who looked into it and then shook his head. "Drink some," she urged. "Ye were just as cold as I."

Again he shook his head. Éabha narrowed her eyes, looked around the room, and then said, "Let it be known to all who stand here, your laird is not a drunkard, nor a man without morals."

The women curtsied, pressed their hands to their hearts and murmured their agreement. The men slapped their chests and shouted their loyalty.

"Ye see?" Éabha grinned. "They know who ye really are, Torsten."

CLAIMED BY THE WARRIOR

CHAPTER EIGHTEEN

This time, Torsten was truly speechless.

In a matter of seconds, Éabha managed to disarm him and gain allegiance from his people. Aye, they'd pledged their loyalty to him, but in agreeing with her, they had also pledged their loyalty to her.

It was enough to make his chest swell with pride, and dry his mouth from the emotion welling up inside him.

The last hour had completely turned him upside down.

This was supposed to be about her. She'd been the one to fling herself into a loch, nearly drowning and freezing to death.

It was all a little much for him. Torsten nodded, drank down his whisky, because to do otherwise would show his men that he did not believe in himself. He was not like his brother. He knew it. And they knew it. The whisky lit a fire on his tongue, and burst into pleasing flames in his empty belly. Lord, it had been a long time since he'd had a drink. Before Cathal had gone off the deep end, Torsten had been a whisky enthusiast, even dabbling in making his own from time to time—they were never as good as those who made it their life's work, but all the same, it was the passion of pursuit that made it fun.

"Thank ye," Torsten said to Éabha.

Then he rose, shrugging off the plaid around his shoulders. He stood in the center of the room in just his linen shirt, nodded again to the few men and servants who stood there. He held out his cup for another dram of whisky. The second time around was just as a smooth.

"I've been blessed with a clan who believes in me," he said, then gave a half-hearted chuckle. "Even when I'm only half dressed. I'd not be able to guide ye without your trust."

And then he was leaving. To where, he didn't know, this was his chamber, but he couldn't stay in there anymore. Not when he had such mixed emotions. Not when the very sight of Éabha had his chest clenching up tight, and the way she'd stirred him and his men...

Torsten marched quickly beneath the doorframe, rounding the corridor and took the stairs two at a time. He walked with purpose when he wanted to run, all the way to his library, where he shut the door behind him and sank into his cushioned chair, his head falling onto the back.

The chamber was dark, only a few slivers of light came in from the shuttered window. 'Twas cold and drafty, last nights fire having long since turned to cool embers.

He didn't move to open the shutters or to light a candle. He preferred the darkness.

What was he going to do about Éabha?

He should send her back to MacDonell lands with a warning to her people not to cross the lines of their property without permission. She was already muddling his mind. Getting under his skin. The best thing for everyone was to let her go.

But he didn't want to let her go.

What would happen to her if he did?

Would she be forced to marry another?

No doubt, she would. She was still young enough. Alliances had to be made. Whoever was going to take MacDonell's place, her cousin George, or another, would need to make a big move, a strong alliance, and getting rid of the old laird's wife who could cause problems was the best way to do that.

An alliance between Mackenzie and MacDonells.

That was the obvious solution, but his own people, they'd never go for it. Not when the MacDonells had already caused them so much pain. They'd never shake hands with the bastards and he didn't blame them. But they had been able to accepted Éabha into their lives. So perhaps it wasn't so unfathomable after all.

A knock came at the door. Gentle and tentative.

"Enter," Torsten barked.

The door creaked open, and soft steps filed in, the door closing with a click. He didn't bother to and see who it was. Probably a servant who'd ask about dinner, they'd light the flameless candles, and try to strike up a fire.

Instead, soft hands fluttered over his shoulders, trembling as they rubbed his tense muscles.

He could sense her, smell her.

"Éabha," he said.

"Aye." Her voice was soft, soothing.

"What are ye doing?" He opened his eyes to see her standing over him, behind his chair.

"What are *ye* doing?" she asked.

He smiled. Obstinate as ever. "Thinking."

"In the dark?"

"I do some of my best work in the dark."

"Hmm. I suppose I do, too. But I believe there is more than simply thinking going on in your head."

"Oh?" Torsten settled further into his chair, leaning his head back and feeling her belly pressed to the chair. He relaxed with the gentle massage of her fingers.

"Ye're afraid," she murmured.

That had him sitting back up, rigid and filled with tension. "How dare ye accuse me of such! I'm never afraid."

Éabha laughed. "Being afraid does not mean ye're a coward."

Torsten grunted. "That is what I tell my men."

"But ye dinna believe it, do ye?"

He grunted again, not wanting to answer. Too many times he'd been afraid and pulled back.

"Ye're a skilled warrior, Torsten. Powerful, too, if ye look at the size of your lands."

"They were not begotten by me."

"But they were held by ye." She yanked him back, continuing to massage away the tenseness he desperately held onto.

Again, he grunted. Was he only able to make animal sounds?

"I dinna expect ye to believe me, or to even listen, I am, after all, your enemy, but the people upstairs, why should they agree with me unless it is the truth?"

"They would not."

"Then ye admit it is true."

"I admit it," he said begrudgingly.

He could almost see her smile as she sighed, and he realized that he *wanted* to see her smile. Reaching for her hand, he tugged her around until she tumbled into his lap and he wrapped his arms around her, expecting her to try to clamber away, but she did not.

"Éabha," he said, not certain how to proceed.

"Torsten." She placed her hands on his shoulders, inching toward the back of his neck and linking them there.

"Ye've changed me," he said.

Had to be the whisky. He didn't normally confess such things. Well, that wasn't true. He'd been confessing things to her since the moment he met her.

Maybe it was the whisky, or maybe he'd grown mushy, he didn't care.

"I've not changed ye." She stroked his hair. "No one can change another person without them letting it happen."

"But ye have, against my will." He chuckled.

She shook her head, and in the dim light he could see the hair tumble loose from her braid, as wild and desperate for freedom as she was. "I have only helped ye."

"Helped me what?"

"The same way ye've helped me."

"I dinna understand, love." He wanted to nuzzle her neck. To breathe in the scent of her hair that moved in waves around her sloping neck.

205

"Ye've opened your mind to new possibilities. Perhaps even forgiven yourself a little."

He tugged her closer. "And have ye?"

"A little."

Torsten slid his hand up her back until her reached the nape of her neck, then tugged a little more, until she was leaning toward him and he could press his face against her skin.

Éabha sighed. "I dinna know how, or why," she was saying. "But as ye mentioned, we are a pair. So much in common, and yet so much that separates us."

She tilted her head to the side and he skimmed his lips over the soft skin at the base of her neck.

"Aye," he said. "I want no other."

And that was true. He didn't want anyone but Éabha, for now and for always, but he couldn't tell her that last part. What he'd said was enough of a confession.

"I want ye, too," she whispered.

An admission? Permission?

Torsten took it as both, his lips claiming hers.

Éabha tightened her hold around Torsten's neck, sinking against him as he kissed her. Oh, but she'd waited so long to feel his lips on hers. Perhaps not so long, since he'd kissed her just that afternoon in the garden. Mayhap, what she'd been waiting for was to let go of all her reservations.

To allow herself to be kissed without pushing him away.

When she admitted that she wanted him, she'd been speaking the truth. She wanted him badly. To kiss. To keep.

To make real love to. To spill secrets in the dark for the rest of their days.

And yet, she was too afraid to share too much, to get hurt.

So, instead, she kissed him deeper. Savoring this moment, this darkness, because someday it would come to an end, and at least when it did, she would have these precious flashes to remember him by. To recall how it felt to be wanted, needed, and not used.

Torsten shifted beneath her, the swell of his erection pressed to her thigh. It made her entire body light on fire, heat searing her skin, lightning whizzing through her veins. She nestled closer, encouraging his roaming hands to keep stroking over her back, her arms, her thighs.

Perhaps it was the whisky, or the need to feel hot when she'd been so cold before, but she started to kiss him with a frenzy, an unbridled need and Torsten eagerly returned her fervor. With his hands on her hips, he lifted her, settling her bottom on his desk, pressing his thighs to her knees and shifting forward so he stood between her legs.

She hooked her calves behind his thighs, tugging him closer, her hands around his waist, pressed to his spine. They moved with fluid need, and ardent devotion. Torsten claimed her mouth with tantalizing intensity. One arm around her waist, the other stroked her ribs, and cupped her breast.

Éabha gasped, wanting his touch but nervous at the same time. Would he like her body? Would she continue to feel this good the entire time he touched her?

The entire time…

Aye, she was going to give herself to him. Right now. Right here. Because she didn't know when she would get the chance again, and she wanted these moments. Needed them.

They were hers.

She whimpered as his thumb brushed over her turgid nipple, and at the same time he pressed his erection against the crux of her thighs.

"I want to make ye mine," he murmured against her lips.

"I am yours," she answered.

"I can never thank ye for giving me all that ye have," he said. "When I took so much away from ye."

"Ye have taken nothing," she said. "Ye have set me free."

Éabha, sensed his hesitation and seeking to give him more confirmation of what she wanted, she gripped her skirts and tugged them over her thighs, feeling the cold hit her skin, baring all of herself to the air, and to him. She tugged at his shirt, lifting until the only barrier between them was gone.

"Make love to me, Torsten." Éabha caressed his hip, gently drawing him forward until his solid shaft touched her damp curls. She gasped at the decadent contact.

"Ye're trembling," he said.

Éabha nodded and with her free hand cupped his face, tilting her head up to kiss him. "I'm all right," she said, sliding her tongue over her lower lip. "I want this. I want ye."

Torsten growled low in his throat, seeming to understand how serious she was. He kissed her deeply, his hands going between their bodies to slide over her folds. She moaned at the same time he did, as his fingers slid over her damp center. And then he was probing, gently pushing a finger inside her as his lips once more pulled from hers to skim over her neck. He tugged on her gown just above her breasts with his teeth, teasing his tongue beneath the fabric to lick her nipple.

"Oh!" Éabha cried out, not realizing a man would do such a thing, nor how much she would enjoy it.

She freed her breasts and moaned again when he wrapped his lips around her nipple and sucked.

"Ye're so beautiful," he murmured. "Your breasts... They are perfection. And your..." He slipped his finger from inside her and drove it in again. "'Tis luscious."

Éabha couldn't breathe, couldn't speak. She was wound tight inside, new and exotic sensations rippling through her. The way he stroked her breasts, between her thighs... 'Twas magical. She threaded her fingers through his hair, feeling the soft locks glide between them.

"I meant what I said, Éabha," Torsten murmured against her breasts, coming up to tug her lower lip with his teeth. "I'm going to make ye mine, and when I do, it's going to last forever."

CHAPTER NINETEEN

Éabha basked in the assurance that this was meant to be. Torsten knew just what she was thinking. They both wanted this moment to last forever.

"Aye," she crooned.

"Say ye'll be mine."

"I am yours." Her head fell back as pleasure coursed through her veins, taking her ability to think straight, even her reflex to breathe, to blink.

She was drunk with desire, need, and excitement. Intoxicated by Torsten's sensual words, his promises of forever, his fingers, lips and tongue.

Torsten gripped his arousal and slid it through her folds, and she cried out at the sweet decadence of it. Holding onto his shoulders, legs wrapped around him, she tilted her hips as much as she could, practically begging for his entry with her movements. She squeezed her eyes shut, waiting for the discomfort of his invasion would cause, praying it would soon be replaced by whatever sensations he'd already stirred inside her.

"Och, lass… Ye have bewitched me."

He notched the head of his arousal at her entrance, her body vibrated with exhilaration, and then he was plunging inside. They both cried out as he buried himself to the hilt, filling her wholly and completely.

She'd expected it to be unpleasant as it had been with her husband. But it was not. In fact, it was the exact opposite.

It felt good. So good. Too good.

Making love to Torsten was everything his kisses had promised.

Éabha gasped, her mouth falling open, she clamped it closed, biting her lip, but she couldn't help confessing, "This is not what I expected."

Torsten pulled his face from the crook of her shoulder to meet her gaze, and even in the dim light she could see his concerned expression.

"Am I hurting ye?"

She smiled, hazy and mildly delirious. "Not at all. Quite the contrary."

Torsten grinned, and stroked her cheek. "Ye're enjoying it?"

Éabha squeezed his shoulders. "Every moment."

Torsten breathed a sigh of relief, withdrawing from her body and when she clenched tight around him, he drove swiftly back inside. She stiffened again, the unpleasantness of bedding drilled into her memory so deep it was hard to forget.

"Relax," he whispered against her ear, tugging her lobe between his teeth and sending shivers racing over every inch of her body. "I would never hurt ye."

"I know." She let her fears go. Let herself sink into this. Alone in the world with nothing and no one but a man who desired her. Cared for her. Protected her. "I trust ye."

And she did, with her whole heart.

"Lay back." Torsten gently guided her to lie back on his desk, skating a palm between her breasts and over her abdomen.

He skimmed his hands up under her skirts slowly sliding the fabric further above her hips, and then he lifted her buttocks, drawing her closer to his body. His touch was confident, knowing, but tender all the same. The way he made her feel... It was amazing. Beautiful. Cherished. Desired. She was going to remember this for the rest of her days.

He swiveled his hips and she moaned at the jolt of pleasure his movements brought. He splayed a hand on her chest, sliding his palm over to cup one of her breasts. Leaning over her, he nuzzled the soft mounds, laving one nipple and then the other. One hand held her thigh, and the other slid from her chest, down her belly and between her thighs where their bodies were joined. He stroked between her folds, a knot of flesh that fired arrows of pleasure from her center outward.

Torsten seemed to know just the right way to touch her, to bring her body to life. He continued to drive his arousal in and out of her, slow and steady, his groans of approval muffled against her flesh.

Éabha waffled between fisting the hair at the back of his head and languidly stroking the back of his neck, depending on the moves he made. When his fingers stilled and he stroked his body in and out of hers, she was floating in a cloud of pleasure. But when he stroked her with his fingers and quickened his pace, her breaths lurched and she felt as though she were racing toward a precipice. He teased her. Taunted her. Switched from fast and hard to slow and soft.

And then it didn't matter what pace he chose, because her body picked up speed, and she demanded he not cease his movements. Torsten laughed, a sensual satisfied sound, scraping against her ear, as he quickened his pace in earnest. His breathing grew deeper, his moans more guttural.

"Kiss me," she demanded, and he did, belly to belly, his mouth claiming hers as he drove deeper and deeper inside her.

Éabha arched her back, lifting her legs higher, then she was crying out, her body shattering in a climax she didn't even know was possible. Or real. Perhaps this was a dream. Mayhap he'd not fished her out of the water after all, but she'd sunk beneath, for it was certain she couldn't catch her breath.

"Och, Éabha," Torsten growled against her mouth.

He slowed above her, lifting her up and cradling her against him.

"Did I drown?" she asked, half-serious.

"I know I did. In pleasure. Decadence. Heaven. Thank goodness the loch didna do us both in."

Éabha laughed, the sound filled with a joy she didn't recognize. When had she ever been so happy?

"Heaven is dark," she said, teasing. The sun must have set as they made love for no light filtered through the shutters.

"We lit it up a moment ago." Torsten brushed his lips over hers.

"Aye, I did not even notice the lack of light."

"Let us go back to my chamber. I will send for our supper."

Éabha shook her head, placing a hand on his shoulder to still his movements. "Nay. I should go back to my chamber. We've been in here too long. They will talk."

Éabha could feel the shift in the air, the stiffening of Torsten's body beneath her hand.

"Talk?"

She cleared her throat, some of the happiness she felt ebbing away. "Aye. Rumors. Innuendos. They will brand me a whore."

"They would never insult me in such a way."

"Insult ye?" Éabha was a little taken aback. "Am I that much of a leper, that a rumor about me being with ye would be an insult?" She shoved at his shoulder, and pushed off the desk, working to straighten her skirts and hair and knowing even in the dark she must look a fright. What had she been thinking giving herself to him? A selfish, senseless whim that was only going to end up costing her.

"Ye misunderstand me," Torsten said.

Éabha put her hands on her hips, wishing there was light so he could see her glower. "How so?"

"I meant if they were to call ye a whore."

"Because ye'd never sleep with a whore?" Tears of frustration stung her eyes. He was ruining all the precious moments they'd just shared.

Firm hands held tight to her shoulders. "Éabha, have ye gone mad again? Will ye not listen to reason?"

"I am beyond reason. This castle is driving me to madness."

Torsten forced her into his embrace, wrapping his arms around her back. And spoke softly. "I was not lying when I said ye'd be mine. Ye are mine. No one would dare to insult what is mine."

"Yours. What does that mean? I am not property." She frowned against his shoulder, still smelling herself on his skin. "It was all well and good in the heat of the moment, your braw words even heightened my excitement and pleasure. I but thought ye meant for the moment. I told ye before I did not want to be beholden to anyone."

Torsten tipped her chin, and kissed her lips. "I meant forever. Ye'd not be beholden to me. I will be good to ye. I intend to wed ye, lass."

Éabha's heart sank. Oh, aye, the idea of marrying Torsten was more than appealing, 'twas a dream come true. But he was only doing it because he'd just bedded her and there were consequences because of it, else he would have asked her properly rather than just assuming it would be so. "But ye didna ask me if I wanted to be wed."

Torsten let out an exasperated sigh. "I assumed by making love with me ye were in agreement."

Well that put a spin on it she'd not anticipated. Still, she needed to know. "And if I wasn't, ye wouldn't have touched me?"

His finger slid along her jawline. "I'm not certain I could have stopped…"

Éabha reached up to still his hand on her face, distracted by his light caress. "I am only newly widowed. Barely a few weeks."

"Were ye ever truly wed?"

She could guess what he meant, in her heart did she think of herself as truly wed, and the answer was nay, but... "In the eyes of the lord and the law, aye."

"Then we will wait. Three months and no more."

"Three months?"

"So your clan is certain ye are not with child."

"I am not. I took precautions... before." Lord, but would he think her evil for having done so? For admitting it? A woman was supposed to do her duty, and she'd blatantly made certain that no child resulted from the abhorrent unions with her husband.

"Ye might be now." Torsten's voice was low and sensual. He tickled her ribs. "For their was no caution in what we just did."

Éabha playfully swatted his shoulder. "Oh, ye brute!" But then she turned serious again. "If I am, then what does it mean?"

"Naught. It would be mine."

"Then why wait three months?"

"Why indeed?"

Her head was beginning to pound. She needed to lie down. She'd almost drowned not two hours before. "Ye toy with me."

"I would never. I simply want to give ye what ye wish."

"How do ye know what I wish?"

"Because, I may have confessed much to ye, but ye have confessed much to me as well. Ye want stability, protection, love, companionship."

She drew in a deep, surprised breath. He'd been listening all this time? "I do," she whispered.

"I know. And I want to give it to ye." Torsten was so full of confidence, strength. She wanted to latch onto it and drag some of it into herself.

"But your clan—why would they ever agree? They think I'm the enemy. Ye came to Strome and captured me. Surely they won't see it as an act of... of..." Love? "They will think ye wed me for political reasons. They will not respect me."

"As evidenced from my chamber, when they all expressed their loyalty to ye, I think not."

She was searching now. Trying to find a reason why they should not be together, because the more they spoke, the more she wanted it, and there had to be a reason it was wrong. Nothing good ever happened to her. "But my clan, they would certainly disagree."

"They will relish an alliance with the Mackenzies since I have declared war on them. Ye are saving them, lass. Is that not what ye wanted to do before?"

"Aye." She chewed her lip. Torsten was offering her everything she ever wanted.

Why would she hesitate? Why should she care what anyone else thought?

She shouldn't!

And she wouldn't.

She was going to grab hold of him and never let go. Her heart lurched and her breath caught. "I will marry ye, Torsten Mackenzie."

"I am honored that ye have accepted." He hauled her up against him and kissed her until she was breathing hard and unable to make sense of the simplest things. "Now, about that supper in my—*our*—chamber."

"Should ye not at least make the contract afore naming it ours?"

"Are ye afraid I'll back out?" He teased.

"Nay." She shifted. "'Tis just that I've lived the past six years with rumors and curses and I dinna want it to be that way here."

"Then what would ye suggest?" He linked his fingers with hers.

"I would suggest supper in the great hall. Proper."

"And then I shall whisk ye up to my chamber and make love to ye the whole night through."

Éabha giggled. "Nay." Och, but it was hard to deny an offer like that.

"Nay?"

"We mustn't. At least not the whole night. I dinna want Mary to come find me in your chamber again. Not until we are wed."

"So we must sneak about like wayward adolescents?"

"Aye."

Torsten laughed. "I actually like the sound of that."

"Supper then. Because I am ravenous."

"I should probably get dressed first. I am only in a shirt."

"I dinna mind." Éabha playfully tugged at the fabric. "I am in a borrowed gown."

"They are not borrowed. They belong to the mistress of Eilean Donan, and that is ye in all but deed."

Éabha didn't feel right about it still. It was all happening so fast. And they'd yet to even declare their feelings for each other. But she supposed that was a luxury she might never have. Torsten was offering her so much, and just freeing her mind from torment was a gift she could never repay.

"Thank ye," she said, not wanting to sound unappreciative. "They are verra nice clothes."

"They were my mothers."

"Oh." Somehow that felt different than when she thought they were his dead wife's. Better. Less *complicated*.

"Before we both perish from starvation, let us sneak from this library. I will rush to get dressed and meet ye in the great hall."

"I will need to freshen up a bit. I'm a little… rumpled."

Torsten chuckled. "Who would have let that happen?" He opened the library door and checked the hallway. "Passage is clear."

Grabbing hold of her hand, he ran toward the stairs, and she lifted the hem of her gown to keep up with him. When they heard the chatter of two female servants, he ducked into a narrow alcove, tugging her with him. They were pressed together from knee to shoulder, and every line of his body was touching hers, even the growing arousal between his hips.

"My laird! Ye must wait," she teased.

"My lady, if I could, I would take ye right here against this wall."

"Ye wouldn't."

"I would." There was a dark, sensual promise in his tone that sent shivers racing through her. And as if to prove his point, he slid a finger from her collarbone, down the center of her chest, over her abdomen and to the very heat of her.

Before she could agree to try it, the servants passed and Torsten was once again tugging her along. They made it up to the top floor, where he insisted on walking to her door, before going to his own.

But when they arrived, Nessa was waiting patiently at a table set for two.

"Papa," she said surprised. "Why are ye only wearing your shirt?"

CHAPTER TWENTY

"I'll be right back." Torsten told Nessa, then turned around and rushed down the stairs.

Well, that was a situation he'd never thought to encounter. He was actually embarrassed, a reaction that didn't happen very often.

Once in his chamber, he hurried to dress, making sure his plaid was pleated to perfection, and securely belted in place. He flung the excess fabric over his shoulder and pinned it with his clan crest. After going over in his mind at least a hundred times how he would explain to his daughter why he'd only been wearing a shirt, he told one of his guards to have his supper sent to the tower room.

His trek up the circular stairs took longer than usual. Mostly because he was dragging his feet. Mayhap he'd get lucky and Éabha would have explained everything for him. But what could she say? That he'd disrobed when he jumped into the loch to save her? That might scare Nessa and he didn't want that either. *Ballocks.*

Torsten stood outside the door, staring at the iron handle for at least a minute before he pushed it open.

Nessa eyed him curiously, but did not mention that he was now dressed.

"Papa, I can share my supper with ye." She patted a stool that Éabha must have pulled up to the table for him. "Come and sit beside me."

Torsten winked at Éabha who smiled sheepishly. "There is no need to share, my sweet, I've had my supper sent up."

"Verra well. Come and sit."

"Yes, my lady," Torsten said to his daughter, taking the stool beside her.

Éabha watched him, a bemused expression on her face.

"There will be many suppers like this," he said softly, calling for the servant to enter when a knock came at the door.

"I look forward to them," she said.

His eyes were caught by the stones around the window. "Ye painted the walls," he said, surprised.

"Me, too, Papa." Nessa jumped from her seat to show him one of the stones that she had painted. It was supposed to be a horse running in a field of flowers.

"Gorgeous, love," he said, but his eye turned to the other stones, painted with such skill.

A horse pawing the earth, as a man brushed its flank.

A child frolicking with a puppy.

Women working in a garden.

A sunset.

A night sky.

A window with a view of the loch beyond.

Everything I can see... Nessa's words returned to him. Éabha had literally painted the lives of his clan.

"Only a few stones are left," Torsten said.

"Aye. I hope ye dinna mind. I found two canvases but I wanted to save one for a landscape I'm doing for Mary and Cook and the other for something special." She shrugged. "Besides, the room was rather bleak."

Torsten grinned. "I dinna mind at all. The room is yours. And soon, if ye like, ye can use it as your painting chamber."

Éabha's eyes welled with tears. "I would like that verra much."

Saints, but he wanted to get up and kiss her. To pull her into his arms and tell her how much she meant to him, but his feet wouldn't move, and his daughter would likely not understand if he did. So, instead, he nodded and stroked her knuckles where her hand rested on the table.

His place set and the servant gone, Nessa raised her cup, momentarily breaking the spell when she said, "A toast, Papa. A toast."

Torsten grinned and raised his mug of watered ale, enjoying his daughter's enthusiasm. It wasn't very often that she didn't eat supper in the nursery. "All right, what shall we toast?"

"Éabha," she said nonchalantly, as though he should have guessed.

And he wholeheartedly agreed. Did his daughter somehow know that Éabha was here to stay? "A toast to Éabha! Our new... friend." Could he tell her already that Éabha was going to be her stepmother?

His intended didn't appear to mind however, and patted Nessa's hand.

"Thank ye, Papa, for saving her."

"Saving?" Torsten looked at Éabha then back at Nessa. He was pretty sure that if Nessa knew they had almost drowned she would be upset about it, that was why he hadn't planned on telling her. And he was ever more sure that Éabha wouldn't tell her anything that would scare her. Especially without his permission. So, what was she on about?

"Did ye see us return today from the loch? Did Éabha tell ye what happened today?"

Across the table, Éabha shook her head.

Nessa took a long sip from her cup and shook her head, though she gazed at him curiously. "Nay, ye saved her. Remember, silly? Ye brought her here."

Torsten's eyes widened. Did his daughter think that when he'd brought Éabha to Eilean Donan it was because he was saving her? Bless her soul, she was a sweet innocent.

"He did save me," Éabha answered before Torsten had a chance to say otherwise. "How did ye know?"

Nessa shrugged and set down her cup. "Because when ye came ye were sad, and now ye're happy."

Éabha smiled at Torsten. "That is true."

"I am happy, too," Torsten said, reaching for Éabha's hand across the table.

"And now I have a mama." Nessa picked up the chicken leg on her platter and gave it a hearty bite.

A mama.

How perceptive children were. He'd known that Éabha and Nessa had formed a bond, but he'd not realized how strong it was. It made him very happy to know that his little lass would have a mother, and that the mother was Éabha.

"I'd be honored to be your mama, Nessa," Éabha said.

"Ye'll be an excellent one." Torsten squeezed her hand. "I trust Nessa's judgment."

"Thank ye, Papa," Nessa said around a mouth full of chicken.

"Eat, before your supper gets cold," Éabha encouraged. He thought her words were directed at Nessa, but she was looking at him. "Besides, I'm starved."

Torsten chuckled, and winked. "I wonder why?"

They ate with as much gusto as his daughter, and when dinner was over they moved to the floor. Nessa told a story in front of the hearth while Bad Lassie gnawed on a bone in the corner.

Torsten had never found the tower room to be quaint or charming, but in these moments, he did. The were creating memories. Becoming a family. And he'd never look at the tower chamber the same way, again. With Éabha and Nessa's paintings on the walls, this room would never be anything other than a vibrant, happy place.

Torsten left Éabha in her chamber and tucked Nessa into bed. One of Cook's daughters had volunteered to act as the child's companion whenever she couldn't be with Éabha. So that was one less thing for him to worry over.

He glanced out the window of his library, taking in the inky black of the night sky. The moon barely showed behind the clouds. And a crackle of thunder rumbled low, followed by a streak of light, and then a melody rain drops. He hoped the crying skies weren't an omen.

He'd spent hours writing a missive to the MacDonell clan, offering them an alliance, having it and a contract ready to be sent off first thing in the morning. He informed them that given the news of their' laird's death, he was going to marry Lady Éabha, and that in doing so, he was extending a merciful hand in their direction. If they were amenable to the alliance, he would send them several wagons full of provisions, a dozen cows, sheep, pigs and chickens that they could breed or slaughter, their choice, but he would not be sending them anymore, nor allowing them to take from him ever again. If they went against his alliance, he would collect what belonged to him—including their land and castle.

He fully expected them to take his offer. They'd be fools not to. 'Twas quite generous given the circumstances, but he offered nonetheless because he wanted Éabha and a peaceful life for all of them.

Torsten sat in his library until the sun rose behind the clouds and then he called for the messenger to take his missive to Strome. He spent the rest of the day going about his duties, checking in on Éabha once but not seeing her about. It had rained most of the day, but now, late in the afternoon, the sun was starting to come out, and he went in search of her again.

"Where is Lady Éabha?" he asked Mary, passing her in the hallway.

"She and Nessa went for a walk in the gardens, my laird, now that the sun has finally decided to shine."

Torsten nodded and headed back down the stairs toward the kitchens and the back door.

"My laird!" Little Rob jogged to catch up with him. Torsten couldn't see his second well in the darkened corridor, but could sense his grim countenance. "The messenger has returned."

Definitely grim. He'd returned too quickly. "What's happened?"

"He's returned missing a finger." Little Rob's voice shook with anger. "He's waiting for ye in the library."

Had he heard him right? "Missing a finger? How the bloody hell did that happen?" Torsten jogged toward his library where Barnard rocked on his heels, holding a bloodied linen to his mangled hand. "What happened? Where is our messenger?"

Barnard grimaced. "He gave our new laird your missive."

"And?"

Barnard shook his head. "He was not pleased. I brought him back, but he's… unable to speak."

"Unable to speak?"

"Aye. He cut off his tongue."

Damnation! "How could he have done such a thing?" Torsten looked at Little Rob. "Go get the healer and have her see to the messenger. Then come back and tell me how he fares." Little Rob hurried from the room. "Why did he cut off your finger?"

Barnard was ready to weep. "Because I tried to stop him from cutting off the lad's tongue, sir."

"That is beyond cruel. I am sorry, lad."

"'Twas not ye that did the cutting."

"But all the same, lairds are supposed to protect their people. Messengers are supposed to be immune to violence. Your new laird does not take our Highland laws into consideration. I offered for ye to stay afore, will ye reconsider now?"

"I would, if the offer still stands."

"It does." If Torsten could save the young man from getting his tongue removed than he would. "Was that his only reply?"

"He did not write a letter. Instead, he gave me a message to give to ye."

"Aye. What was the message?"

"Ye'd best return the lady unwed because she's been promised to another. And every day that passes, more of your villages will be pillaged."

Torsten gritted his teeth. "Who is he, the new laird? Is it George?"

"Aye. He is nephew to the old laird MacDonell."

"The man he promised her to, was it himself?"

"He didna say."

Torsten slammed his fist against the table, splintering the wood, and slicing his knuckles. This was an act of war. And he'd treat it as such.

"My laird." Little Rob returned, his face pale. "He's alive, but the healer is not certain he'll make it through the night. He's lost a lot of blood, and has started a fever already."

"Dammit." Torsten raked a hand through his hair, rage storming through his blood. "We ride. We will line ourselves up, making camp along our borders, and when they try to cross, we will cut them down one by one until there are no MacDonells left." Torsten pressed his lips together and shook his head. "What is it about the bloody MacDonells that makes them so damned obstinate?"

"Cathal might have something to do with that," Little Rob offered.

"What could Cathal have to do with it?"

"I dinna know," Little Rob said, wiping sweat from his brow.

"I do," Barnard said. "At least I think so." He winced in pain. "The MacDonell said something to one of his men when I was leaving, something about how they would never let what Cathal did to the laird's brother go unpunished."

"The laird's brother?" Torsten shook his head. "I have no bloody idea what that means."

What he did know was that Éabha's father had been brother to Donald MacDonell. He didn't know what happened to her father, only that both her parents had died when she was young. He assumed before her marriage took place. Could it be that Cathal had something do with Éabha's father's death, and George sought to avenge him?

Éabha may be the only one who knew the answer to that question.

"This new laird wants a fight." Torsten glanced at Little Rob who nodded. "'Tis a fight he shall receive."

"And he'll lose." Fury was mirrored in his friend's eyes.

"Aye." Torsten nodded to Barnard. "Go and see the healer. Ye've done well and ye will be rewarded for your duty to our clan. Your new clan."

Once the messenger was gone, Little Rob drew closer. "Your plan to line the border is a good one, my laird, but have ye thought about the long term repercussions a marriage to the MacDonell lass will have?"

Torsten furrowed his brow, keeping in mind that Little Rob only had the clan's best interests at heart. "I have, and the good far outweighs the bad. They have been holding a grudge against our clan for far too long. I had thought we could make an alliance, but they do not want it. They are damned foolish."

"Aye." Little Rob tugged out his *sgian dubh* to pick at his nails. "Their foolishness will be their end."

"Even if the MacDonells try to appeal to the king on the pretense that I am just as bad as my brother, there are too many that will say I am not." Torsten moved to his desk. "I need to write a missive to the king. He needs to know what has happened."

"Ye have strengthened our alliances over the years. The king will support ye."

"Aye. I have provided our king with many men to fight the English."

"The MacDonells have some claim to noble blood, but they've never been able to build up enough power to make use of it. Do ye think that is why they want the lass? Is she the tie?"

Torsten shrugged. "Could be. Doesna matter. They will not have her. She is mine."

"May I speak freely, my laird?"

Torsten blew out a breath, ready for Little Rob to try and knock some sense into him, though he couldn't see about what. "Go ahead."

"What if Laird MacDonell was not dead? What then? Would ye still try to keep her."

Torsten frowned. "I would desire that." He answered without hesitation. "But such a move would have caused pain to many parties. 'Tis lucky I am that the man is dead, for I might have..." Lord, could he truly confess to Little Rob that

230

he might have run away with her otherwise? Or that he might have seen the man dead to have her? Did this speak to his true nature? But then he knew. "She wouldn't have had me though. The lass is too pure. She'd have sooner leapt from a window than commit another sin."

"Another?"

"Aye. She repents for the sin of incest."

"She would not be the first," Little Rob pointed out.

"Nay. And if she'd denied me, I'd have spent the rest of my days trying to seek her comfort."

"Ye love her, my laird?"

Love. Torsten's gut twisted, his heart swelled beneath his ribs making it impossible to breathe. *Love...* "I care for her deeply," he confessed, though in his mind, he knew he was head over heels in love with her. But Little Rob would not be the first to know. She needed to be.

"As do we all."

Torsten grinned, pleased beyond measure that his clan had grown to love Éabha. "I'm not letting her go."

"Neither would I. Though, what do I know, as she said, my brain is rather small."

They both got a good laugh out of that. Éabha had certainly stormed into their lives with a vengeance and left her mark on nearly everyone.

"We'd best prepare the men, and send messengers to the villages. Everyone needs to be ready for the impending attacks."

"Aye, my laird."

"And, Little Rob, for what it's worth, your brain is not so tiny."

Little Rob snickered. "I dinna care what the size, as long as I can fight with skill and honor, then come home to bed my wife, that's all that matters."

"A man after my own heart." Torsten slapped Little Rob on the back, and they left the library to prepare the men.

After setting everything in motion, Torsten made his way up to the tower room. He knocked softly at the door, but before he could even finish it was whipped open. Éabha grinned at him with excitement in her eyes.

He hated to be the bearer of bad news. So, instead of telling her right away that he was leaving, he pulled her into his arms and kissed her. Kissed her with all the love and passion he felt. Kissed her to remember the taste of her lips, the scent of her hair.

When she pulled away from him, he felt bereft and she looked it, her blue eyes shimmering with unshed tears.

"What's wrong? Something's happened," she said. "I can feel it."

Torsten didn't know whether to be irritated that she knew him so well, or grateful that he'd found someone whom he shared such an emotional connection with. She could read him like a book, and sense his feelings. That could be good or bad.

"I have to leave for a little while," he regretfully admitted.

She chewed on her lip, studying his features before asking, "Does it have anything to do with the man with the bloody hand?"

Torsten glanced toward the window. He should have known. She spent much of her time gazing out at the world, perhaps gaining ideas and subjects for her paintings. "Ye saw him?"

She nodded. "From the window. What happened?"

"He was the messenger I sent to Strome." He held back about the injury, not wanting her to know just how dark her clan had become.

She took a step back, her face falling, eyes hooded. She was prepared for disappointment. Then she met his gaze, her intelligent eyes boring into him. "Tell me what happened. Are they the ones who hurt him?"

He couldn't lie to her. They'd promised to be honest, to trust each other. "Aye. They have declared war on us."

"They did not accept your proposal of an alliance, of our marriage, did they?" Her tone was resolute, as though she already knew the answer and that tore at his heart.

Torsten pressed his lips together, wanting only to give her good news, but knowing she deserved the truth. "Nay."

Éabha rubbed her arms, but he didn't miss the shiver that stole over her. "What… did they say?"

"Only that they planned to attack." He couldn't bring himself to tell her that they wanted her back, to marry her to another. But… what if she desired that, too?

"They are attacking because ye plan to wed me?" She looked confused.

Torsten reached for her, but she backed away, and met his gaze with penetrating eyes.

"Tell me the truth, Torsten. If we plan to wed, then we must always be honest with each other, and I can tell ye aren't telling me everything."

Torsten blew out a long breath. "Ye're right. And I'm sorry." He had to tell her. And if she chose them over him, then they' weren't meant to be. He'd have to accept it. Stop living in a dream world and move on. "They demanded your return, else they'd attack. They plan to wed ye to someone else, mayhap the new laird himself, your cousin George."

Éabha shook her head hard enough that her hair came loose of its plait. Her hands fisted at her sides. "Nay. Nay. Nay. This canna be happening. I will not."

CHAPTER TWENTY-ONE

What was George *doing*?

How could her cousin demand her return?

She and George were raised together at Strome. He was the son of her father's sister, and was a few years younger than Dugal and one year younger than her. Her aunt had been widowed at a young age, and moved home to give birth to her son. George was rash and filled with impertinence. Never followed any sort of rules and rebelled against everyone and everything. He'd often stomped his foot and thumbed his nose at their uncle Donald—but didn't get punished for it. 'Twas odd really. Then again, her aunt had a temper that rivaled Satan, so it was easy to see why no one would want to cross her, even her own brother, the laird.

George had always been jealous of her and Dugal.

He'd chased after them, thrown rocks at Éabha and poured salt in Dugal's ale. He'd steal something and blame Dugal,

235

then laugh when Dugal was given a thrashing. He'd even opened the pen and let all the pigs run rampant in the bailey, blaming Éabha when the castle erupted into chaos.

She and Dugal had their hides tanned on more than one occasion because of George and no one ever believed them. If they ever tried to get back at him, the rascal had howled as though he was being murdered, and once more they'd find themselves with reddened bums.

"He's irrational," Éabha whispered, trudging over to the tower window. She scanned outside, looking out over the sloping moors, and the mountains rising in the north beyond the loch. The cattails and reeds waved gently on the shore. Perhaps she was looking for George, just as she always had as a child, finding him laying low, watching the chaos he'd created unfold.

"I'd say he's more than irrational." Torsten followed her, setting his hip against the wall, his arms crossed over his chest.

She chanced a glance at him, seeing the concern creasing around the edges of his eyes.

"Ye dinna understand. George has never been rational. Ever. My uncle only made him the gate master because he needed to give him a task that could settle his rage. Something to keep him occupied else he wreak havoc."

"Rage?"

"George…" She shook her head, trying to find the right words. "Ye've thought I was mad on occasion, but George is truly mad, in a vicious sort of way. He's gotten what he wanted for so long, he doesna know how to be any other way. He wants what he wants and he gets it."

"Not this time."

Éabha sank against the window frame, wishing she could believe Torsten. "I wish it were true."

"I need to ask ye something."

Torsten's expression was tense, his body drawn just as taut. She wanted to massage the stress from his shoulders, to forget this whole thing with her cousin. When they'd decided to wed, she just knew it was too good to be true. And it seemed she was right.

"Ye can ask me anything," she said.

"Do ye think… Or do ye know… Did my brother Cathal have something to do with your parents' deaths?"

His question stunned Éabha. She shook her head. "Nay, nay. 'Tis impossible."

"Are ye certain?"

She closed her eyes for a moment, pressing her hands to her temple trying to remember that day. "They were nowhere near Eilean Donan. They'd gone to Stirling Castle on an errand for Donald. Your brother would have been no more than a child, or an adolescent, aye?"

Torsten frowned, his brow narrowing, lips pursing. "Aye. So why would your cousin blame him?"

Éabha shook her head. "George has always been able to come up with an explanation behind his actions, even if they were complete falsehoods, machinations of his own making." Oh, why did this have to be happening? She stared up at the gray sky, watching the clouds fighting for space, much like how she felt. She shivered. George was an adversary she'd never been able to shake. "If he's got a notion in his mind, one in which he thinks validates his decision, he will stop at nothing."

"He will stop at me, I swear it." Torsten entwined his fingers with hers and brought them to his lips where he kissed her. His voice was strong, his eyes filled with conviction.

She wanted to believe him. She really did. But George... he was the worst kind of enemy to have. The one that snuck up from behind and cut, cut, cut until there was nothing left. She couldn't let him do that to Torsten. To his people. To Nessa.

"Nay." She returned her gaze to the ripples gracing the surface of the water, her mind set. "Ye've done enough for me already. Ye've lost enough people because of me. I will not let ye lose anyone else. I am going back to Strome."

Torsten reached for her, but she stepped back.

"Please, dinna," she said. "My heart is breaking. I wouldn't wish this life on anyone."

"Then dinna wish it on yourself. I can and will protect ye, love. There is no need for ye to go back to Strome, ye'll not bend to that man's will."

What was this awful pain in her chest? She felt as though a thousand daggers stabbed at her heart and water colder than the icy loch was being forced into her lungs. She pulled her hand away from Torsten's feeling as though she were being shredded from the inside out. "Do ye not understand? I have no choice. I simply canna be the cause of more pain, more loss."

"Does my pain, my loss, not matter?" Torsten asked, his brows and lips drawing low.

Oh, she could barely look at him. It took everything she had not to burst into tears. "Not when ye're the laird. The loss of me, one person, is not so great as the loss of another village."

"We can beat him." He grabbed her hand, taking the other one, too, and holding them aloft between them, like a bridge she just needed to cross to be safe. "We are going to beat him. Together."

Éabha shook her head, and tore her hands away, metaphorically breaking the bridge. "At what cost?"

"The cost is irrelevant." Torsten reached for her but she backed just out of grasp.

Éabha pressed her hands to her heart. "But it matters to me."

"Ye are worth it, Éabha. And I'm not the only one who thinks so." This time when he reached for her hands she let him take them, if only to feel his warmth and strength one last time. He tugged her all the way to him, resting her head on his chest so she could hear the heavy pounding of his heart.

She drew in a shuddering breath to keep her tears from spilling. "Ye are sweet, Torsten Mackenzie. Dinna let anyone tell ye otherwise. These past weeks with ye should have been the scariest of my life, but it has ended up being the most joyful. I will cherish them always."

"Ye'll cherish them and many more memories to come— more memories ye create with me, for this is not the end. I'll not let ye go." He wrapped his arms around her, holding her tight, and she let herself sink into his warmth.

If only it could be just as he said…

"I'm begging ye, dinna prolong the inevitable," she murmured. "It already hurts so much."

Suddenly Torsten was stiffening, putting her at arm's length, eyes boring into hers with an intensity that sent the hair on her arms to stand on end. "Tell me the truth. Were ye ever going to marry me, Éabha?"

"What?" She blinked up at him, startled. "Of course. How could ye ask such a thing?"

"Because, for a woman who had decided to spend her life with me, and agreed to be a mother to my daughter, ye have given up verra easily. Was it all a ruse? Did ye plan to escape the entire time? Tell me I'm wrong."

He was right about one thing, even if he was wrong about the rest. She was giving up too easily. Perhaps that was why it felt as though she'd just been punched in the gut. All the air whooshed from her lungs, and she took a step back.

"I care deeply for Nessa. For ye." Her voice shook as she spoke. "How dare ye say such?"

"Yet ye'd leave me, her, so easily."

Éabha shook her head. She had to stick to her plan. Remain strong. "I am saving ye both from heartache."

"Ye're such a martyr are ye not? So selfless."

He was mocking her, she could hear it in his tone. "Perhaps I am. For I'm willing to give up my own happiness to save the lives of your people."

"Ye've no faith in me. Ye doubt that I can win."

"I have every faith in ye. I know ye can win. That is not why I want ye to give up."

Torsten held out his arms in exasperation, staring at her as though she'd grown four extra heads. "Then why will ye not just trust me?"

Éabha hugged herself tighter, tears stinging her eyes. She'd not be able to hold them at bay much longer. "I do not want anyone else to die because of me."

His hands came to his hips and he hung his head low, swaying it back and forth before looking up at her sharply.

"They will not die because of ye, lass, they will die because they are willing to protect ye."

"But they barely know me."

"They trust me."

"Ye barely know me." Even as she uttered the words, she knew they were a lie. She'd shared more with him these past few weeks than she had with anyone else in her entire life.

"I know ye well enough, Éabha. Better than I know some of the men in my clan, and they've been around since I was a child. Ye can lie to yourself and say we are strangers if that makes ye sleep better at night, but that doesna change the truth. I have lain awake with ye, shared my dreams with ye. Shared my fears, and I have heard yours. I have grieved with ye over your loss and I have prayed for the Lord to wipe away the sins ye think mar your soul. Dinna tell me, I dinna know ye."

She didn't answer, couldn't speak. His words were too moving. Perfect and enthralling. And most of all the truth.

She did want to stay. Wanted to tell him she was sorry for even suggesting that she leave. But she couldn't stand the thought of bringing pain to anyone else. And if she stayed, that was what would happen. How could she be so selfish?

"Give me a chance, Éabha. Please, lass. Dinna give up a chance at happiness because one evil man demands it."

"How could I? How could I ask it of anyone?"

"Ye'd not be asking them do something they haven't already agreed to. Just give me one chance. Just one. And if I fail, we'll do things your way. I swear it."

She chewed her lip and turned away. She couldn't look at him; he muddled her brain. One chance. One chance to prove himself. One chance to be rid of the strife of Strome. A chance for true happiness. She thought of Nessa. Of how much the child would be hurt to see her leave. She thought of the friends she'd made. She thought of Torsten, of his touch, his kiss, his laugh. All of it would be gone, and she'd be thrust back into the dark, a prison within her own soul. Mayhap, one chance was what she needed. One chance to be herself.

Éabha cleared her throat and twisted to face him. Torsten's expression was grim, emotions she'd not seen before glaring bright in his eyes.

"All right. I will give ye one chance."

He blew out a breath he must have been holding. "Give *us* a chance."

"Aye. Us." She swiped at the tears tracking hotly down her cheeks. "When the first Mackenzie falls, ye'll come back here. Ye'll surrender and I'll go."

The way he frowned, narrowing his eyes into slits she could practically hear him shouting, *I never surrender*, but he did not shout it, nor did he deny her terms.

Torsten held out his arm. "Agreed."

Éabha gripped his forearm, squeezing thick muscle.

"Ye'll not marry George, or return to Strome unless it is what ye truly wish," Torsten said, not letting go of her. "I will succeed. Ye have my word."

"I believe ye will try with everything ye possess."

She could tell he didn't like her response, but what more could she say? George was the devil incarnate and nobody beat the devil.

"I will prove it to ye." Torsten hauled her up against him and brushed his lips lightly over hers.

She kissed him back wanting to get away from him, and wanting to hold on to him all at the same time. She liked touching him. Liked the security she felt when she was around him. The warmth of his body. The promise of happiness.

His kiss was tender, loving, and over too quickly.

Torsten glanced around her chamber. "Ye barely touched your meal."

The bowl of porridge Mary had brought her sat cold and congealed on the table beside a full bowl of dried fruit.

"Ye're changing the subject," she said.

He nodded, then gently rubbed her arm. "Because, the other topic was much too unpleasant."

She agreed, but still said, "Not all things in life are pleasant."

"Truth. But it's a beautiful day, and I only want to see the amazing woman before me smile." With the pads of his thumbs he rubbed the last of her tears away. "I dinna like to see ye cry."

"Ye're verra good at distractions, but it will not work. This is something we canna brush under the rushes, even if we want to. When ye came up here"—she gestured toward the door—"ye had a plan in place. Share it with me."

"Ye are not one to mince words."

"Never. But ye knew that."

"'Tis one of the things I like so much about ye."

She rolled her eyes. "Ye are a master at changing the subject."

Torsten chuckled, wrapping his arms back around her middle. She leaned her chin against his chest and gazed up at him.

"I can see ye will not let me off the hook," he said. "And so I must concede. Since ye so graciously are allowing me a chance to prove myself, I shall endeavor to do so."

"By all means, dinna let me keep ye from it."

Torsten plucked her on the nose. "Always keeping me in line."

Éabha pursed her lips and tapped her foot. "I'm still waiting."

"All right then, bossy lass. My men and I are going to ride to the border. We are going to engage anyone who deems it a good idea to cross over the border in order to enact on Laird MacDonell's threats to our villages. We will pick them off one by one if need be."

Éabha nodded. "That makes sense. But your lands are vast, even if ye decided to make a fence of men, ye'd not have enough to cover the border."

"We will have to patrol it."

"And what if he crosses into another clan's lands in order to get to yours? Will ye have men on all sides, not just the side that borders MacDonell lands?"

Torsten frowned, obviously not having thought about it like that before. "Ye have a point. Our lands are vast. But we will have to make due with what we have." He eyed her curiously. "Ye know your cousin. Perhaps ye can shed some light on his tactics."

Éabha nodded, approaching the table to take a sip of the now warmed ale. Och, but it did not go down so easily like that. She offered a cup to Torsten who shook his head.

"I do know him. He fights dirty. He will sneak up on ye, slash the backs of your knees and be gone before ye can turn around. George is the worst kind of opponent."

"And your clan will follow him?"

"They will be too afraid not to."

"Hmm," Torsten said thoughtful, changing his mind and pouring himself a cup of the warmed ale.

"That is not going to taste good," she offered.

"Does it ever?"

"Nay, it does not."

He laughed. "Yet another thing we can agree on." He set the cup back down after a long gulp. "So what ye're saying is George will likely cross onto another clan's lands in order to get to the Mackenzies. That seems the sneakiest way."

"Aye, that is the least expected, for he'd have to travel twice as long."

"But ye think he will?"

Éabha shrugged. "I would not put it past him. And if I were the one trying to find him, that is what I'd guess. Unless ye can think of a shiftier way to get to the Mackenzies."

Torsten frowned and then rubbed his furrowed brow. "From the inside."

"Infiltrating from the inside?" She nodded. "Aye, he would do that, too."

"But through who?" He eyed Éabha, a slight grin curling his lips. "Ye?"

"Ye're jesting. Ye are the one who stole me away, do ye not remember? For if ye need a reminder, I've kept quite a catalog of insults that seemed to bother ye most." She tapped her temple.

"Och, I remember. No need for ye to remind me, I just have to ask…"

Her heart started to pound as his grin faded. Why did he seem to stare at her harder.

"I've been here all this time and sent no letters," she said.

"That I know of."

Her mouth fell open. Was he actually accusing her of sending letters in secret? "Do ye seek to offend me? The woman ye wish to marry? If ye dinna—"

"Cease your nagging, woman." Torsten tucked her against him to dull the pain of his rebuke. "I trust ye. 'Tis simply a question I had to ask given my men will likely ask it of me. I hated doing so and beg your forgiveness."

"I understand. And I forgive ye." She pinched his arm satisfied when he yelped.

Torsten brushed his lips feather-light over her forehead. "I'll need to have two plans then. One in which my men are on the northern border, and one in which we are prepared here."

"Aye. I think it would be safest to do such."

"I want to crush him." She could feel his fingers around her back curling into fists.

"He will be difficult to crush."

"For the safety of my people, and the woman I wish to wed, I would fight the devil himself."

"Ye'll be getting a dose of it. Though, George is a mite too impulsive. He will make mistakes." Éabha thought back on the years, the very rare times that George had made a mistake, how quickly he'd recovered with few people the wiser. "He's cunning, Torsten. This will not be quick and easy."

"A trait that must run in the family."

"If only I were cunning enough to get out of this mess."

"But ye are, love, ye've given me two new ideas I'd not thought of before. Ye see, we truly are a good match. Good partners. Clan Mackenzie will flourish with ye by my side."

If only…

CHAPTER TWENTY-TWO

"I dinna like the idea of dividing the men, but I trust ye with my life, and the welfare of this clan," Torsten said to Little Rob.

They stood around the table in Torsten's library with a map of his holdings, stones showing where he thought the MacDonell's might cross and where Little Rob would be waiting with his men.

His second towered over him, his face grim. "I will do right by ye, my laird. Ye can count on me to see that the MacDonell's dinna cross onto Mackenzie lands."

Torsten slapped his hand on Little Rob's beefy shoulder. "I couldn't do this without ye. Lady Éabha has enlightened me to some of George's strategies, and I want to cover all our bases. I'll remain here, fortifying the castle and making certain to keep an eye on anyone who could be working for the MacDonells, attempting to infiltrate from within."

Little Rob nodded, and Torsten was shocked that the man did not suggest Lady Éabha was the mole. She wasn't, and it made him proud to know that his people believed that, too.

Little Rob patted him on the back. "Our clan would not have come out of the shadows without ye, my laird. We were in a dark place with Cathal. He left us in shambles. We were heading for war with our own king. Many of us feared for our lives. We didna believe in Cathal's mission. Ye have relieved our fears, proven to our king that we are loyal to him and to our country. We are Scots, Torsten Mackenzie, and ye've reminded the world of that."

Torsten nodded grimly, his chest swelling with pride. "And now we go to battle with an enemy that threatens the stable hold we have."

"Aye," Little Rob said, rubbing the stubble of his beard.

Torsten cracked his neck. "And we will show them that we are not beaten, that we will not bend to their will."

"Ye did the right thing, my laird."

"To what are ye referring?"

"When ye saved Lady Éabha. When ye brought her to us."

"Saved her," Torsten mused. That was not what he'd done initially, but even Éabha had alluded to such, and Nessa, too. "'Twas not so innocent at the start, and ye know it. Ye were there. I sought to use her as a pawn in my thirst for revenge."

"Not revenge, my laird. Ye were protecting your lands. Ye were retaliating against the abuse the MacDonells forced on your people. And aye, ye did seek to use her as a pawn, but ye never kept her as a prisoner. Ye treated her well from the start." Little Rob chuckled. "Even if she did prove she could take down a man with her venomous tongue."

Torsten laughed, too. "That she did. Must have been at least a dozen of us that were ready to leave her at the closest village." His contemplation turned serious. "I thank ye, Little Rob, but I dinna need ye to make excuses for my actions. Ye're a good man and I value your loyalty."

"Ye're an honorable man and a good leader. Ye have my loyalty and my sword for life. "

"Unless—"

Little Rob held up his hands, shaking his head. "Pardon my interruption, my laird, but if ye say unless ye turn into your brother Cathal, I might be pushed to challenge ye. Ye'll never be that rat bastard. Never."

Torsten smiled. He should challenge Little Rob himself for taking such a tone with his laird, but he couldn't. He needed to hear it. And he needed to accept it. He needed to believe it.

"Ye're right. I am not my brother. I've had every chance to prove otherwise. I am my own man."

Little Rob nodded curtly. "High time ye believed it. When did ye want me to leave with the men?"

"Within the hour. Take fifty warriors with ye and gather fifty more from the various villages. One hundred strong on the border should be enough against the MacDonells. They are smaller and not as well trained or equipped. They will not have surprise on their side this time. Send word as soon as ye have eyes on them."

"Aye, my laird, we will."

"Be wary when ye spot them. I believe if George brings his men to the northern border, he will not approach ye head on. He will seek to ambush ye."

"I'll be certain to keep our men on their toes. No way will the MacDonells take us by surprise."

"Good." Torsten headed to the sideboard and poured a dram of whisky into two cups. "Now, my friend, a toast."

"A toast, my laird?"

"Aye, because we know Donald MacDonell is dead. And because ye will help see us to victory." Torsten did not say what he was really thinking. That since they were heading off to battle, this could be last time he ever saw his best mate, and he wanted to toast him. "A toast to ye, for your loyalty and your bravery."

"And to ye, my laird, for bringing prosperity back to our people."

They raised their cups and then swallowed the whisky, the amber liquid burned a path from Torsten's tongue straight to his belly.

"Damn, but that was good," Torsten said.

Little Rob laughed and clapped him on the back. "Glad to have ye back."

Éabha watched from the window as the men rode out in a long line over the bridge that led to the castle. She counted fifty of them, and at their lead was Little Rob. But not Torsten. She searched the men, looking for one with the same width and breadth of shoulder, the same steady line of spine, and the confident tilt of his dark-haired head.

But none of them matched.

Where was Torsten?

Did he remain behind? If he did, it was because he was convinced that George or one of his minions would attack the castle.

She shivered with fear. George… terrified her. He always had. Even now she could feel the sting of a switch on her rear from their governess. But Torsten, he would be here. That knowledge gave her a sense of relief she wasn't aware she needed. Perhaps the idea of losing the man she'd come to love before she'd even had a chance to tell him so, didn't sit right, understandably.

Love.

Her heart swelled, lodging in her throat, making her feel teary eyed, but in a way that she wanted to leap for joy. She loved him. Loved him immensely with every breath in her body, every fiber of her being.

Éabha hugged herself tight as she watched until the warriors shrank from view, blending in with the woods beyond.

"Please let this work," she murmured, pressing her hands together in prayer.

A soft scratch and a yip sounded at the door behind her, immediately bringing a smile to her face.

"What are ye doing?" Éabha asked, opening the door to find only Bad Lassie on the other end. "Where is your little lady?"

She stepped into the corridor, expecting to see Nessa leap from somewhere, another game they liked to play, but it was completely empty.

"Nessa," she called in a singsong voice, but only silence answered her.

Éabha scooped up the puppy and tapped her on her tiny, wet nose.

"Shall we go and find your lassie?"

The pup licked and nibbled her chin.

"I'll take that as an aye."

Mayhap this was a new game. Nessa had brought the puppy down, and then ran off, waiting for Éabha to find her. Nessa's carefree spirit called to her, and made her heart feel light, filling her with joy. She thanked the stars every night for bringing Torsten to her. And she prayed that they were able to defeat George, for that was her biggest worry. She'd given Torsten one chance, because she couldn't *not*. She wanted this life so badly.

Éabha carried the puppy to the end of the hall, but the little thing wiggled and waggled until she set her down. The hound bounced down the stairs and out of sight. Shaking her head, Éabha followed, exiting off the floor below and heading toward the nursery, expecting to see the puppy there, but the room was empty.

"Nessa? Bad Lassie?" Éabha called. "Are we playing a game of hide and seek?"

Nessa was very good at it, and even Bad Lassie had grown quite skilled. The child would remain silent as a ghost until found, and Bad Lassie would lay in wait until she could leap out and pounce on Éabha's toes.

Éabha tiptoed into the nursery, quietly getting down to check under the beds, finding only dust motes and the wooden dog she'd grabbed up for Nessa in the cellar weeks ago.

"Ye are so good at this game," Éabha said, sneaking toward the tapestry of a unicorn to pull it back. "Ha!" she called to an empty wall.

She couldn't help laughing at herself. Nessa brought out a side of her that could laugh and play and be silly without reservation. A part of her that had been buried since she was a child, and even then kept reserved most of the time. Éabha slinked to the next tapestry, and yanked it back, then nearly leapt out of her skin.

"Saints," she screeched, hands coming to her mouth.

A man knelt, holding Nessa hostage. She was pinned to his side, an arm behind her tiny head, his dirty hand over her mouth. In his other hand he held a blade out toward Éabha.

Why did he look familiar?

"Back away slowly," he said.

"What are ye doing?" Éabha held up her hands, complying with his words, and assessing how many weapons he had and how Nessa fared.

"What I was paid to do," he growled.

Éabha swallowed, gathering the strength to keep from shaking, trying to remain calm for Nessa's sake. Inside she was screaming. "By who? George?"

The man smiled and nodded. "He said ye'd know that."

George was playing games. How long had his plan been in place? "What does he want? He doesna want the lass, take me."

"He said ye'd say that, too." The man looked awestruck by his leader, and such devotion turned her stomach.

If this man worshipped George, then he, too, was completely mad. Madmen were unpredictable.

"What else did George say?" Éabha hoped to distract the man while she remembered who he was and tried to figure a way out of this.

"Only that ye were a mouthy wench, and would probably make me want to slap ye. And he was right on both counts."

She narrowed her gaze. "Well, it doesna matter. Let the lass go. Take me in her place."

"I'm not to do that. George wants the lass."

Éabha ignored his words, keeping her eyes locked on his. "Ye've been here for awhile now, haven't ye?"

The man cocked his head, assessing her. He squinted his eyes. "Mayhap. What's it matter?"

"I've seen ye before." Éabha kept her emotions at bay, talking steadily, trying to keep the man distracted from his true purpose. Subtly steering their position into her control. "Ye've been working with the smithy, haven't ye?"

His eyes narrowed further, and he tightened his hold on Nessa. "Why do ye ask?"

Éabha held out her hands, shaking them slightly, her body language telling him *nay*. "There's no need to hurt the lass." She kept her voice calm. "I only asked because if I've seen ye, then others have, too."

He loosened his hold on Nessa, and waggled his sword at her, his eyes crinkling as he tried to figure out what she meant. "What's your point, wench?"

"They'll know who ye are, and given ye're working for George, they'll know where ye're headed. Ye'll not get far with the, lass. Take me, and no one will notice for some time."

"Who's to say they'll figure out where I'm taking the lass?"

"I will tell them."

"Not if I kill ye."

Éabha shook her head. "Ye canna kill me and hold the lass at the same time, and ye canna put her down because she'll run off. The safest thing is for ye to simply leave, or take me in her stead."

"And if I dinna?" His tone turned cocky, the slight jut of his chin just as arrogant.

He wasn't going to comply. And he wasn't going to make this easy. *Bastard.*

Perhaps she needed to change her tactics. She shrugged, acting as though she could care less. "There is the small fact that the laird is likely to chop ye to pieces when he finally reaches ye. He loves his daughter. So, I wouldn't put mutilation past him. He's going to be right mad when he finds out. Madder than ye will be, for he has more at stake. Laird Mackenzie will be filled with blood lust. More so than ye, seeing as how ye're only being paid and he'd be protecting his own."

His face paled a shade but he still blustered, making circles at her with the tip of his sword. "What's all this nonsense ye're spewing?"

Her words had resonated somewhere in his small mind. Good. He was getting flustered and less able to concentrate on his task.

"On the other hand, I'm simply a captive, we have no blood ties. Take me and tell George the lass was unobtainable. I daresay if the Mackenzie caught up with ye, he'd not cut ye to ribbons over me."

The man moved to stand, his lips pulled back from his teeth. "Lies. I heard the rumors. Ye're to marry the

Mackenzie bastard. I ought to gut ye right now for your treachery."

Saints, news traveled fast. Well, still, she couldn't let him know that she mattered. Éabha shrugged again, going for nonchalant, praying he thought she didn't care about Torsten. "Brides can be found by the dozen. He won't miss me. But ye've given me an idea." She tapped her chin. "I'll not let ye leave this room without a fight, and ye've made it clear ye'll not change your mind. So, how about ye set the lass aside, and once ye're finished battling with me, ye can leave."

The grimy soul looked at her as though she'd grown three heads. His mouth fell open, and then suddenly clamped shut into a wide grin that fit a cat who'd found a mouse. Greedy. Hungry. And way too confident that he'd win.

"Ye canna be serious," he spat.

Bad Lassie took that moment to enter the nursery. Animal instinct kicked in, and she was immediately growling, the hair along her spine standing on end.

Éabha still remained calm, refusing to show any sort of emotion, lest he get an insight into her mind. "But I am. I see ye have an extra sword." She nodded to the one hanging on his sword loop. "Let me have it so we're evenly matched— well, by weapons that is."

He grinned, and she allowed him to think that he had the upper hand. But this man was not going to be evenly matched with her. Éabha took one look at him and knew she could wipe him off the face of the earth. And she was going to.

George had been one of the reasons she'd insisted on training with her cousin Dugal. She wanted to be able to protect herself. Even at a young age she'd had an inkling that one day, she'd need to know how to use a sword against her cousin.

"It's going to be all right, Nessa," Éabha crooned as the man slowly uncovered the child's mouth, leaving red imprints on her skin from where he'd held her. "Go and sit over there with Bad Lassie, and dinna watch. Sing that song ye sang for me the other day about the loch and the rainbow. I liked that one." Éabha started to croon the tune, soft at first then louder. Nessa walked toward Bad Lassie, and scooped her up, then buried her face in her fur. Just looking at her, so scared and defeated made Éabha's blood boil. She couldn't wait to slice into the bastard, to make him pay for the torment he'd caused. She'd said that Torsten would be the one to slice him to ribbons, well, she was going to do her damndest to see it done.

"Have ye any last words?" the outlaw ground out.

"Nay," Éabha said, for they would not be her last.

When he tossed her the sword she let the hilt slap her palm before she dropped it, pretending not to have a decent grip. His grin was as wide as his face, showing off a few rotten teeth.

She was going to enjoy besting him.

Éabha wrapped her fingers around the hilt, measuring the weight, then lifted the hem of her gown so she wouldn't trip over it—wishing that she was wearing one of the borrowed ones that were several inches too short.

"Are ye ready to die?" he growled.

"Is one ever ready?" she quipped.

He lunged forward, and she ducked, scooting to the side, then backing up a step. She could have sliced him across his back when he stumbled forward, but she didn't want him to know the extent of her skills. *Just yet.* When he turned around, rage cutting over his already gruesome features, she acted surprised.

Taking one look at her, he lunged again, expecting her to stay put this time. *Fool.* Éabha disappointed him once more, and this time when he stumbled past, she kicked him in the arse causing him to fall forward..

He whirled around, catching himself a lot faster this time, and swung his sword in a reckless arc. She bent backward, the edge of his blade missing her chest by an inch.

Nessa screamed. The child had turned at some point to watch.

"'Tis all right, Nessa, dear. Turn back around. Hug Bad Lassie."

Nessa cried all the more and the puppy barked nonstop, but Éabha tuned the noises out. She couldn't afford any distractions. She had to win.

"'Twill be over soon, I promise," Éabha said. And she needed to make good on that promise, because she wouldn't let Nessa suffer any longer.

The cur swung again, and Éabha ducked low, twisting and thrusting upward, her blade sinking between his ribs and piercing his heart.

"Any last words?" Éabha whispered.

The bloody bastard glared down at her, eyes wide in pain and surprise.

"Bitch," he murmured, as a trickle of blood slipped from the corner of his mouth.

"That is not a good way to present yourself to your maker."

Lord, why was she worried for his soul? He was where he belonged. At the gates of Hell. And she'd sent him there. Her hands shook and bile rose in her throat. She'd never killed anyone before. It was terrifying, and though he was a bad man, and would have killed her, or hurt Nessa, she still repented. "Atone for your sins."

"Fuck ye," the man croaked, as he slumped forward.

Éabha dropped the sword.

"May God have mercy on your soul," she muttered.

"Éabha!" Nessa cried out.

She ran to Nessa, grabbed her up and held her tight, swinging her around so she couldn't see the body. She pressed her hand to the back of Nessa's head, stroking her hair and kissing her temple over and over.

"Ye're all right now," Éabha said, her voice shaking, tears stinging her eyes. "I'll not let anyone hurt ye. It's going to be all right. I promise."

Nessa wrapped her arms around Éabha's neck. "Ye saved me," she whimpered. "I knew ye would. I love ye."

"I love ye, too."

Out in the corridor, boots pounded on the floorboards and then several guards rushed into the room, with Torsten at the lead. "What's happened?" he bellowed.

Éabha met his gaze, watched him flinch as he took in the dead body, then whipped his gaze back to the both of them. So much emotion passed through his eyes that it stole her breath. Her knees shook and she was dangerously close to collapsing.

"From the inside," she whispered.

"Bastard." He rushed forward and grabbed Nessa, holding her just as close as Éabha had.

"Merrick," one of the guards muttered. "He was the smithy's apprentice."

"Apprehend the smithy for questioning," Torsten ordered. "In fact, close the gates. Everyone will be questioned."

"Papa! I was so scared." She buried her face against his shoulder. "Éabha saved me."

"She's an angel," Torsten said. "Ye were meant to be here, Éabha. I can never thank ye enough for risking your life." He wrapped one arm around her, pulling her and Nessa close.

"I'd do it again." She leaned her head against his shoulder, breathing in his scent, and trying hopelessly to calm herself. She needed a drink. She needed to lay down.

"I pray ye dinna have to."

"He won't be the only one," she said, clutching her arms around them both. "George would never entrust his plan to a single man."

CHAPTER TWENTY-THREE

Torsten spent the next several hours storming his own castle. They caught two men sneaking out the postern gate, bags of goods tossed over their shoulders, and when they were tackled to the ground, they confessed to being planted there by George. As soon as they'd heard about Merrick's death, they'd tried to escape.

Too late. Torsten wasn't letting anyone out.

Right now, everyone was a suspect.

The servants were clearly shaken. Those who'd been loyal for years were thoroughly questioned. No stone was left unturned. Most of them weren't offended, just angry, and vowed to help find any traitors.

When Torsten questioned Fergus, the smithy, he found out that Merrick was related to him through his mother, and had used that relationship, however distant, in order to gain work. Fergus was outraged that his relation had been the one to threaten the life of the laird's daughter and betrothed. He'd knelt before Torsten and vowed to take any punishment he deemed worthy for allowing the man inside Mackenzie walls. Torsten had pardoned the smithy, convinced that he had nothing to do with it.

The two men caught at the postern gate had bribed a crofter into letting them tag along when he made a delivery that morning. No one had ever seen them before. The crofter was found unconscious behind the barn. And when he woke up, he said the two men promised they weren't going to hurt anyone, that they only wanted to meet with the laird, and seeing a shiny handful of coins, he couldn't resist. He was just another pawn in the game George was playing. He might think he's smart, more fit to play the game, but Torsten was smarter. And had more to lose.

As punishment for his betrayal, the crofter was given additional lands to harvest for the laird's table. And Torsten made it clear that if he was ever so down on his luck that he would resort to treachery, to come to him for help. Knowing he could have been hung for his disloyalty, the man was happy to accept his penalty.

The other two men were locked in a cell until their trial. They admitted that George awaited them at Strome, which meant he was not going to cross the border, but it didn't mean his men wouldn't. Torsten could have hung them both, but since they ran and didn't hurt anyone other than the crofter, he was considering two days in the stocks instead. He also had them bury Merrick, the dead vagrant, in the woods. Torsten did not think that anyone else had infiltrated the castle, but they were still on high alert.

The following morning, Éabha knocked on his library door to bring him breakfast.

"I heard ye'd not eaten yet," she said.

He stood, took the tray from her and set it on the table. "Will ye eat with me?"

"Aye."

They ate in silence, and when they finished, Torsten asked what she was thinking. "How do ye feel about all this? Do ye think George will try again or do ye think three attempts will be enough?"

"For now." Her green eyes looked haunted and she'd taken to rubbing her arms as though a permanent chill had settled in her bones. She pushed away from the table and went to the window, looking over the bailey below.

Torsten came up behind her and placed his hands on her shoulders, gently massaging. "Thank god ye were there for Nessa. I'll never be able to repay ye for saving her from that madman."

Éabha's smile was tired as she leaned her head back on his chest, looking up at him. "Ye dinna need to repay me. I'd do it again in a heartbeat."

"I feel like a fool. Three men were able to breach my walls with me none the wiser."

"George plays dirty. He'd not have sent in three armed men. Better to send men ye'd never look at. A smithy's apprentice. A couple of crofters. Why would ye think they'd be the enemy?"

"He has ruined me. I will now be suspicious of everyone. Even the most innocent of people."

"Aye. But ye'll never be taken advantage of again."

Torsten tucked her head beneath his chin and sighed. He wrapped his arms around her waist and held her close. "When I came upon ye. Nessa in your arms, the bastard bleeding…"

Éabha stroked his arms. "I love Nessa as though she were my own. I wasn't leaving that room without her."

He was still in shock from what he'd seen. The man's bleeding body, sword still deep in his abdomen. Éabha holding tight to his child, a lioness and her cub. "Ye risked your life. I should tell ye that ye're foolish. I should punish ye." He turned her in his embrace, gazing deep into her eyes. "But I canna, because I'm too damned grateful. Your stubborn hide, your fiery nature that I fought against when ye first arrived, it saved her. Ye saved us all."

"I am also the reason she was put in harms away." Éabha laid her head against his chest, breaking eye contact, her arms squeezing tight around his middle. "'Tis my fault."

"Nay, nay, nay. Dinna think that." Lord, but she sounded so bereft. He wanted to scoop her up and hold her tight forever.

"But it is." She nodded, her head bumping his chin. He stroked a hand down her back. "If I wasn't here, then George would have had no reason to infiltrate your walls."

"He would have eventually. I would have brought war to his door, for I see him walking in your uncle's footsteps. Today, tomorrow, a week or year from now, we would have come to this."

Torsten tilted her chin up, staring into her glistening eyes. "Tell me ye agree," he said.

Her eyelids lowered, and he had the distinct impression she was trying to hide her feelings.

"Dinna hide from me," Torsten urged. "Speak the truth."

"I did." She glanced up at him with tears shining in her eyes. "I still believe what I said. Ye may have defeated him today, but he will not rest."

"That is why I must take men to Strome." He was more determined than ever to put an end to this. "I must confront him man to man. This must end."

"I do agree with ye on that point," Éabha said. "It must end."

Relieved that she agreed, Torsten bent to kiss her. He planned to leave that night, but not before he made love to her one more time. Deepening the kiss, he stroked the backs of his fingers down her ribs to her hips, gripping them tight and tugging her harder against him so she could feel his arousal, wanting her to know his intent. She sighed against his lips.

"I want ye," he said. "I need ye."

"I need ye, too," she murmured, wrapping her arms around his neck and dragging her fingers through his hair.

Torsten whipped off his plaid and laid it on the floor, guiding her down. "After last time, and this, I dinna think I'll ever be able to work in this room again. I'll only be able to see your cheeks flamed with color, your eyes filled with passion, and your body writhing beneath mine."

Laying to the side of her, he slowly glided the hem of her skirt up to her hip, then bent down to kiss her knee. Éabha sucked in a breath.

"I see your wicked glances, your roving lips and hear your sensual words whenever I close my eyes. I canna escape ye," she murmured.

"And ye won't have to, for we'll be married as soon as I return from Strome."

Torsten kissed her knee again, shifting his body lower, and trailing his lips up her thigh as he revealed inch after inch of her flesh. Her skin was silky smooth and her legs went on forever, but at last he uncovered her hips and the glistening curls between her thighs.

"I dinna think heaven can be a sweeter place than right here." He cupped her sex, watching her back arch, her eyes roll, lips part. "I love to watch the way ye respond to me." He parted her thighs, sliding a finger along the glistening seam, and delighting in the shiver that stole over her.

Torsten knelt between her thighs, bracing himself on his arms, and kissed her on the mouth, drinking in her sigh of pleasure. He worked his way over her neck, to her breasts, tugging at the lacing of her gown until the soft globes were free, and her taut nipples peeked at his lips. But he didn't stop there. Nay, Torsten wanted to taste her. To commit her essence to memory and the sight of her writhing, her thighs tight around his head.

"Torsten," she murmured. "Stop. Ye canna."

"Oh, aye, and I am." Spreading his fingers over her inner thighs, he dipped his head to her heat, running his tongue between the slickened folds.

"Oh… aye, this… is…" Her fingers grappled for hold on his shoulders.

"What is it?" he asked, flicking his tongue over the swollen nub of her pleasure and enjoying the buck of her hips that went with it.

"Amazing."

"Infinitely."

Torsten licked and teased and sucked her sensitive spots until Éabha was crying out with pleasure.

Before she had a chance to recover from her climax, he moved upward, gripped her hips and drove his cock inside her tight sheath. Heaven surrounded him in heat and pleasure and love. She wrapped her legs around him, tugged him toward her for a kiss, and moaned against his mouth.

Their passion collided with their bodies. Skin to skin. Heat to heat. He drove deep inside her again and again, his pace urgent and shaken. When he felt the first tremors of a climax begin within him, he ceased moving, sinking his face to the crook of her arm.

"Dinna stop," she said.

"I have to. I dinna want to finish without ye." He nuzzled her neck, licking a drop of sweat from her skin.

"Without me?" Her voice was deep, throaty, filled with sensuality.

"I want ye to climax with me."

"Oh… I think I might. I feel so… on fire. I am shaking. And my insides are pulsing…"

Still inside her, he felt the walls of her channel tighten around him. Torsten groaned, skimmed his teeth over her collarbone.

"Ye felt that?" she asked.

"Aye."

"It felt… verra nice," she murmured.

"Verra," he moaned.

It was too much. He sensed how close she was, and he couldn't breathe without moving. Slow at first, he pushed in, pulled out, but she continued to pulse her muscles around his shaft and he was lost. Torsten drove deep inside her, passion, pleasure and sensation taking over, until they were both crying out with release.

Late in the afternoon, Éabha feigned being tired, assuring Torsten she was fine, and with a wink that something must have worn her out. Because of the earlier events of the day, no one questioned her insistence on a quiet nap without being disturbed.

Though she was truly exhausted, Éabha didn't stay in her bed for longer than five minutes. As soon as the sound of footsteps on the stairs faded, she leapt from her bed and scooped up her plain brown wool blanket to use on the journey she'd be taking.

Torsten planned to leave at nightfall for Strome, and she had to be there before he arrived. She simply couldn't risk Nessa or anyone else's life again. Though Torsten believed all would have eventually played out this way even if she'd never been involved, Éabha didn't think so. Taking Éabha from George had been a personal insult, even though Torsten didn't know it. George had intended to strike Torsten at his core. His child.

And she couldn't allow it to happen again.

Éabha wrapped the blanket over her shoulders and tucked it over her head. The servants would be heading home soon, and she intended to blend in. The guards were on high alert for anyone entering, but she hoped they'd not think twice about a servant leaving. She lifted up the basket she'd swiped from the kitchen. It was filled with herbs and a jug of milk. So, if anyone stopped her, she'd smile and say she was bringing it to Mary's niece whom she had overheard was sick.

She checked the blade at her calf, feeling slightly remorseful about having swiped it from Torsten after they made love earlier in the day. But she needed a weapon, and one that she could conceal.

Éabha opened the door to her chamber. Seeing no on outside, she crept toward the stairs, which were empty as far as she could tell. She slid along the wall at a snail's pace, not wanting anyone to hear her footsteps, who out of curiosity might check to see who she was.

On horseback the trip wouldn't take more than four hours, but on foot, she was looking at closer to eight. She'd need to get a horse somewhere along the way, or she'd never make it before Torsten caught up to her. Too bad she'd promised never to steal one of his horses.

At the bottom of the stairs, Éabha leapt into the shadows before she was seen by two passing guards. They were in an intense discussion and quickly moved passed her, not seeming to notice her presence in the least.

She slipped unseen through a servant's entrance near the kitchen and into the gardens beyond. The ladies in the kitchen wouldn't be leaving anytime soon because they still had supper to serve, then cleaning and preparations for the next day. She'd be leaving with some of the maids, but there were none about. Mayhap it would be better to insist on delivering the basket...

Just then, two maids exited the castle wearing similar wool plaids pulled over their heads and holding baskets in their hands. Éabha's luck could not have been any better. Thank the saints she'd spent so much time studying the habits of every person that passed through the bailey.

Keeping only a few feet between them she followed them toward the gate. They waved to the guards and passed through with Éabha on their heels. Every step over the bridge seemed to pound through her ears. At any moment she expected someone to shout for her to stop. To hear Torsten's bellow above the din of her heartbeat. But no one stopped her. Not at the other side of the bridge, or in the village. She walked all the way to the end, before slipping into someone's barn and saddling their horse with them none the wiser. Whispering an apology, she slipped unseen into the woods, and rode at a quick pace. Escape was easier than she'd ever imagined.

If she'd ever wanted to escape before, seems it wouldn't have been too hard.

And here she was, headed back to the place that kept her shrouded in darkness, and filled with shame. She didn't want to go back, but she didn't want Nessa to be harmed even more.

She had to choose the lesser of two evils. There was no other choice.

CHAPTER TWENTY-FOUR

"My laird!" The scout came rushing to Torsten in the bailey, sweaty and coated in dirt.

"What is it?" Torsten was immediately on high alert. Another intruder? He was already dressed for war, weapons and armor donned.

The scout bent over, hands on his knees, sucking in a breath. "'Tis the lady. Lady Éabha. She… I swear, I just saw her riding through the woods. Headed back toward Strome."

Torsten's blood turned cold. He pressed his lips together to keep from bellowing. "Are ye certain?" The lad had to be mistaken. Why in the bloody hell would Éabha be riding through the woods? He'd just left her chamber not long ago. She was going to take a nap…

"Same golden hair, my laird, and, she kept glancing over her shoulder. But I will not swear my life on it. Could have been a trick of the eyes."

"Was she alone?"

"Aye, my laird."

"Search the castle," Torsten ordered several guards, scraping a hand over his face. "I'll check her chamber."

He stormed through the castle doors, up the stairs, half in denial that she would betray him and half racking his brain to figure out why she would have done so. They'd just made love that morning. She'd teased him about needing to take a nap because she'd exhausted herself. She'd *saved* Nessa.

Why would she run?

Why would she leave him?

The sensation rushing through his chest was one he'd not experienced before. Not even when his wife had passed away, or when he'd found out that his brother had betrayed him, their clan and their country.

He felt as though he was being ripped apart from the inside out, gutted by a thousand miniature swords.

Stopping halfway up the stairs, he leaned for a moment against the wall. His heart pounded in his ears, ears that burned. Teeth clamped tightly closed, his jaw muscles started to hurt. He closed his eyes, then blinked them open, taking deep breaths and trying to regain some composure.

Was this what it felt like to have his heart broken?

Was this what it felt like to be betrayed by the one you loved?

With his brother's betrayal, he'd seen it coming, perhaps not to the degree in which Cathal presented his perfidy, but it was a downward spiral that could only have ended badly. And with Anna... She'd been sick for so long it seemed the whole world expected her to perish at some point, as sad as that realization was.

But, Éabha…

Ballocks, but this hurt deeply.

He'd not seen it coming. He'd been blind-sided.

It couldn't be true. The scout couldn't have seen her. It had to be someone else. He *loved* her. Wanted to spend his life with her. They were going to be a family.

How had she so thoroughly duped him? Dear God, if this had been an ambush he wouldn't have been more surprised. A brilliant move on her part.

Torsten raced up the rest of the stairs, shoving open her chamber door without knocking, an apology on his lips, because she had to be sitting there at the window.

He took a step back, outside the room, the breath knocked from him.

Her chamber was empty.

Empty.

She was gone.

The painted walls a mocking echo that she'd betrayed him.

Still, Torsten couldn't believe it. He shook his head, punched the door hard enough to make the wood splinter and whirled around. She was in the kitchen. Or the gardens. The nursery. Not in the woods. Not headed back to Strome.

But only Nessa, her companion and Bad Lassie were in the nursery. She wasn't in the kitchens either, and the garden was empty save for a few wild cats and the birds that taunted them.

"She's gone," he said to himself, the knowledge leaving his blood cold.

The guards confirmed it, no one could find her.

Éabha had left him.

But, why?

Her passion, her laughter, the feelings they'd shared, they couldn't have been made up.

Torsten gritted his teeth. Well, she might have left him, but he refused to believe she'd betray him, not unless she told him so herself. There had to be another reason for her to flee. Just as she'd picked up the sword against Nessa's attacker, perhaps she was attempting to save him, too. Well, he wasn't going to wait around to find out.

"I'm going after her."

Though the sky was dark, Strome was lit up with torches and the guards kept watch, walking along the walls. By the look of things, George fully expected the enemy to knock on his door, only further proving his treachery. Part of her had hoped that it was a misunderstanding, nothing more than a handful of clansmen going rogue in order to please their new laird.

After having taken a moment to relieve herself and splash water on her face by the loch—well enough away that no one could see her—she'd continued the last quarter hour practicing what she'd say when she saw her cousin. But the sight of the castle seemed to somehow wipe her mind clean.

Éabha approached with caution, fear making her tremble. She gripped the reins of her horse so tightly her fingers had gone numb. The four hour ride from Eilean Donan had been uneventful. She'd encountered no one, though she made certain to keep herself hidden. In fact, she considered it quite a miracle that she'd arrived unscathed. She was also surprised that no one from Eilean Donan had caught up to her. When she was just beyond the village, she could have sworn she was spotted by a scout.

She slowed her mount as she continued her approach, not wanting to alarm the guards into shooting their arrows before asking who she was. But even still, she regarded them wearily, taking note of a subtle shift in their stances when they finally saw her.

"Who goes there?" A guard's voice thudded dully on the heath surrounding her.

She opened her mouth to talk, her throat dry despite the water she'd sipped not too long ago. Her voice wouldn't cooperate, coming out in a small croak.

"I said who goes there?" His voice had grown irritated, and more of the guards now gathered on the wall to stare down at her.

Éabha cleared her throat, forcing herself to calm, to let her voice be heard, else they decide to shoot her after all.

"Lady Éabha MacDonell," she called.

The guard did not answer. Instead there was more movement, several guards shoved aside and then a tall figure loomed above. She stopped her horse a fair distance from the gates, and observed one of the men who'd made her life hell. His blond hair was slicked back with a queue, his beard just as light and coming to a point. Though she couldn't see his eyes from here, she imagined them, light blue and soulless.

"Cousin," she said, unable to hide the bristle from her tone.

"Ye will address me as laird," George growled. Even from down where she was, she could see the way he gripped the wall tightly, as though he were wringing her neck. "Open the gates," he called.

Éabha shuddered, tempted to kick her horse into a gallop in the opposite direction. She'd have a chance of getting away if she left now. Och, but she couldn't. Éabha gritted her teeth. Departing now would leave everything in limbo. Nay, she had to see this finished.

The gates were opened, the portcullis raised, and beyond the opening, a line of guards waited.

Éabha drew in a breath that only caused her to become more lightheaded. *Come on. Ye must do this. Be done with it. Be done with him.*

This was for Torsten. For Nessa. For herself.

With those reminders in place, she clucked to her mount and rode forward. A stable hand met her in the stony, cold bailey, and the faces of the guards were not at all welcoming. The gates remained open behind her, mocking her desire to escape.

"Why have ye returned?" George demanded.

"We had a visitor at Eilean Donan," she answered.

"We?" he mocked, winging a brow.

"Ye know verra well that I was to be married to Laird Mackenzie."

George snickered. "I know he tried to steal ye away from us. But this is where ye belong." He stabbed his finger toward the ground.

Éabha dismounted from the borrowed horse, standing at her full height, which was only a few inches shorter than her cousin. "I dinna belong here. Nor do I belong to *ye*. Ye're a fool not to have taken the offer of an alliance."

George laughed, looking at his men who joined in the laughter, though she could tell many of them were forcing it. This was not the first time he and his cronies had mocked her. She was tunneled back to years before, standing in this very spot as a young lass, her cousin goading his friends into tormenting her. They'd flung mud and prodded her with sticks, calling her Lady Piggy. Dugal had whipped a few of the boys, bloodying George's nose and they'd all gone to bed without supper.

Anger burned within her belly, and she clenched her fists at her sides. He was not going to win this time.

"I challenge ye, George MacDonell," she seethed.

"Ye"—he pointed at her, a gawk of pure derision overtaking his features—"challenge *me*?"

"Aye." She held her ground and waved to a guard. "Give me your sword."

The guard took a cue from George, who shook his head, and then crossed his arms over his chest.

"Ye're serious?" George asked.

"Deadly." Gaze steady on his, she didn't waver, and suddenly her trembling ceased, and the anger that clouded her vision cleared. This was how it had to be, and she needed to focus on ending this, one way or another. "If I win, ye will let me go. If I lose, then do with me what ye will."

George sneered, a fierceness in his eyes that made her belly sink. "I accept. Give her a sword."

Éabha barely had enough time to reach for the sword that was tossed at her, and it came dangerously close, so close that whoever threw it obviously hoped to hit her with it, perhaps to please his laird as they all seemed completely under

George's cruel spell. She didn't frown though, to hell with giving him the satisfaction.

The sword was heavy. The guard who'd loaned her his weapon was large, his sword made to match that size. She wrapped her long fingers around the hilt and lifted it, feeling her muscles strain.

"Ye're going to be mine." George sounded excited, greedy and just plain mean. "And trust me, I *will* do whatever I want with ye, whenever I want, how I want, and ye're going to take it. All of it."

Flashes of herself being tormented by George tried to shove their way into her mind, tried to hijack her courage, because truth be told, a future with him was terrifying.

Lord, she had to win this fight, because he meant every word he said. And she'd rather die then suffer through a life with him.

Éabha kept quiet. She needed her wits. Couldn't let her fear or his taunts distract her. Her life was at stake. And Nessa's. And Torsten's. God help her…

George began circling as a hungry animal would his prey. His sword was held out, that same arrogant sneer on his face that he'd had since she walked through the gates. His eyes were filled with such malice that she found it hard to keep his gaze, but to waver would be deadly.

Éabha started to shift, one foot crossing over the other as she rounded the imaginary circle George outlined. She was glad she'd donned one of Torsten's mother's gowns rather than her own. With the shortened length, she didn't need to hold the fabric up, and could use her arm to block any blows she couldn't thwart with her blade. A blade which seemed heavier and heavier as the minutes passed.

"What are ye waiting for?" George taunted. "Ye wanted this. Ye make the first move."

She didn't want to make the first move. Whoever started a battle was always at a disadvantage, at least that was how she felt, indeed what she'd learned—and George had, too.

He wanted her at a disadvantage.

Well, she wasn't going to give in. Though her weapon was heavy in her hand, and she was struggling, she wouldn't dare let George know it.

She'd have to hold it with two hands. Fisting it with both, she held it to the right, knowing full well she was already at a disadvantage.

George seemed to like that, and he didn't wait for her to make a move. He swung toward her left and she swiveled her sword, blocking him at the very last second. But he was strong, and she was already tired from lack of sleep, her four hour journey, and the heavy sword.

He held her in that position, making her arm strain even more, showing her just how much stronger he was, and then he jumped back, laughing.

"Are ye certain ye want to continue?"

She couldn't resist. "Did I tell ye how your minion died? I killed him."

George laughed some more. "A fine story ye've concocted."

Why had she bothered to speak? She should have known he would mock her. Laughter surrounded her.

"What is going on here?"

Éabha jumped at the sound of Torsten's voice.

Nay! What was he doing here? He wasn't supposed to be here for hours. Why couldn't he just have stayed put and let her take care of George? She guessed that the scout had in fact informed him of her escape. To get here just on her heels he must have ridden hard and fast right away.

"Torsten?" She started to turn, but the moment she did, George moved.

She saw him from the corner of her eye, raising his sword, and she tried to raise her own, but everything seemed to be moving in slow motion, and deep in her heart, she knew that even if she did manage to rise up in time, to block the blow with her blade, the strength of his sword arm would crush her. She closed her eyes and prepared herself for the pain. Hoped it would be swift. And was forever grateful for the time she'd spent at Eilean Donan. For finding love, happiness and peace.

Something whizzed passed her, shifting the wind. She blinked open her eyes to see George had stopped moving. A blade protruded from his chest. But his sword was still arcing straight for her. Torsten's bellow cut the air. Éabha barely had enough time to leap out of the way before George's sword sank deep into the dirt beside her.

Éabha gaped in revulsion at the blood staining the bailey from her cousin's wound, her gaze slowly moving up to meet his. He wasn't dead yet. He blinked in confusion, staring at her and then looked down toward the hilt of the dagger protruding from his torso.

"What the…?" George whispered.

George's knees buckled, and he dropped them to the ground, staring up at her. His breathing became labored as blood poured from his mouth, but he gathered enough strength to point at Torsten.

"Attack." His order came out no more than a mutter, and none of his men made a move to do so. "Get him," he said weakly, blood trickling from the corner of his mouth. He held onto the dagger lodged near his heart and seemed to be debating whether or not to pull it out.

George blinked slowly, staring around the group of unmoving men, confusion on his face and then dawning knowledge lighting in his bleak eyes.

"Ye have... betrayed me," he panted. "All of ye."

His accusation was met with silence.

Éabha stared with a mixture of horror and awe.

George was beaten.

Torsten had saved her.

Her future awaited, but the knowledge didn't seem to reach her fully.

Legs knocking together, hands shaking uncontrollably. She dropped the sword and her legs gave out, but Torsten caught her in his embrace before she hit the ground. She clung to him, clung to his strength.

Stroking her face, he whispered, "Ye're safe, ye little fool."

"How did ye know?" she asked. "That I was here?"

"A scout saw ye leave. I guessed ye might have come back to Strome to settle things yourself. I admit, at first I thought ye'd betrayed me, but my heart wouldn't believe it."

"Never. I would never."

"I know." He brushed his lips over her forehead. "I love ye, lass. I want to marry ye, to share a life with ye. Please, dinna ever do anything so rash again."

Éabha buried her face in his chest. "I love ye so much. I will never tempt fate again."

"At least not by yourself, love. We're in this together. We will fight our battles together."

His words made her heart soar. In the face of so much tragedy, she was eternally blessed to have Torsten on her side. Happiness and love were hers. And best of all, Torsten loved her, for *her*. She was free to be herself.

Seeing the Mackenzie warriors filling the bailey, the MacDonells dropped to their knees in surrender.

"Nay, stand," Torsten ordered.

"I want to go home," Éabha said. "This place holds nothing for me."

"But we are surrendering to ye," one of the clansmen said. "Ye're the only surviving kin of the old laird."

"We are leaving," Éabha said, finding the strength to stand on her own. "Ye were unkind to me while I was here. But I will show ye mercy in the face of your cruelty. Ye are your own people."

Torsten stood tall beside her, her rock, her wall. "Vote in your next laird, but beware, ye will leave us in peace. None of ye should step foot on my land without permission."

"Aye, Laird Mackenzie."

James, a man who'd been by her uncle's side since she was a child, stepped forward, to nominate himself as laird, which would only mean more of the same. But to her surprise, a younger clansman, stepped up as well.

"My name is Angus and I nominate myself. I will respect your lands, and our alliance, Laird Mackenzie. I worked my way up through the ranks of men. I know how to fight, I've been to battle, I've protected these walls," said Angus.

"But I served our laird Donald MacDonell for nigh on a dozen years. I've more experience and knowledge in ruling this clan," James argued.

Many of the clan elders piped in their agreement that Angus should be laird, though several balked, thinking her uncle's second-in-command the best choice. And besides, she didn't see James giving up his claim to the lairdship.

"Let us leave," Éabha whispered to Torsten. "I care not what happens, as long as I have ye."

Torsten chuckled. "I wish it were that easy, love, but since I am here already, they need to vote on their laird now so we can leave with an alliance in place."

Éabha nodded, understanding that it was best to wait, but wanting to run all the way back to Eilean Donan anyway. The gates were still open wide, and freedom waited just beyond the wall. It was so close she could taste it.

"James is a bad choice," she murmured to Torsten. "He loves raiding as much as Donald did."

Éabha feared the vote would cause the men to come to blows, but it seemed most were in favor of Angus. While they balked, James challenged Angus to a swordfight. Éabha definitely did not want to watch the poor lad be hacked to bits by the angrier older man, but just then Torsten spoke up.

"I vote for Angus, and since ye have surrendered yourself to me, to my betrothed, I suggest ye take my opinion seriously." He pointed to James, though he spoke to all the MacDonells. "I speak for us both when I say, if that man becomes your laird, war is inevitable." He held out his arms. "And I've already got my army right here."

James seethed, but Angus grinned, and so did those supporting him.

"Ye've no choice but to surrender your claim," Torsten said to James. "Else it's war, and the annihilation of your clan will be on your head."

James growled and stormed off. Knowing what was best for them, no one followed, instead they knelt before Angus, swearing their loyalty. Torsten shook the man's arm, and their alliance was agreed upon.

"I'll have a formal alliance drawn up," Torsten told Angus. "And we can enjoy many years of peace, I pray, between our clans."

"Aye."

Torsten then turned to Éabha and said, "Now, we can go home."

He lifted her into his arms and carried her beneath the gate toward Lucifer who waited dutifully for his master.

"I love ye," Torsten said again. "I'll never get tired of saying that."

Éabha stroked his stubbled cheek. "I love ye, too, and I canna wait to say it every day for the rest of my life."

EPILOGUE

Three months later…

"Come, I want ye to see your surprise, husband." Éabha could barely contain her excitement. She bounced through the door of their bedchamber and leapt onto the bed.

Grabbing hold of Torsten's hand, she attempted to tug him from the bed. They'd made love well into the night, and when he'd fallen asleep, she'd been too excited to follow. She'd spent the remainder of the night in her painting chamber, finishing the project she'd begun a month prior, snoozing just before dawn and waking to a beautiful stream of light shining on her masterpiece.

"Did ye not sleep at all?" he asked, grumbling, but the curve to his lips and the twinkle in his eyes showed his pleasure.

"A little. But I assure ye, I'm wide awake." And she was. Energy coursed through her—especially odd given her need for naps lately. She suspected that moments after presenting him with her surprise that she would be asleep at least until noon.

Torsten tugged her back into the bed, wrapping her in his warm embrace. "Can it wait?" he nuzzled her neck, sending shivers of desire racing over her skin.

She considered it for a minute, wanting very much to feel his weight on her, his body sliding in and out of hers.

"Normally, I would say yes." She turned in his embrace to kiss him. "But I am too, excited. Ye must rise and come with me."

Torsten chuckled, and climbed from bed. He tugged on his shirt, and grabbed a pair of breeches. He'd taken to wearing them these past couple of months, and she thought it might have something to do with how easily they tugged on, given he was without his clothes more often…

"What have ye been up to?" he asked, blue eyes bright and mirroring her excitement.

"Ye will see."

They raced up the tower stairs, hand in hand, with Torsten tickling her from behind until they reached the door. She stopped, turning to face him and blocking the way.

"Close your eyes," she said.

Torsten wiggled his brows and leaned forward for a kiss.

"No peeking, and no tricks," she said, giving him a quick kiss and then backing away with a stern look.

Torsten exaggeratingly closed his eyes. "Ye'll have to lead me, else I trip."

Éabha laughed. "Ye could walk the length of this entire castle blindfolded."

He started to open his eyes and she slapped her hands over them. "No peeking!"

When she was certain he couldn't see, she lifted the handle and pushed the door open. The chamber was bright with the morning sun, the gleam of light shining on the easel he'd built for her. And there was her surprise.

Sitting up on the easel was the canvas she'd been saving for months until she could find a project that seemed worthy. The landscape she'd painted for the servants hung proudly in the kitchen.

Éabha led him into the room until he was only a few feet from her masterpiece.

"All right, open your eyes."

Torsten blinked several times, his eyes focusing where the sun shone on the canvas.

"What's this?" He walked forward to study the painting closer, a bemused smile on his face.

Éabha had spent the last month painstakingly outlining, sketching, painting and repainting some parts. 'Twas of Torsten standing before the hearth in the great hall, dressed in his plaid. She'd even gotten down the details of his rabbit-fur sporran, his silver brooch and the gleaming hilt of his sword. Beside him, she'd painted Nessa dressed in a tiny plaid gown, Bad Lassie in her arms, and the mischievous smile she wore most of the time depicted on her face. The painting was a surprise, but the biggest surprise was what she'd painted Torsten holding in the crook of his arm—an infant wrapped in a Mackenzie plaid—one green eye and one blue because she didn't know which their child would have.

"'Tis ye," she whispered. "And Nessa." She chewed her lip, feeling her belly do flip after flip.

Torsten stared at her, one eyebrow curved in question, a smile of hope curling his lips. He walked forward and pointed to the infant in the painting. "And who is this?"

She smiled, her face flowing with happiness. "That's a bairn."

"I know 'tis a bairn. Why am I holding it?"

Éabha found it hard not to give up her secret. "Would ye take issue in holding a bairn, husband?"

Torsten raked a hand through his hair and studied her with keen interest, his eyes roving over her middle. Éabha had been hiding the news for weeks. Weeks of pure torment! Ever since they'd met, she found it hard not tell Torsten everything. But, she wanted to present it to him in a way that was different, a way that embodied her. He'd been so supportive of her art, and she thought this was the best way to honor their love.

"'Tis your bairn," she said with glee, clapping her hands. "Ours."

"Are ye…" He trailed off, but nodded his head in her direction, taking a tentative step forward. He pointed to the bairn again and then back at her belly.

"Am I what?" she asked coyly, cocking her head to the side, hands on her hips, arching her back and sticking out the tiny ball of her belly. "Happily wed? Aye. Verra."

"Nay, lass, are ye…" Torsten reached for her, rubbing his hand over her abdomen, his grin growing as he felt the small swell. He knelt before her, both hands on her stomach, pressing his lips to the spot just below her belly button. "Why did ye not tell me? How could I not have noticed?"

Éabha laughed, and pressed her hand to his over the life that grew within her. "Truth is, I'm not surprised ye did not notice."

"Oh, really? How's that?" He stood up, stroking her cheek and tucking a loose lock of hair behind her ear.

Éabha wrapped her arms around his waist and leaned up on tiptoe to kiss him. Och, but she loved to kiss him. Loved to sink against him, feel the heat of his body on hers, the shivers he always produced. Within moments he was kissing her deeply, holding her securely in his embrace. Then just as suddenly, he pulled away, chuckling.

He raked his gaze hotly over her, a devilish glint in her eyes. "I see now how ye've distracted me."

"Do ye?" She stroked her hands up over the muscles of his back, wanting to wrench off the fabric of his shirt and show him just how she planned to occupy him this morning. Her nap could wait.

"Och, aye. And I'm more than happy to oblige ye whenever ye need it." He nuzzled her neck. "Ye've made me the happiest man in all the land."

Éabha was certain her happiness rivaled his. When he'd taken her from Strome, he'd not only set her free, but given her the independence to find herself, to love herself, and in turn love him wholeheartedly. "I love ye so much, husband."

"I love ye." He rubbed her belly, then leaned down to whisper, "And ye, too."

THE END

Eliza Knight

If you enjoyed **CLAIMED BY THE WARRIOR**, *please spread the word by leaving a review on the site where you purchased your copy, or a reader site such as Goodreads or Shelfari! I love to hear from readers too, so drop me a line at* authorelizaknight@gmail.com *OR visit me on Facebook:* https://www.facebook.com/elizaknightauthor. I'm also on Twitter: @ElizaKnight. If you'd like to receive my occasional newsletter, please sign up at www.elizaknight.com. *Many thanks!*

CLAIMED BY THE WARRIOR

Eliza Knight is an award-winning and *USA Today* bestselling indie author of sizzling historical romance and erotic romance. Under the name E. Knight, she pens rip-your-heart-out historical fiction. While not reading, writing or researching for her latest book, she chases after her three children. In her spare time (if there is such a thing…) she likes daydreaming, wine-tasting, traveling, hiking, staring at the stars, watching movies, shopping and visiting with family and friends. She lives atop a small mountain with her own knight in shining armor, three princesses and one very naughty puppy. Visit Eliza at http://www.elizaknight.com or her historical blog History Undressed: www.historyundressed.com

MORE BOOKS BY ELIZA KNIGHT

The Conquered Bride Series
Conquered by the Highlander
Seduced by the Laird
Taken by the Highlander (in the Captured by a Celtic Warrior anthology)
Claimed by the Warrior

Coming soon…
Stolen by the Laird

The Stolen Bride Series
The Highlander's Temptation
The Highlander's Reward
The Highlander's Conquest
The Highlander's Lady
The Highlander's Warrior Bride
The Highlander's Triumph
The Highlander's Sin
Wild Highland Mistletoe—a Stolen Bride winter novella
The Highlander's Charm
A Kilted Christmas Wish – a contemporary Holiday spin-off

The Thistles and Roses Series
Eternally Bound
Promise of a Knight

Under the name E. Knight

Tales From the Tudor Court
My Lady Viper
Prisoner of the Queen

Ancient Historical Fiction
A Day of Fire: a novel of Pompeii
A Year of Ravens: a novel of Boudica's Rebellion

Made in the USA
San Bernardino, CA
29 September 2017